Darkness at Sunset and Vine
Trilogy

Ginger Mayerson

The Wapshott Press

Darkness at Sunset and Vine Trilogy

Published by
The Wapshott Press
PO Box 31513
Los Angeles, CA 90031

The Wapshott Press
www.WapshottPress.com

This trilogy has appeared on the web and an adaptation of the first part was performed at the University of Texas at Denton in 2008, see www.DASAV.com for more fascinating information.

ISBN: 978-0-9825813-8-4

06 05 04 03 4 3 2 1

Wapshott Press logo by Molly Kiely

Darkness at Sunset and Vine
Trilogy

Table of Contents

Also by Ginger Mayerson

Dr. Hackenbush Gets a Job

Dr. Hackenbush Gains Perspective

Electricland

The Pajama Boy

Introduction

I think I can claim the distinction of being this book's first, biggest fan.

I read the manuscript for the first time sometime between 2004–2005. As a director, I immediately could see the text's wonderful potential for performance. However, the story had to marinate in my imagination for a few years before I was brave enough to try to stage it. Even as late as the fall of 2007, I had made plans and announced that I would be directing an entirely different production. My mind kept coming back to "Darkness" though, and the conviction that now was the time to articulate the feelings and ideas I could express by staging the then unpublished novella that said such beautifully ugly things about the United States.

I hesitantly asked Ginger Mayerson if she'd give me permission to adapt the text for performance. Either not knowing or not caring about the violence adaptation can do to authorial intent, she enthusiastically agreed. In the spring of 2008, I gathered a cast and created a production that had audiences standing and cheering for the bloody exploits of Miss Nellie Gail.

[Note: My production covered only the events that took place in Part I of this book. The title of the segment I worked from has been changed from "Darkness at Sunset and Vine" to "The Way We Live

Now at Sunset and Vine." However, the themes of the first part of the trilogy carry on, and do they ever, throughout the rest of the trilogy.]

When at talkbacks for the production, respondents asked why I chose to direct "Darkness at Sunset and Vine," I always replied that my decision was based on the fact that "Darkness" was such a perfect election year piece. Joking aside, it is an incontrovertible fact that my dissatisfaction with the George W. Bush regime and anger at the attitudes prevalent in this country that aided and supported the aims of that administration were at the heart of my decision to stage this particular text at that particular time. Ginger Mayerson says that she wrote the novella in 2003, "in a fury after Bush's "Give me $87 billion so I can start to clean up my mess that never had to happen" speech." Do you remember that one? So much happened both before and after that now it's hard to pick out just one blood-boilingly outrageous event from that disastrous presidency, isn't it?

"Darkness at Sunset and Vine" is set in near-future Los Angeles in the aftermath of the total collapse of the rule of law in the U.S. and the government turning the greatest military in the world on its own people. "Nellie Gail" is the *nomme de guerre* of an agent on disciplinary leave from the Rumsfeld Stasi section of the CIA for having accidentally blown up Dick Cheney and Condoleezza Rice. "Darkness"—to radically simplify the plot of my production of the first segment of this book— is her first person account of a case she is coerced into taking on as a private investigator.

The title "Darkness at Sunset and Vine" is a play on *Darkness at Noon* by Arthur Koestler. That novel tells the story of Rubashaov, a 1917 revolutionary who is imprisoned and tried for treason by the Soviet government he once helped create. Like Rubashov, Nellie is fully aware that she was part of the creation of the hell she now tries to survive in, a cog in the machine now trying to destroy her.

"Darkness at Sunset and Vine" draws on conventions and stock characters from several genres such as comic books, anime, and action-adventure movies. For me, the most important influence on the structure of the novel is the tradition of Film Noir. As in a classic Humphrey Bogart movie, "Darkness" gives us the first person narrative of a jaded private investigator in Southern California, navigating his/her way through a jungle of violence and moral bankruptcy. As in the classic Noir film or Raymond Chandler novel, the heart of the story is not about solving the case. It's about the journey the protagonist takes to get there. "Darkness," like a good Noir film, is sort of a *Pilgrim's Progress* in a landscape with every scrap of moral certainty removed.

In their 1955 book, *Panorama du film noir American*, Borde and Chaumeton listed the five primary attributes of the film noir as being oneiric (dreamlike), strange, erotic, ambivalent, and cruel. I think the novella with its comic book style hyper-violence, bizarre villains, and protagonist who is equal parts hardboiled detective and the most fatal of *femme fatales* certainly embodies all these characteristics.

In my production of the text, my cast and I consistently made staging and adaptation choices that highlighted the strange, cruel, and oneiric qualities of the novella. Visually, the production wallowed with perverse, giddy glee in blood, guns, and death. The wild, violently dreamlike quality of the novella was also reflected in my choice to have the whole cast on stage continually for the whole production since this meant that cast members played characters who died grisly deaths only to immediately rise and play other characters who killed or were killed again… and again… and again.

The oneiric quality of the novella was also highlighted some of the choices we made in selecting material to include or cut. Though, in general, we followed an action-adventure movie model of "show–don't tell," choosing to trim dialogue to the bone to keep a headlong pace for the plot, there were several moments where this kamikaze-style forward motion was broken up by narrative digressions. Before the collapse of civilization, Nellie was a scholar specializing in the study of genocide. We preserved several of her ruminations on the cannibalistic collapse of her own civilization in the form of "image-sculpture" pieces. We gave them names like the "SoCal Post-Apocalypse Infomercial," the "Lincoln Heights Animitronic," and the "Genocide March."

I choose a collaborative directing style for this production. This meant that I shared responsibility for generating staging, adaptation of the text, and assignment of the lines with my cast. As in previous collaborative efforts, my cast came up with ideas that I would not have. Because of their contributions, the production had a richness and complexity it would not have had otherwise.

I particularly wanted to use a collaborative technique to create this production because of the text itself. In "Darkness at Sunset and Vine" although mindless groupthink facilitates the fall of civilization, working collaboratively for the greater good is hope for humanity.

Well, well, well... As always with "Darkness," I start out with rage and end up talking about hope. Guess it does spring eternal...

Dr. Kelly S. Taylor
Associate Professor
Department of Communication Studies
University of North Texas

The Way we Live Now at Sunset and Vine

I think it all officially went to hell when the President, for lack of a better title, stopped giving speeches and hired an actor to do them. It had been going to hell for years, but this seemed to be the official announcement that life as we once knew it was over and was never coming back.

I was working late that night at Universal Insurance; sometimes a girl's gotta put in a little overtime if she's gonna surf the web at work most of the day. Being a data entry drone was a safe gig for now. I still had my PI license, but the Company, as the Rumsfeld Stasi part of the CIA was still called even after his fatal car accident in a parked car, told me to cool it for a while. No better place to be invisible than a seedy insurance company in Hollywood. Still, the least those bastards could have done was get me a better job or any job. I had to dig this one up myself in the LA Times want ads. Since all publishing was banned, the LA Times is little more than a crappy zine with the Internet Broadcast schedule and want ads. Nevertheless, I hate newszines; the newsprint gets all over your hands. You'd think science could do something about that. But there wasn't much science anymore, so I was out of luck, as usual.

But when the Company tells you to cool it, you do, or you end up in the deep freeze. Or staring brain-damaged into your LCD with big empty eyes, waiting for the next task prompt. You dig? Yeah, I thought you did.

So, there I was, being a good little wage slave and data entry drone with the IB on because data entry will kill you if you focus on it. Scientists will tell you that it causes your frontal lobe to dissolve if you actually concentrate on the numbers. On my penultimate Company gig, we used it for interrogation at MegaCorpInc when the CEO tried to call his lawyer. He hadn't heard that our Supremes gutted *his* Miranda rights along with all the other poor devils. Hooked the bastard's shriveled dick up to a car battery and put him to work on an Excel sheet. Every error got him a little jolt. I still smile about that as it was highly amusing. Too bad we didn't know about the frontal lobe problem. Or maybe it was a cerebral hemorrhage. Dead guys with blood leaking out of their orifices are just as dead whatever the reason. We cleaned up and made it look like the CEO bolted with a bunch of cash. Paid a few debts, bought a Mauser 9mm with a matching silencer, and had a nice little vacation after that. Rather wish I'd saved some; three hundred thou a year don't go far in Hollywood. At least not in this new currency we got.

I hate working late. I hate data entry. So you can just imagine how interested I was when the IB announcer said in those annoyingly well-modulated and well enunciated tones:

"And now please welcome Mr. Daniel Bland, who will be delivering this evening's Presidential address."
I must say that Daniel Bland, he of the epic space drama wherein he, as Captain Lula, bravely captains a starship

into the unknown, did a great job with that speech. He was reassuring, fatherly and, unlike the weasely little rat we had foisted on us twelve years ago, he was... Presidential. I wonder how many people could remember Presidential and were having a Bill Clinton flashback as they watched this actor. After all these years of President Whistle-Ass and his handlers, it was soooo nice to see some command mojo on the screen that night; reminded me of the good old Clinton admin days, even made me wet.

But wet or not, I've spent too many years listening to confessions through screams of agony not to hear what old Captain Lula was saying on behalf of our permanent-for-our-own-good government. He was saying, in a roundabout way, that the Internal Intelligence Agency had rounded up and executed another cell of terrorists masquerading as the renegade underground MIT linguistics department, including professors emeritus.

'Hm,' I thought, 'that should make some renegade, underground Berkeley linguists happy.'

The speech went on and on with high praise for the continuing efforts of the IIA to make America a safer and happier place for everyone.

"Everyone that doesn't piss the IIA off, that is," I added, wondering why they still bothered to tell us zombies anything. To scare us? Can't scare zombies, you fools.

The actor representing the POTUS continued, in reassuring tones, that the IIA would be redoubling its efforts on the West Coast to catch the Dissidents Superior League, the dreaded DSL, which would make America an even safer place. God bless us all. The Marine Corps double amputee choir began the Hymn of

America, signaling that we could all go back to whatever we were doing before our government fucked up our evening entertainment viewing. In my case, it went back to the live webcast from my favorite slaughter house — "Abattoir Tonight" — which was the only reality show I could enjoy. Since Max and his "Dr. Max's Live, Nude Economics" show vanished, there just wasn't much on the Internet for me anymore. I even had an email thing going with him for a while before he disappeared. What a shame. I always felt so smart watching Max explain money and power, but being smart isn't worth much anymore when even being useful won't keep you alive for long.

But my thoughts were not on Max or the enhanced sledgehammer-wielding Schwarzenegger lookalike, or the throat-slashing Steven Segal bad plastic job who kept missing the stunned cow's jugular. Foolish of me, but sometimes I just can't help rooting for the victims.

No, as I absently hummed the Hymn for America, my thoughts were on the DSL. Twelve years ago, in a pants-crapping spasm of terror orchestrated by, well, my department at the Company, we convinced most of America to begin being inoculated on a weekly basis against Ebola pox.

Most of America obediently lined up their families for this free injection against a disease that didn't even exist. This injection was primarily composed of Thorazine, a little souped up thimerosal, and a little Lophophora juice mixed in for body. There was a shot of heroin to keep them coming back, too. This little cocktail, administered once a week, did exactly what it was designed to do: It killed the elderly in a matter of months, it caused brain damage in children, but most importantly it made the vast majority of able-bodied Americans into passive, paper-pushing, keyboard-tapping, manual-laboring beasts of burden.

I say most Americans because there actually were quite a few who told the government to fuck off. Very nasty—we in the government (even we on disciplinary leave from the government) do not like to be told to fuck off. First we tried fear—a few festering, pustule-covered Ebola pox victims in major metropolitan areas, obviously the work of terrorists. That worked on a few skeptics, but not all. Then we tried coercion—the inoculations were not optional, they were mandatory. That's when the huge numbers of people, many of them linguists, who would later be named the DSL, went underground.

I blame the internet for sounding the alarm and, um, telling the truth. There, I said it: The government was lying and the wackos on the internet were telling the truth. We caught a lot of dissidents before they vanished, got them into a course of injections, strapped down and screaming blue murder. Most wanted to die and I personally obliged a few. I can be a nice gal if you catch me in the right mood. But quite a few got away, aided by a network of killjoys on the internet who posted routes to safe houses that changed hourly.

The Company could not keep up. We finally ended up trying to pull the plug on cyberspace and found out we couldn't because we couldn't take down the telephone system. It would result in chaos and you can't keep the herd in line in chaos. For ourselves, we used the internet for our own purposes—to amuse, to terrorize, to send email reminders to make sure people got their weekly inoculation fix. We used the internet to misdirect and suppress information. We felt spreading it, like manure, was a perverted use of such an excellent propaganda tool. We could blank out what we could find, but the internet is like the ocean—you have to know what you're looking for to find it.

This was used against us so much, and made the Company look so bad, that the Advisory Board on Terrorism, the ABT, formed the Internal Intelligence Agency. The IIA was independent of everything, including domestic law. They were once governed by the ABT, but last time I checked, the first director and his assistants were the board of the ABT. At least that's who it was eleven years ago, when you could still get information like that off the internet.

Around eleven, I decided to call it a night. "Abattoir Tonight" was over, so no real reason to hang around anymore. The data entry could wait.

I checked the street before I went down the stairs, quiet as usual. We didn't have any police in Los Angeles anymore, especially not in this hard-ass part of Hollywood. There was no money because the late "Governor Schwarzenegger" further cut the shit out of the already insufficient property and business taxes.

I have no sympathy for property owners or businesses because I have neither property, business nor money. You get what you pay for and civilization and infrastructure are two of those things. I suppose I could toss in "rule of law" and "continuation of life", but that probably falls under civilization. But we haven't had much civilization here in LA since the invasion and occupation, which is actually fine with me.

They want us to forget that when the recall election failed, the one, true Governor Davis mysteriously could not be found. Kevin Shelly, our last, late and very brave Secretary of State, declared Bustamante, who'd gotten the most votes to replace

Davis if the recall succeeded, our new Governor. Well, we couldn't find Davis, and some of us were REALLY looking (but not so he could be Governor), so Bustamante would have to do. But then the Federal Government declared California a martial law state. Me, I couldn't care less, but this very seriously annoyed many of my neighbors. The ensuing riots had decimated what police we once had and when it was over, there was no money for new ones. The Chief and a few dozen uniforms huddled in various station houses around town, occasionally defending them because, after all, they lived in them, too.

Only Hollenbeck was leveled, mainly because the Police changed sides and fought the Federal troops alongside the community. The worst street fighting had been in Lincoln and Boyle Heights, the oldest parts of the city, and they were finally subdued in an afternoon of carpet bombing. On breaks from interrogations, I watched it all from Dodger Stadium, high on the hill across the Golden State Freeway, where the captured dissidents/protesters/freedom fighters (you pick one, I don't care) were penned up. The bombing took out Cal State LA. I was almost an alumnus, and it bothered me briefly that this bothered me not at all.

Since then we've had eight appointed Governors, several periods of martial law, but no Federal funding for anything. We have lights and water because the Department of Water and Power runs a tight, well-armed ship. Pretty much the DWP is the government of Southern California. They were and are the only operation together enough to do it. Why they'd want to is a mystery, but to each his own addiction. Seems like they made an alliance with AT&T, which re-assimilated Pacific Bell, and Greater Los Angeles has all the things its slaves need to survive.

I got emails for phone bills and electric bills, but somebody else was paying the water (so far). These amounts were deducted from my DWP bank account, which I'd never opened and into which my pay check was automatically deposited. Cash no longer existed; I used a DWP credit card for everything. I never applied for it. It was on my desk with my first pay stub and a bank statement for an account I cannot close or amend. I don't miss cash. Or rather, I don't miss the monopoly money the US Mint, Inc. is printing up. I miss the portraits of the weird-looking white guys, but this new currency is as ugly as it is worthless. Money only has power because we believe in it, and no one believes in this neon colored synthetic paper crap.

So no one bothers to stick anyone up anymore either. Crime is now no longer about gain, it has attained a purer form; it's only about violence.

As crappy as my home, my job, my city, and my country are, I can always get off work at eleven PM and go out and kill a few people. I'd hunt them through the mazes of Hollywood, sometimes as far afield as Brentwood. Brentwood was a little tricky, because sometimes the target would breach the security of a gated home and I'd have to kill my way through the security squad to get to my target. As I said, all crime was now sport or insanity or both by then, but sometimes, if they had some nice portable electronics, I'd give them a new home while I was at it. The scavengers very politely waited until I was on my way before they moved in. Brentwood is dotted with ravaged mansions with dead and eaten gardens, housing dozens of half-dead hulking, useless humans. This is not all my work; as the half-dead communities grow, they expand. And there is no one to stop them. .

But tonight all I wanted to do was go home, drink some absinthe, and think about Captain Lula delivering our "president's" speech. There were nuances and subtleties here I wanted to ponder. Was "President" Whistle-Ass dead or incapacitated? He had a part time job teaching pre-school that was broadcast from 10-2 PDT; I'd tuned in briefly and he looked fine this afternoon. Perhaps whoever was running the country these days just decided since no one really cared, they might as well hire somebody who could pronounce all the words the speech writers wrote. That struck me as efficient—sick, but efficient. I hoped they'd further streamline the process and just email the text of the speeches to us. Eventually they would simply issue edicts and this would save everyone from the pretense that our government was anything other than our masters. Edicts that were tersely worded, so we could all get back to our Internet Broadcasts that much more quickly.

Down in the parking garage Paulo was guarding the vehicles. I'd wondered if Paulo was part of the DSL, since he seemed a little too alert for one of the inoculated. And he was a little too old to have missed the inoculation program, which stopped after three years, due to having enough fucked-up workers and needing workers who could almost function. That's when we all started getting absinthe delivered to our doors: it was optional brain damage, as opposed to the mandatory vaccination kind. I suspected the IIA was behind it all. I'm sure one of them realized they'd need a new generation of slaves eventually, so in addition to stopping the inoculation program, they got all forms of birth control banned. This was a mixed success. For every healthy baby, three people got AIDS. This fucked-up planning was what made me think it was the IIA behind it; they couldn't plan their way out of a paper bag.

"Evening, Miss Gail, nice evening," Paulo mumbled as I handed him half a cheese sandwich I'd saved from my lunch. Because he lived in the parking garage and it was relatively safe with the gates down, it probably wasn't necessary for me to tip him, but I didn't want the rest of that sandwich anyway.

"Yeah..." I said, digging the keys to my Electrocatti out of my pocket. "Nice."

My jacket gaped open and Paulo's eyes lit up seeing the butt of my titanium Colt, but went out again. Made me wonder about him, but maybe he just had good taste in guns. This lightweight .45 was one of the last goodies I twisted out of the Company before I was put on leave. I told them I lost it and they never asked for it back again, suckers. In addition to my Mauser, I liked to carry it for day wear because it was so light and efficient; it blasts anything it hits to bits. It's not the most accurate gun in the world, but I didn't do much target shooting on my way home, usually just had to blast my way through an ambush now and then. Not lately, though, as I think the word is out that I'm deadly and just trying to get home. Eventually you get to know people by sight on your route home. It's only the first few trips that can be difficult, when neither side knows what to expect.

And even if I did get ambushed, what would they get? A titanium gun and an electric scooter. It was a honey, though, I thought as I unplugged it from the recharger socket. Assembled in Mexico, where most of the skilled labor fled when the trade unions were banned, designed by the rocket scientists, who'd fled to Mexico when NASA became part of the DARPA Space Weapons Program (now defunct for lack of talent), and produced by Ducati motorcycles after they purchased Electrolux vacuums and moved the plant to Mexico. Fast, quiet, and ran like a gazelle for days on a single charge, thank God, because only the very rich and the government could afford gasoline these days, and I am neither. It even had cunningly designed (oh, those Italian designers!) solar panels, so it charged on its own when it could be left out in the sun. Which was never, because there were no Police, as I said earlier, and I can't afford vehicle security thugs on my salary.

However, I did have an Auto Defense System, which was merely electrical current, a lot of it, for anyone touching my ride. As long as DWP kept the current on, no one was going to get anything but fried for messing with my scooter. I clicked the system off and unplugged the charger cord. My fingers slid over the raised letters "Heche en Mexico", where all the good stuff came from. If you could work out the barter. To get the Electrocatti, I'd killed a couple of troublemakers for the supply guys who were tired of paying them protection money. Greed takes everyone down eventually. I'd worked the same deal for my titanium-guarded leather jacket and all my other Mexico goodies. It wasn't always murder—sometimes it was just guarding a UPS convoy from Mexico through the wasteland between La Jolla and Santa Ana. When Camp Pendleton mutinied, the worst fighting had been along the coast, but also inland when 29 Palms and March Air Force Base joined in the rebellion against the Federal troops. It was ugly, but didn't get to LA, so I couldn't get very worked up about what I saw on the IB.

11

I did get a little queasy the first time I went down the Interstate Five to Mexico on a shipment escort job. Someone, maybe DWP, maybe San Diego, had fixed the highway, but nothing would fix the burned up land around it. Some of it looked like scorch, some of it looked like chemical burns, but all of it looked dead, like sterile, like it was never going to be alive again. Even eight years after the last jar head rebellion, which was the last time I was down San Diego way, there wasn't a blade of grass or even mold anywhere, just silence and dust. That was always the most unnerving part of the trip. Shooting my way through Fullerton, Compton, Commerce and back into town was refreshing after that. But nowadays, all the goods come up the coast on ships, so there's not much for me to barter with. The importers still need protection when they're in LA, but not as much and not as often since things have pretty much settled down here. Nobody has the time or energy to riot and all the Federal troops are busy in Iraq, Iran, Syria, Saudi Arabia, Jordan, Afghanistan, Uzbekistan, Tajikistan, Pakistan, Algeria, Morocco, Libya, Israel, Canada, France, and parts of Siberia. The Federal troops were actually way over-extended. There are always ads for mercenaries in the LA Times, looks like great pay and perks, but I hate to travel, so I'm ignoring them (for now).

There was a fortress-like natural gas and solar powered MTA bus lumbering down Sunset when I pulled out of the garage. It could hold off a siege and anti-tank weapons, not to mention crush me and the scooter like a bug. I knew this because I'd fought one to a standstill once, but not even I am a match for cannon turrets and fender-mounted machine guns. I let it have the right of way. For myself, I just wanted to get home

12

and think about why an actor was giving our president-for-life's speeches now. I mean, not even a body double, but a completely different guy. Should we call him President Simulacra? President Representation? It was a huge subject for me, so huge and engrossing, I didn't see the kid throw the hunk of metal at me. Little bastard; I'm just trying to get home and you're just trying to get killed. I chased him on the scooter up to what was left of the Hollywood branch of the LA City Library. My, this city had been proud when that branch opened. Last time I was here in the daylight, there was an old guy standing in front of it, crying his eyes out. Eh, it was just a wrecked building that used to be full of books you could borrow for free... there was so much else to cry about, but I sort of dug his pain. But now it was just a good place for an ambush. I parked the scooter behind a burned-out SUV and flipped on the battery defense system. I didn't figure to be too long. These punk kids are stupid and I was in the mood for an easy kill. It would have to be a quiet kill, too, so I drew my other gun, a Mauser, and screwed the silencer on it. I put on my Infra-RayBans so I could see, and watched the rubble for a few minutes to get my bearings.

Most of the books and furniture had been used for fuel by now, but anything that wouldn't burn was strewn around the building shell. I used as much of it for cover as I could. I was quiet in my Capezio boots—designed for speed, stealth, ass-kicking, ankle and arch support. I wished I'd worn darker stockings because my legs and face gave me away even on this moonless night. It didn't matter, I shot two punks right away: one who ran at me and one who ran away. The third came at me from the left and the stick he threw at me bounced off my jacket. Not that it wouldn't leave a bruise on my left tit, but it would be nothing compared to the hole I blasted in the kid's chest.

I seemed to be done. If there were any more live ones in the library, they were face down and barely breathing. I picked what hit me and it turned out to be one of those knife sharpening rods. 'Fool,' I thought. 'Only good if you can get close enough to ram it into a major organ, if then.'

But you were quick or dead in LA, and now there was a kind of intelligence hygiene going on. Only the fast and the smart were living much past puberty these days. I stuck the rod in the back of my ti-tandex mini skirt, but kept my gun handy just in case somebody else thought it was a good night to die.

I lived south of Echo Park and east of Little Tokyo in what was left of the Good Samaritan hospital complex. It was on a hill, of sorts, had good views and breezes and was defensible when necessary. It had not been necessary for a long time because all the hard cases lived there and kept the neighborhood neat. A healthy community of kiosk businesses had taken root in the old parking lots and I stopped by my favorite fruitas guy for a bag of apples and a half pound of pistachios.

"Somebody in your place, Miss Nellie," Arlo said as he swiped my DWP debit card. "They got the lights on, but you ain't home."

Story of my life. "Yeah? How long?"

I shut up because we were no longer alone. A guy dressed in a baggy, filthy black suit, he looked like a scarecrow with a bad case of caffeine jitters had joined us. "You Nellie Gail?" he asked.

"No," I said.

This puzzled Mr. S. Crow, but he recovered. "The boss wants to see you. Mr. James."

14

My old boss from the Company, the guy who put me on disciplinary leave four years ago. What the fuck did he want? Well, I'd find out. I took my groceries and brushed past the scarecrow and into the livable wreck I called home.

I had two small rooms in what had once been a lab so there was an abundance of sinks, counter, cabinets, and outlets. I'd thrown a futon and an orange crate into what I used for a bedroom (I don't sleep much), and there was an overstuffed armchair and a lamp in the main room. There was also a low bookcase full of books I'd scrounged and bartered for over the years. One of my books, Dwork and the Van Pelts' *Holocaust: A History*, was in Mr. James' bony paw when I came in. Standing behind him was a beefier scarecrow in a black suit who wasn't reading anything. He did have a gun in his hand. He used his other hand to take my guns and give them to James.

"Good to know you're still reading in your field, Nell," he said. "We like our agents, even those on disciplinary leave, not to lose their edge."

"What do you want?" I knew he wasn't interested in me or my unfinished history degree.

"I've got a job for you," he said.

"My old job?"

"No, private job. You've still got your PI license, haven't you?"

"Sure," I said and waited.

"My daughter's gone missing," he said, and handed me a photo of a plump, blond teen. "Her name is Sara Lee James. I think she's with the DSL here in LA."

"Why do you think that?"

"I would have found her by now if she was

anywhere but in this hellhole."

"When did she blow?" I asked, laying the picture on the sink.

"A few weeks ago, right after the IIA picked up that MIT linguistics terrorist cell."

"I thought that just happened."

"No, the IIA had to make sure they had the right people," he said, wincing a little. "They were tough linguists, and the interrogations took longer than they thought. My daughter got wind of it on my secure home computer. She was interested in studying linguistics, so some of these people were heroes to her. She cut and ran."

I couldn't say I blamed her.

"I want you to find her, Nell, and keep her in one piece until I can get to her," he said to my silence. "I'll... deal with the situation from there."

He'd probably deal with it with a couple of Ebola pox shots, how fucking fatherly. Kids—you give them every chemical advantage and they kick you in the teeth anyway.

He didn't haggle over the price, which made me suspicious of ever getting paid. Or ever living to ever actually get paid. The clincher was when the bodyguard brought my Universal Insurance boss in from the bedroom. My boss was bound and gagged and based on the color of his extremities, he'd been tied up for quite a while.

"And just in case you were thinking of saying no to me," James said, and put a bullet from my Mauser into my boss' head. Just to be thorough he also shot him at close range with my Colt. Messy, very messy, and very, very loud; the neighbors would not be amused. "There are still police, courts, and prisons outside of

Southern California, Nellie, the courts don't really need evidence to convict, but it's never a bad thing. Not even you would last very long in lockdown." He turned to his bodyguard and told him to wait just outside the door. He must have been worried, even though I was unarmed. Except for the sharpening rod that he didn't know about.

James had never made a pass at me; he was so sexless, it seemed incredible that he could have a daughter. Maybe he wasn't the father, or maybe I couldn't care less.

"Tell me something, Nell, as a historian, why do you think the Third Reich failed?"

"They were bad at logistics." People asked me this a lot, this was my standard answer.

"Just that? Don't you think they were morally wrong and evil and therefore doomed?"

"They were very powerful and at the same time wasteful of their resources, unable to re-evaluate their positions and change course, and they didn't listen to their own experts. I don't know if that's morally wrong and/or evil. I do know it's stupid." This was my standard elaboration on the standard answer.

"See any similarities in our government?"

I shrugged. "What government, James? All we've got now is martial law and presidential speech givers." He looked embarrassed so I changed the subject. "What about my Company job?"

"Let's see how you do on my private job."

I didn't like the sound of that. "I think enough time has gone by…"

"Nellie, you took out Cheney, Rice and the entire Strag Plans office, including the building. It was tough to convince State you made a simple mistake."

"You sent me the wrong picture. And too much C-4."

"It was supposed to look like an accident."

"I accidentally used too much C-4," I said. "And you sent me a picture of the wrong guy."

"Dick Cheney looks nothing like Paul Krugman. Anybody who reads news off the Internet knows that," James said.

"I wasn't..."

"I know, you don't get out much, I managed to explain it away. And in some ways it worked to the Company's advantage. Cheney's visits were getting on our nerves and Rice was useless from day one," he said. "That's why you're still among the living even though you gave Krugman a chance to get to Mexico. I hear he and Saches are tearing the place up down there."

I must have looked puzzled at the idea of economists tearing a place or anything up.

"They've got the economy humming right along, trade deals all over the world, universal education from pre-school through a PhD for anyone with the brains and will, and universal healthcare," he continued. "Supposedly, Mexico is a great place since Gates and Soros bought it."

"I didn't know Bill Gates was in on that deal. I thought he was still on the run in the tropics." I casually stretched back and got hold of the long, metal rod I'd taken from the punk in Hollywood. I needed James to let his guard down, just a little. I had pretty much decided I didn't want this job and a simple no was not going to get me out of it. And having him in my face again just reminded me how little I liked him in the first place.

"Yes, well, Gates is just hedging his bets and

lying low in case things don't go his way in the U.S. again. He didn't like his company being nationalized, not that the product improved any. It was the principle of the thing." He gave me a hard look. "Soros, Sachs, Krugman and their crews are serious about making a better world without the U.S. They've written us off, Nellie, they've left us behind. The bastards." He seemed distressed by this.

But not for long. I knew he was wearing body armor, but not on his face, so I buried the rod into his left eye and jammed it into the back of his skull. I stepped over his flopping body and grabbed the Mauser. James' idiot bodyguard came in at the commotion and I dropped him with a head shot. I prefer chest shots because they are the bigger target and more efficient, but I was pretty sure he was wearing body armor and I was in a hurry.

Mr. S. Crow saw his colleague fall and decided not to be a hero. He could also run faster than I could. I chased him out of the building and through the kiosks, even into the rubble beyond them before I gave up. I think I winged him, though, I heard him yelp, but I figured the scavengers in the rubble would get him, especially if they smelled blood. On the other hand, some well-concealed scavengers were throwing rocks at me and, as irritating as I found this, I was not in the mood to fight a guerrilla war just then. There were probably too many to kill and I was also way too tired.

On my way back through the kiosks I stopped at the Limo Brothers' recycling and burger stand and asked them to get the three bodies out of my apartment. They sent some of the younger generation up while I had a cup of chocolate with the fruitas guy.

"Tough night?" he asked.

"Nothing I can't handle," I said. "As long as the Limo Brothers are in business."

We smiled grimly at each other. The Limo Brothers were called that because they delivered freshly butchered meat in a solar/electric golf cart they called "The Limo" to anyone who could afford it. Or wanted it. No one ever saw a cow or pig anywhere near the mini-abattoir behind their kiosk. They also did a brisk bar-b-que and burger business, 24/7. I never ate there. Or never more than once a week.

James had recruited me when I was at Cal State LA. I'd scored high on the sociopath scale on some mysterious tests the State wanted us to take to get our degrees that year. A test is a test, but these were damn weird: they asked us to make moral decisions dressed up as IQ testing. Not long after that James contacted me and my brother, who was doing a PhD in linguistics at Berkeley because we'd both scored "well" on those tests, by Company standards, and the Company was hiring. We'd both refused, but James had our family and our dog killed, our scholarships cancelled and got us evicted from our places. We had nowhere to go but to him, so we did. He gave us new names—I got Nellie Gail because Laguna Woods was taken. I went into terror and interrogations and my brother into logistics and long-term planning because I was only ruthless, but he was ruthless and smart. But maybe not smart enough. Five years ago he'd vanished on a project in Houston. I could never find out what happened to him. James said he didn't know and maybe he didn't. He even let me look for him as much as I could because the Company doesn't like losing their investments for any reason.

But that was five years ago and this was tonight and I was very tired. The Limo Brothers body disposal did a thorough and fast job on my place. You'd never know there had been three messily killed bodies in it, they'd wiped it down so well. I lit the photo of Sara Lee, the girl I would not be finding for her father, and let it burn in the sink. I figured someone had Mr. Scare Crow for dinner, so there was now no evidence whatsoever that Mr. James of the Company or his goons had ever been in my neighborhood. I slept better for knowing that.

I went to work the next day and no one noticed that our boss was missing. Around noon his secretary stuck her head in my office and asked me if I'd seen him. I said no, but that he was calling in for messages. She said, "Oh," and came back five minutes later with a handful of message slips. I handled most of them in an hour and the others after lunch. This made me wonder just what my late boss actually did here at Universal Insurance.

Against my will, I found myself wondering about the late Mr. James' wandering daughter. It took some moxie to rebel these days, especially if you were raised with every advantage, in a gated community, and educated privately.

But linguistics had fucked up better minds than could ever be spawned by James. My brother had once been a normal guy, and then he became passionately, obsessively engrossed in the way the letter "T" was palatized in different languages. Every conversation ended up on that subject and then you couldn't get him off it with, well, twenty pounds of C-4. He said it was where the language was going that was important. Nothing was more important than where the language was going: It Was The Future.

He used to laugh at me, said I was always looking

back, that I majored in history because I was afraid of the future. Well, considering the present we now got, yeah, maybe I was afraid of the future. But I wasn't always looking back; I was looking over my shoulder because I knew the same mistakes were gaining on us in the here and now, that it was only a matter of time...

Oh fuck it. My throat got tight when I thought about my big brother. History was a safe subject, but my own past was a minefield.

I emailed a grocery order to Trader Joe's and told them I'd be there in ten minutes. A few years ago a clerk in the Eagle Rock store "politely" lipped off at me and I took the sarcastic little motherfucker out. I was so pissed off, I took out the whole store, including the customers. After that Trader Joe's management asked me to just email my orders to whichever store and they'd have the surliest clerk they could find give them to me at the door. Surliness I can handle; sarcasm makes me homicidal. This arrangement is fine with me because I hate to shop. And the Hollywood Trader Joe's had some way surly clerks. I think they were aspiring actors, so they could really do surly.

I stopped at the fruitas guy for a large carrot juice to go with my peanut butter pretzel entrée and Trail Mix Vegan cookies for dessert.

"Strangers around today, Miss Gail."

"Again?"

"One was limping. Another was helping him. With a gun."

"Skinny limping guy? Like the one I was chasing last night?"

"He was not limping last night, but, yes, it is him."

I was mulling this over when the very distinctive

sound of two shotguns being pumped distracted me. The fruitas guy, raising his hands and backing away was even more distracting.

"Glenn wants to see you."

I looked over my shoulder to see who had the deep basso voice. There were two, one was a bad imitation of Mr. T and the other looked like Don Knotts on too many steroids. I nodded, picked up my groceries and my drink and headed for my place. No one spoke, so I never did know which one had the deep, deep voice.

I figured it was Glenn sitting in my arm chair with my copy of Balakian's *Black Dog of Fate*. He was mean and bureaucratic-looking. Mr. Scare Crow was sitting on the floor next to him, looking very, very scared. Another guy with an alarming resemblance to Leonard Nimoy was standing over him with a riot gun. Don Knotts took my Trader Joe's bag and put it on the sink. I sipped my carrot juice and waited for developments.

"Do you believe this Armenian genocide bullshit, Nellie?" Glenn snarled by way of greeting.

"Yeah."

"Why?"

"A million and a half Armenians disappeared between 1915 and 1923. That many people don't just vanish."

"Not easily, no."

He seemed lost in thought so I decided the history discussion was over. "Who are you and what the fuck do you want?"

"I'm with the Internal Intelligence Agency and I want you to find this girl." He handed me a photo of a pudgy, red-faced, squalling toddler. "She was last seen with this girl." He handed me a photo of Sara Lee.

"Know her?"

"No."

"Whoa, Nellie, don't you know her? Her father was here last night."

Since Mr. S. Crow was in the room, I figured an outright lie was not going to wash. "So?"

"So? So what did he want?"

"He wanted my opinion on the Third Reich." This seemed to throw him into a funk.

"Didn't Hitler mention the Armenian Genocide?"

"Yes." I waited until he was back on track.

"I want to hire you to find the toddler. Her name is Millie. The girl's name is Sara Lee James, in case you forgot in the past 24 hours."

"What makes you think they're in LA?"

"James was here looking for his daughter," he said. "Hiring you to look for her. Millie was last seen with Sara."

"What makes you think I can find either of them?"

"This is your town, Nellie," he said coolly.

I scowled. "What's this job pay? Or am I working for the IIA now?" I asked. The IIA had great benefits.

"It's a private job. A million for the kid, alive and in good shape."

"And for Sara Lee?"

"I don't give a good goddamn about Sara Lee," he said, and to punctuate his point, he took a sleek Beretta out of his coat and shot Mr. S. Crow in the head. Twice. "This gun is registered to you." He laid it on the bookshelf. "Can I borrow this?" He waved "Black Dog of Fate" at me.

I said no; I never lend my books because there're

no publishers anymore to replace them. Glenn shrugged and put it on the bookcase, next to my new gun. "How do I find you for updates?" I asked.

He put a business card on the book and stood up. "I'll be in touch." He turned back at the door. "Oh, and we think the kid is with the DSL, if you need a hint."

They left and I emailed the Limo Brothers that I had a pick-up for them, a single. I decided to take my peanut butter pretzels and carrot juice outside while they tidied up. Don-Knotts-overdosed-on-steroids stole my fucking pretzels, the bastard.

This just was not my day.

At least I got a nice new gun out of this mess. I'd always wanted a Beretta, too. It was the only bright spot in the whole scenario and I wondered if Glenn would want it back when I failed to find Pookie-Boo or whatever her fucking name was. Millie, yeah, Millie. He was probably going to kill me whether I found her or not, so it was moot really.

I was considering this between data entry and calls from the main office of Universal Insurance, asking me what my very absent boss wanted to do on certain matters. I said whatever came into my head and they seemed to think that made my boss brilliant. Well, maybe it did, what do I know?

If, and it was a big fucking "IF", this Millie kid was with the DSL there was no way to find her. The DSL was everywhere and nowhere. There were even urban legends that they'd all morphed into cyber-spirits and were living in the Internet, appearing in visions to the faithful. Well, that sounded like the faithful got a bad hit of Ebola pox vaccine to me.

The other question I had was WHY did the DSL have her IF they had her? And WHY was the IIA involved, and HOW was SARA LEE, I mean, Sara Lee involved? And WTF was I supposed to do about it? I figured I could stall for about 24 hours and then run like hell. In the meantime, I surfed up some gossip on the net about the DSL in LA, just so if Glenn wanted an update, it would buy me some time.

There wasn't much out there. As there was no law in LA, only loose guidelines, there were no criminal investigations or official arrests. Well, the IIA couldn't criminal investigate their way to their own ass and their idea of arrest was spelled immediate execution. I did find it interesting that when I ran the string "Sara Lee" and Millie and "MIT Linguists" and IIA and .gov – "Baked goods" –Chomsky –terrorists, I got whitehouse.gov and a page about Bush I's dog, Millie. Well, this made no sense to me, so I ran it without the .gov parameter and got a dead link to Dr. Donald Monroe's page at MIT or what used to be MIT linguistics. I hit the cached version of the page.

Ghosts and more ghosts. Monroe had been a legend among linguists—no one could understand his theory of meta-languages, it was too amazing, not even my brother could comprehend it; he had been huge. Unlike his colleagues, he didn't go underground with the DSL, he'd gotten a cushy government job; close to, if not in the White House. No one knew what he did there (no one knew what anyone did in the White House anymore) and I hadn't heard about him in a long time. I dug Glenn's card out of my purse and emailed him to email me a secure chat room. A few seconds later there was a discreet ding on my computer.

:::what?
:::where's t monroe, phd?
:::why?

:::maybe a lead

:::he's dead

:::when?

:::two months ago

:::how and why?

:::he was in the raid that picked up the mit renegades. he thought he was leading us to them. he'd served his purpose anyway

:::is he connected to sara lee?

:::fuck her

:::pass, was he?

:::he was her mentor

Hm, Sara Lee was that close to the White House, yuck, no wonder she ran.

:::ARE YOU FUCKING HERE?

:::yeah yeah, monroe and the DSL, wtf?

:::he crossed over or tried to, we had a chip in him, it was the trade-off for not being inoculated

:::do you know why he crossed?

:::no. did you find millie yet?

:::working on it. over and out.

I decided right then to take a page out of Sara Lee's book and get the fuck out of Dodge, or at least the U.S. I didn't have any friends in Mexico or anywhere really, but I did have some people I could scare into giving me a start in Baja.

There were a few things I wanted from home. Not much—I'm not sentimental—but there was a photo of me and my brother, and a copy of *The Protocols of the Elders of Zion*, which was always good for a few laughs. Southern California had been the sixth, maybe even fifth, largest economy in the whole fucking world. It had had flocks of the most brilliant thinkers, herds of beautiful men and women, a string of great universities, two and a half of the greatest cities in the world, and more joy, more hope, and more love than you could shake a stick at, all of which translated into megabucks for some reason I could never understand. Where crazy women like Catherine Ponder and Louise Hay had had the guts to say there was more than enough for everyone, more than anyone could ever want in the world, just go out there with love in your heart and get it. Now there was only rage and fear. Most of the state was now wasteland or jungle-like cities. There was no GSP, no money, and damn little hope. Why would any sane person running the world, let alone the Illuminati, destroy one of their biggest money makers? This is why I knew the Jews were not running the world—historically, they were not a wasteful people. And, from a historical point of view, at least mine, what was going on in the U.S. was more like Crusader thinking: don't like it, let's kill or enslave it, thereby rendering it useless and non-threatening whether or not it was ever a threat in the first place. I have nothing against Christianity, but, historically, it's done almost as much harm as good, if anyone still bothered with those kinds of distinctions.

Hah! Not me! I was on my way to old Mexico and out of this mess for good. I tied up a few loose ends at my desk, made a few more decisions for my dead boss, gave Paulo a big smile and a pastrami sandwich I no longer wanted and hit the road for home.

They were waiting for me. I knew this because they left Glenn's, Mr. T's and Don Knotts-OD'd-on-steroids' heads neatly lined up in front of my door. I saw red, and it wasn't just blood. Enough was fucking enough. I wheeled on the goon coming up the stairs behind me. I caught him in the chest with both Capezio boot-clad feet and rode him down the flight of stairs. I had my new gun out by then and shot him. I fired wildly at movement to my right. There was a scream and a thump. I ran to the left.

I could hear them coming. I ran through wrecked wards parallel to the hallway I knew they were in. It was the hallway to the outside. I needed to be outside, I stood a better chance outside. I wasn't fast enough or there were too many of them. I dove for cover and started firing at whatever moved. Their guns were noisy and messy. I put the Mauser away and drew my titanium Colt. The debris around me shattered into a million shards. I put on my Infra-RayBans to protect my eyes. I emptied the Colt and wished I had more bullets. I stuck it in the waistband of my skirt and drew out my other guns, emptying them at whatever moved out there. I slid another magazine in the Mauser; it would have to last. I rolled for the blasted windows, hopped the balcony railing and slid down the fire ladder. I had the hospital between me and the kiosks. There was shooting in my general direction, but I was in the shelter of the overhang, creeping around the side of the building. I figured they'd figure I'd go for my scooter in the parking garage, but I was going for the cover of the kiosks. If I could lure whoever the fuck this was into that snare, once they started firing, the vendors would defend themselves. This would give me cover to get to my scooter and get the fuck out of there. If I wasn't dead by then.

I took a deep breath at the corner of the building. Once around it, I had a dash across open space to the kiosks. If I could just make it across the open space... There were pounding feet behind me, so I knew I only had a few seconds. Guns drawn, one empty, I came around the building like a hurricane.

Directly into the black helicopters between me and the kiosks. There were also half a dozen guys with bigger guns than mine. Their colleagues came around behind me, making it an even dozen. I hadn't even heard the helicopters, but then the only noise they were making was a low hum, like a window air conditioner.

A guy wearing a nice blue suit and an AK-47 strolled up to me and said, "Boss wants to see you." He pointed the gun at my head, while another guy in an equally nice herringbone pattern took my guns. "Let's go, Miss Gail," he said, herding me back into my own home at gunpoint. I went quietly; I was getting used to it.

They were a tidy crew. The dead guys were already gone from the stairwell and even the blood was cleaned away. It was worthy of the Limo Brothers, but I knew they'd be defending their kiosk until the shooting died down.

Someone had opened the drapes. Or tried to. They were in a dusty tangle on the floor, probably disintegrated from heat and disuse. The sun was slanting through the dirty window and lighting the dinginess to a new low.

For this reason, I tried never to see my flop in natural light. It just made the well-dressed thugs and the tall, pacing guy look as bad as they probably were. The guy stopped pacing and looked down at me. This must be the boss, since he was the only one who didn't have a gun in his hand. He had a samizdat copy of a treatise on neo-fascism in his hand, my copy to be exact.

"For a historian you read very crappy stuff," he said.

"I'll try to reform," I said, figuring there was no point in arguing. "Who are you?"

"Oh, just call me Rush," he said, waving the samizdat pamphlet at me and smiling.

It was kind of nauseating. His namesake was wandering around the East Coast, mostly brain dead, not that anyone could really tell, except that he was no longer on the radio every day. He'd patriotically and publicly taken his Ebola Pox inoculations to encourage others to take them. No one in the know tried to stop him; he'd served his purpose. We in the Company called him Mr. Judas Goat. However, his deteriorating condition on TV, and cable (when there were such things), the IB, and his even more incoherent broadcasts tipped the more alert citizens off that maybe these inoculations weren't such a great thing to get.

But I just nodded politely and waited for him to go on. Or kill me. One or the other seemed inevitable.

"Have you found Millie yet?" he asked, pacing again.

"Not yet," I said. "And since Glenn's head is on my doorstep, I don't have a client anymore."

"I'm your client now."

"I was thinking of retiring."

"Find me Millie and you can retire," he said. "I don't care what you do after you find her."

"Why does everyone think I can find this kid?" I asked. "You've got more firepower and muscle, you find her."

"She's not where we can go," he said, still pacing my tiny parlor. "She's in Lincoln Heights, at County with the DSL."

"Forget it," I said. I'm tough but not psychotic enough to start looking for the DSL in the rubble of County Hospital.

He stopped pacing and faced me. "Do you know

what's holding this country together, Nellie?" he asked with a snarl.

"Greed?"

"Will. A few people with the will and vision to guide America," he said, getting this weird, beatific look in his eyes. "An elite class, the natural leaders of America."

"And who might they be?" I asked, trying to sound awed. I must have succeeded, because he smiled, and it was disgusting.

"Do you believe in the Ulluminati?"

I forced my eyes not to roll. "Ah, no, I don't believe in the Illuminati any more than I believe in Santa Claus or the Easter Bunny."

"I didn't say the Illuminati," he snarled mere millimeters from my face. "I said the Ulluminati."

"I see." I wondered which one of us had the pronunciation problem.

"I don't believe in the Illuminati either," he said more calmly. "But admire the concept. My people have modeled ourselves after the Illuminati, except we're Protestant."

"Southern Baptists?"

"Episcopalian. University-educated, business-minded, heterosexual, and fed up with Democracy." He resumed pacing. "We never cared for it in the first place."

I wondered how long this lecture was going to go on.

"Sara Lee took one of our most precious children and we want her back," he continued. "We want you to convince the DSL to give her back."

"Why me?" I asked.

"Fyodor Chandler is involved," he said, watching

me.

I didn't flinch. I'd trained myself not to flinch or think about Fyodor Chandler. "Fyodor Chandler is dead."

"No, he's not, he's in Lincoln Heights," he said. "Get us the girl, and we'll let him live."

"I have no idea how to find him," I said, keeping my voice steady.

"Your file says that once you have an objective, you focus on it to the point of monomania," he said coolly. "Now that you know he's alive and where he is, you'll find him, if only to kill him yourself. We don't care, we just want the girl."

I didn't say anything. He was staring too hard at me. I thought if I opened my mouth, he'd try to grab my tongue.

"Tell me, Nellie, do you think this Orcinus guy got it right about the transmitters?" he asked, waving the pamphlet at me.

"Yes and no."

"Oh? Tell me."

"Yes, the conservative radio people and journalists were getting their lines from the extreme right, fascists, if you will, but the white trash militias and the Christanists were never the real danger because they had no real power, just rage and the ability to kill a varying number of people. As we know, they were the first ones to volunteer to be inoculated and were the first sacrificed."

"And, what do you think was the real danger?"

"People who'd been in the top one percent income bracket for more than two generations, isolated by their wealth and out of touch with this country," I said. "The danger was always that the rich would use whatever means to seize power and use it to get what they wanted."

"Which was?"

"Everything. And what they didn't want, or couldn't understand, or were afraid of, they threw away. Like Los Angeles."

"And why do you think we, I mean, they did that?" he asked, deadpan.

"Because you, I mean, they had, by normal standards, everything, but it was not enough and you, I mean, they would do anything to make sure you, I mean, they, kept it," I said.

"And we, I mean, they, have succeeded magnificently!" He slapped his thigh with the pamphlet. "Mission accomplished, one could say, with a caveat or two."

I thought about the last guy who said that and it wasn't true then either. The war on everything exploded, hundreds of thousands had died, were still dying, and it still wasn't even close to over yet. But I kept my mouth shut. This wasn't the right time to make sense.

"I wonder, Nellie, as a historian, what do you admire about the Third Reich?" he asked.

I've been asked this question before, but never with so many guns on me. "That they lost."

"Oh, I agree," he said, nodding. "A complete waste. Either win conclusively or annihilate everything when you go, that's the ticket."

I thought about asking him what the Ulluminati's policy on that was, but the moment passed. He took out a lighter and set the pamphlet on fire.

"You're not supposed to have this," he said, waving it closer and closer to my head.

It occurred to me that I'd just download another one and print it out. Someone always had one online somewhere. But this was not my biggest worry after he singed off half my hair. "I'm going to have a tough time finding your girl with my head on fire, Rush," I said, gritting my teeth and patting out the sparks.

"Eh," he said, tossing the still burning pages into the sink. "It's a new look for you."

Heine once observed that "where one burns books, one in the end burns men". I didn't know if this applied to pamphlets and female PIs, but it seemed apt for the moment.

"Rush" handed me a PDA and told me all his contact points were in it. It was secure and wireless. I was impressed until I noticed the "Heche en Mexico" on the back and wondered who he had killed to get this.

"The clock is running, Nellie," he said, brushing past me.

I asked what the job paid.

"It's a living wage," he said on his way out. "You get to live."

Ba dum bum bum. Asshole.

I ran some water over my head, just to be sure my hair was completely out. I put the three heads in a garbage bag and took them downstairs. I figured I'd put them where the scavengers would find them when they came out right before dawn, which was the best time to be locked in your own cage around here. On my way by, the fruitas guy waved me over and asked about my new look.

"My latest visitor set my hair on fire."

"Just the right side?"

"So far." One of the Limo Brothers' kids—I never knew which kid belonged to which brother, it was such a flock—came over and damn politely asked me if he could be of any assistance. Actually said:

"Excuse me, Miss Gail, may we be of any assistance tonight?"

"It's slim pickin's, kid, all I got is these three heads," I said, holding the bag open.

He said they'd find something to do with them and thanked me. Then he looked at my hair and asked if I wanted his sister to cut the rest of it off because they could use it, too.

I almost asked what for, but I just didn't want to know, so I said sure. A nice little teenage girl came over with the biggest pair of shears I'd ever seen and cut my hair so it was about an inch all over my head. At least it would be easy to take care of until it grew out again. If I lived that long.

A week ago, my life was simple, boring and predictable. I brooded away the rest of the afternoon and was no closer to having any idea of what was going on now or why I was in the middle of it. Nevertheless, I figured I better shake a tailfeather and get my ass down to Lincoln Heights. Due to the condition it and I were in, I thought I'd dress for trouble. I don't worry about fashion much, give me a ti-tandex miniskirt, a tank top and a leather jacket coated with titanium guard, and I'm all set. Titanium guard is a spray that makes whatever it's used on fire-proof, water-proof, puncture-proof, and scratch-proof. This jacket had saved me several times and it still looked like new. I would have to see if there was some kind of titanium guard for my hair, or what was left of it. I surely could have used it this afternoon.

So I put on my snakeskin patterned ti-tandex body suit. It was the finest fusion of support hose and body armor technology and the height of fashion in

Mexico City last year. I could slide under a truck on broken glass in it and come out without a scratch. I added a black mini skirt and a sleeveless turtleneck for modesty. I always wore my leather jacket and Capezio boots because they were lightweight, quiet, and fast. The soles had a lot of bounce in them, but also a lot of punch. They were flexible on the inside, but, based on the number of chests I'd jumped on in them, chest-crushingly hard on the outside. I also knew this because I dropped one on my own foot once, and limped for days afterwards. I had no idea what they were made of or where they came from, maybe France, because though they were chic, it was not in the Mexico City style. I got them from a kiosk on my way to work one morning.

No stealth outfit was complete without a black ski mask. They were standard issue from the Company, even though no one in the US skied anymore. I did interrogations in this ski mask, too, I thought it was lucky for me. I'd need luck tonight because I didn't have a clue and probably not a prayer, but I was going to Lincoln Heights anyway.

The final touch was my Infra-RayBans. They were a little clunky, but there were no street lamps where I was going, so I'd need them. On my way out, I caught sight of myself in a dark window—I had achieved a look somewhere between Acquanetta the Eel Woman and a horse fly. It was perfect and I hopped on my Electrocatti with a lighter heart. As Kierkegaard said, a woman in fashion fears neither man nor God because She Is In Fashion. I wish it could all be so simple that he could be right. Though he's useless for someone like me, I rather like Kierkegaard.

But all the philosophy I need is at the end of a gun. I'm no good with a knife, so it has to be a gun.

However, I did have several knives and I strapped them in easy to reach places, just in case I needed to reach them easily. I had all my guns with me, a pocket full of speed-loaders for the Colt and several magazines each for the Beretta and the Mauser. Considering I had no fucking idea what I'd do at County when I got there, I felt reassuringly well-prepared.

Lincoln Heights had once been a thriving, mostly Hispanic and Asian community. They all had jobs, and many had small businesses and employees. They sent their children to Lincoln High or Sacred Heart and put "Proud Parent" bumper stickers on their cars. Their children went to East LA College or Pasadena City College and then got Bachelors degrees from Cal State LA or Cal State Long Beach and the next generation could live a bit better than the previous one. They made progress for themselves, small, careful, measured steps toward the life they wanted. There were no get-rich-quick schemes in Lincoln Heights, there were no blazing superstars; it was the land of hopeful realists. And they did have hope, they had it by the yard, but now all they had was rubble.

The people of Lincoln Heights, and Boyle Heights, too, would not accept the occupation and so they fought back. Many of them had lived in Asia and Central America, so they knew, better than the rest of us, what was going to happen. They knew soldiers in the streets are never a temporary condition, but herald a profound change for everyone. They had seen it all before and this was their stand, their last stand, because it's better to die on your feet than live on your knees.

And they lost. The battles raged from Figueroa in Highland Park all the way south to the 60 freeway. The final siege was at the County/USC Medical School and

Hospital complex. It was one of the places the community was most proud of and they defended it to the last man, woman and child. County Hospital was built after World War I, when steel was plentiful, and so it withstood most of the ground assault. The aerial bombing and tank assaults finished it off, more or less; it still rose above the rubble on the rise it had always been on. It was where the poor had always taken refuge; it was where doctors cared for everyone without prejudice and loved healing the sick; it was where researchers toiled for better patient care and the advancement of science; and when it fell, it ripped the heart out of eastern Los Angeles.

I had watched the fireworks from Dodger Stadium between interrogations and felt nothing. My heroes were dead before I was born. Poland had fought and been savaged and I knew Los Angeles didn't have a chance in hell. Our own government had turned the greatest military in the world on their own people. Without the ideals our country was founded on, we were all dead, even the living. The American experiment was over. We could only be slaves now.

Those of us who truly understood that did various things. Some were suicide bombers, some just killed themselves, and a few became freelance assassins or snipers. What armed and organized resistance there was was put down fairly quickly. Many of us shut off our consciences and worked for the government in one capacity or another. I had a particularly nasty, but rewarding (for me) government job until I was put on disciplinary leave. Quite a large number went underground as the DSL and got to Mexico.

But Lincoln Heights had fought and been crushed. And, unlike the Warsaw Ghetto, Los Angeles did not pave over the scene of this rebellion. So the streets were still a wreck. But nature doesn't philosophize, it just sends up saplings in the bombed out streets and grass shoots in the shattered pavements.

I'd picked up a tail on Sunset and was looking over my shoulder to make sure I'd lost it when I got smacked in the face—by a tree. A sapling, to be exact, but it still smarted and worse, rattled me because I should have seen it. Well, it was just a tree, and a little one at that; I left it behind me.

It was very dark in Lincoln Heights. DWP had restored the power citywide, but they never repaired the street lighting in this part of town. If anyone was in these mashed buildings, they had their lights off or blacked-out from the street. I didn't blame them; light meant people and in this part of town, people meant food.

The silence around the rubble of County Hospital is very creepy. There was nothing there to make noise anymore, and even the light breeze had nothing to rustle or make sigh. I cut the scooter's quiet motor and coasted into what looked like the remains of a parking garage, looking for the darkest corner to stash my scooter, preferably behind some rubble. I shot two scavengers crouching there and looked around for more. There weren't any; I had heard that the County complex was no man's land, even for the scavengers. They might pass through it, but it was no one's territory. That was the rumor, and I never knew if or how it was true. But the bright spot was the recharger station glowing in the darkness. I walked my scooter over to it and plugged in. God bless the DWP. I set the scooter defense system and left it charging behind a mound of concrete and steel rebar.

I paused to get my bearings. It would truly wreck my night if I couldn't remember where I parked my scooter. I moved through the rubble as quietly as possible. If the DSL and Fyodor really were here, where would they be? Fyodor had been pretty crazy the last time I tried to talk to him. If he was crazier now, it made sense that he'd be here in this hell, and might be anywhere. If it were me, I'd hole up in the ruins of the hospital itself. It looked like there were lots of places to hide and lots of exits. And lots of places for an ambush. I stayed in the shadows and considered the choices before me on Zonal Street: County Hospital on the west side, USC Med School on the east.

On a whim, I swung east and up through the Med School. Fyodor had been a library freak once and might still be, and there had been a big one called Norris up there. I wound my way up the small rise and into what was left of the main plaza.

There wasn't much left of Norris. The south side of the first and second stories had pretty much been crushed, as if a big fist had decided to make the rectangle into a triangle. I had lots of cover up there and was able to circle the library, looking for a way in.

Movement on my left caught my eye and I froze into the shadows again. Had it seen me? No... scavengers weren't stalkers, they were chasers. But I wasn't sure this was a scavenger, since it seemed to be looking for something. For me? Would someone be crazy enough to tail me here? It couldn't be the tail I shook on Sunset. I was sure I'd lost them.

For the moment, I was stuck. I had my back to Norris Library and I was facing what was left of the Cancer Hospital. I wondered if I could outwait whatever was out there. Dawn was only a few hours away and the scavengers would find places to hide during the daylight hours. I also needed a better, if only more comfortable, vantage point. The Cancer Hospital seemed like a more likely spot. I skulked across the small space between the buildings, using a burned-out SUV for cover. I tiptoed along the wall, looking for a way in. I wanted to get to the second floor for a better view. I found a promising break in the rubble and went in.

There was the occasional stairwell or undamaged hallway for me to use, but there was also a lot of climbing over things. I wasn't sure what floor I got to, but I finally found a view of the plaza I liked. I adjusted my weapons and got comfortable.

There was someone out there, looking for something, and not randomly. They were tracing my steps, more or less, as if they could guess what I'd do. Well, I was doing what a sane person would do and in this insane place, there weren't many options. My stalker slipped into the shadows again, flashed out and disappeared behind the SUV below my aerie. I saw the figure come forward, just enough, to see me if it looked up. I drew away from the ledge, even though I knew, black ski mask et al., that I was invisible. Unless those things on its face were night goggles. I stopped breathing. Scavengers don't have night goggles. Who the fuck was down there?

I drew my Mauser and put the silencer on it. I figured I'd better scope out my line of retreat before I fired, just in case whoever that was had a partner. I wandered down a hallway and turned a corner.

I smelled them before I saw them and would have made tracks if the floor hadn't given under me. I slid down in a shower of linoleum and ceiling tile, right into a convention of scavengers. There was a hallway at my back, which I hoped to God didn't lead into another group of monsters. I ran. They chased me.

I could hear them falling over things behind me. If I could find my way out, I might be able to out-run them, simply because I could see what not to fall over. I still stumbled over broken furniture and decaying bodies. I clambered down a stairway and into another hallway, a long one. I could see double doors at the end, and I hoped they were open.

They weren't. I pulled my Colt and shot the lock, but the doors still held. I turned and emptied it into the mob in the hallway. Falling over the dead slowed them but didn't stop them. I got my Mauser and Beretta out and fired for all I was worth. There were too many and I wasn't willing to be torn apart. I figured I had one shot left in the Beretta. I put it to my head and pulled the trigger.

I can't even fucking count anymore.

I raised the empty guns to bash a few heads before I went. It wouldn't do any good but it would make me feel better.

At that moment, the doors opened behind me and I fell on my ass. I was looking up at three guys firing reloadable riot guns into the scavengers. Empty shells fell around me as the cartridge belts jitterbugged through the guns. There was a lot of screaming, and some of it might have been mine. One of the guys hauled me back a few feet and the others slammed the doors. They shoved buttresses against them. I figured this was why blowing the lock off hadn't worked. They pointed their guns at me. They were all wearing night goggles.

"Let's go, Nellie."

I got to my feet and handed over my guns when I was asked to. I was getting a lot of practice at this. We proceeded down the hall, one of them in front and two behind me. We were very quiet and they seemed relieved when we were out of the building. They herded me across the plaza, over Zonal and into the County Hospital complex. I caught flashes of movement in the ruins around us, but my escort seemed okay with it, so why should I worry?

We went into the ruins of a building behind County and into a biggish, dimly lit room—might have been a conference room once, it had a table half buried in the shadows to prove it. I had my hand on my knife. If this was rape, I'd hurt them as much as I could. I leapt back and got my back to the wall, knife out and looking like I might know what to do with it.

But they didn't attack. In fact they let their gun barrels point at the floor instead of at me.

"Who the fuck are you guys?" I snarled. I hate small talk.

"I'm with the DWP," a muscular guy dressed in khakis and a work shirt said.

"I'm with the Chinatown Defense League," an Asian guy all in black said.

"And you?" I practically yelled at a tall, dark guy slouched against the door.

"Hollenbeck."

Representatives of the doomed police department, the DWP and the CDL. I was in the room with what passed for civilization in Los Angeles. And they were all looking at the far end of the conference table. I figured there must be something to see there. There was. And he looked just like he did on "Live, Nude Economics".

"Hello, Max," I said, putting away my knife and pulling up a chair. "I heard you were dead," I added, pulling off my Infra-RayBans and ski mask.

"Not dead, Nell. Not even resting," he said pleasantly, leaning forward so I could see his shaggy grey head and tanned, craggy features. "I've been south of the border."

"What brings you to Los Angeles?" I asked.

"Fyodor Chandler."

"He's dead."

"Oh, he's very much alive and causing as much trouble as ever," Max said, folding his hands on the table. "Who else could bring the Company, the IIA, and the Ulluminati down on the City of Angels?"

"Somebody named Sara Lee?"

"She's just a pawn."

"And Millie?"

"Just a tool."

I decided I didn't even want to know what was going on. "Well, Max, it was great to meet you in person at last," I said, getting to my feet.

The men by the door raised their guns.

"Sit down, Nell," Max said softly. "I need you."

"Why me?"

"Because you're in the middle of this. You're the center of attention, the star of the show," he said with some heat.

"Oh, yeah? How'm I doing?"

"Don't quit your day job," he said. "You're my best shot at solving what's become my worst problem."

"Then you're way fucked, Max," I said, tipping my chair back. "Because I can't find Sara Lee James or this Millie kid. And if they're here, and my evening so far is any indication, somebody has eaten them by now."

"I know where they are," he said. "And of course you would pick the wrong side of the street. This side, County Hospital, is controlled by the DSL. The Med school side is all scavengers."

It figured. "Where do I fit in?" I asked.

"I need you to convince Fyodor Chandler to bring his people to Mexico with me."

"Why?"

"Fyodor Chandler was one of the most brilliant minds the Company ever recruited. Anything he planned went off without a hitch. He made all you agents look good, real good. And when he vanished or, as you thought, was murdered, mission risk went through the ceiling. It was a lucky break for us. Keeping you people on the hop gave the DSL a chance to get most of their people to Mexico. Especially the economists; can't do anything without economists these days," Max said. "Fyodor is still a genius, Nell. Crazy as a loon, but still one of the best minds in the country," he added.

"That's not saying much, Max, all the best minds are in Mexico now. Or dead."

He ignored me and continued, "Fyodor is leading an army of healthy, educated people into harm's way. And I'm here, not to stop them, but to divert them to where their skills can be put to more constructive uses. In Mexico City."

"Ah! Mexico, how wonderful. And why do you think he'll listen to me?"

"He loves you," Max said. "Even though you probably want to kill him for leaving you."

I let that pass. "How do Sara Lee and Millie fit into all this?"

"Sara Lee kidnapped Millie from the White House

and brought her to the DSL here in LA. James really was just trying to find his daughter."

"Who's Millie?"

Max looked uncomfortable. "She's the bastard love child of Arnold Schwarzenegger and Jenna Bush."

This was no mean feat. Schwarzenegger had been dead for eight years and Jenna Bush in an alcoholic coma for six. "How old is this kid?"

"She's four." He held up a hand to stop my obvious question. "She was cloned."

"That's illegal."

"The Bush family considers itself above the law."

"But why do it?"

"As you know, this country's current leadership has no imagination whatsoever," he said, pedantically. "They want to rule dynastically and this is the best they could do. To us, it's pathetic, but after they installed Schwarzenegger as governor, he grew in their minds as the next president."

"I thought you had to be born here to..."

"To be elected, yes, but the Bush gang doesn't bother with elections or laws, my dear."

"How did Sara grab her?" I asked, my opinion of James' little girl rising slightly.

"She was helping Donald Monroe in the White House," Max said.

"Doing what?"

"Millie can't speak, so the Bushes brought Monroe in to teach her."

I didn't even ask why anyone would hire a theoretical linguist to work as a speech therapist, but it was typical wrongheaded Bush family wastefulness.

"And when Monroe saw the disaster the Bushes had planned, he freaked and ran to the renegade MIT linguists. Led the IIA to them, in fact, which is a shame because they were on their way here," he continued. "Some of them made it. Sara was able to hook up with them and she had Millie with her."

"Revenge?"

"Not really, I think the thought of having another gibbering idiot Bush as President for life was too much for her," he said. "The one we've got has finally gone over the edge. That's why we have an actor delivering Presidential addresses. Things are bad, Nellie. When the whip comes down, we can only hope the military will side with us."

"What military, Max? They're all stuck in third world countries getting their asses shot off over nothing," I said. "You better get your invasion trip together before Canada or the French Foreign Legion beats you to it." I sighed heavily. "So, okay, like, who the fuck are the Ulluminati in all this?"

"Second-tier nouveau riche posers," he scoffed. "They think if they return the heir, the Bush family will cut them in on the action. The problem is, things have gone so far into hell outside of California that the Bush family can barely hold onto the power they have and there is no action to cut anyone into. We're waiting for the right moment to invade and retake the United States, but we need Los Angeles to stay stable until we do. This will be a major base for us. But not if Fyodor leads a rebellion that will bring in Federal action."

"How did you know I was involved?"

"James was quiet about it, but the IIA and the Ulluminati make a lot of noise wherever they go," he said. "God knows who else knows they're here and why."

"MI6? KGB?"

"WTO, IMF, RIAA. Maybe worse than that."

I wondered what could be worse than the RIAA, but really didn't want to know. "What a fucking mess." I scowled. "All right, I'll convince Fyodor go with you. But in return, I want this Millie kid. I'll need her to buy some time and save my life."

"I don't care what you do with her," Max growled. "The IIA and the Ulluminati have a small army in LA for this."

"And you want me to take them out?" I asked, wondering how much C-4 I could get out of this.

"No, I want Fyodor Chandler and his people." Max waved at the guys with guns by the door. "Your city wants you to take out the IIA and Illuminati as a warning to others."

"All by myself?" I asked, wondering how much C-4 and House Special Chow Mein I could get out of this.

"We had some thoughts on that," the DWP guy said softly.

He outlined a plan. I told him it stank and outlined a better one.

"I always knew you were good for something, Nell," Max said, impressed.

I also had a list of demands, all of which I thought were doable if I was going to risk my life for... for whatever all this was about. I got nods, which I took as a good sign.

"Okay, where's Fyodor?" I asked.

The DWP guy said he'd show me the way. He led me out and over to the ruins of the hospital and then underground.

"How do you know Max?" he asked.

"From the Internet," I said.

Paulo from the parking garage stepped into our path and I didn't have a half a sandwich for him.

"He takes you from here," the DWP guy said. "I'll be here when you get back."

I followed Paulo down the hall. We didn't speak, but he kept shooting nervous glances at me. For myself, I was trying to think of what I'd ask him. I once did interrogations, but usually with people I'd studied enough to interrogate. I also don't cope well with surprises — at least, not the ones I can't shoot.

We passed through several rooms full of weapons, including anti-tank guns, mortars, and bazookas. Even I was impressed by the stash, but also knew it wouldn't last five minutes against the IIA, let alone the hired guns of the RIAA. Fool, Fyodor, always a mad, dreaming fool!

Paulo rapped softly on a door and was told to come in. We stepped into a dark room with a circle of light around a man at a computer. He looked up at me.

"Hello, Alison."

What heart I have beat a little faster. "Heya, Larry." I walked over and put my arms around him. He nearly crushed my ribs returning the embrace. "Long time," I said, trying very hard not to cry.

He wasn't even trying not to cry. "Yeah, well, I've been busy..."

"Yeah, me, too..." We stood there crying like idiots for a few moments before my innate professionalism kicked back in. "Larry, listen, I seriously have to talk to you."

"I don't want to go to Mexico, Al."

"I know, I know, we both scored high on the self-destruction scale," I said, referring to our Company employment tests. "But it's not just you, is it? It's you and a bunch of people depending on you."

"They understand."

"That they're going to die for nothing, when they could live to liberate their country?"

This got his attention. "Like... how?"

I ran it down for him: exile in Mexico until the invasion, rest, training, recovery, planning, and best of all—logistics! "You could be like Moses, Larry."

"With Curly and Shemp?"

"No, I said Moses, Larry, not Moe." I scored really low on the humor scale so even when I got the joke, it wasn't funny.

"I'm not a coward."

I dredged up a line from some crappy novel I read long ago: "Sometimes living takes more guts than dying." I heard Paulo sniffle behind me. At least I was making progress with one of them. I started to pace to clear my head. "Look, Larry, the world needs brains right now, yours mainly. As fucked up as LA is, as we are, there is a better life out there, for you and your people, in Mexico. I don't make the rules, Larry, here I've found you again when I'd given up all hope, and I've got to send you away from me. But there are just some things that are bigger than you and me and this whole crazy mess we call life. So, please, just fucking go to Mexico with Max. Please? Do it for who we used to be, how we used to be, long ago, and once upon a time."

Now Larry was sniffling. He looked past me at Paulo, who stepped forward and put his arms around him. Hm, Larry must be batting for the other team now. Anyway, they murmured at each other for a little while (I was too polite to overhear), and eventually Larry looked up at me and said one word:

"Okay."

"There is one little detail," I said, feeling three hundred years old.

"What?"

"Millie."

When we were done working the details out, Paulo walked me back down the hall. I stopped in the weapons room and suggested he give this stuff to the DWP guy since he and Larry wouldn't be using it.

He thought that was a great idea. He turned to go, but I stood still. "How long have you been in charge, Paulo?"

"Only on his bad days," he said, not looking at me. "Which are many. I think he'll be okay in Mexico, once the pressure is off." He looked up at me, almost defiantly. "He still loves you, and when we came to LA, he asked me to keep an eye on you."

"I'm glad he has you," I said quietly.

"Even though I've... I've taken your place?" he asked, probably expecting me to kill him.

This puzzled me, so I had to ask, "As his sister?"

Paulo's jaw hit the floor. "You're his sister?"

I nodded, wondering just how much these guys talked to each other. Oh well. Love—it's wonderful. "Let's go, kid."

He led me back to the DWP guy and we three had a long talk with Max and the CDL rep. The Hollenbeck police officer had business elsewhere keeping order, because there was no law. We adjusted my original, and brilliant, plan to fit a few new wrinkles and left on fairly good terms. As good as people who wished they'd never met and hope never to see each other again can part.

I said good-night, but Max had a parting shot.

"Dr. Krugman sends his regards," he said. "He

knows you got the right picture."

"No, I got the wrong one," I said. "That's my story and I'm sticking to it."

The DWP guy walked me back to my scooter, which was not only still there, but all charged up. Rather amazing, because there was a charred body next to it. Obviously the burned body does learn the quickest.

"I'm going to need a heavier, faster ride," I said, unplugging the Electrocatti.

"A Harley?" he asked.

"Too heavy. A Suzuki or Honda will do fine. More guns, too. Like those flat, lightweight flexible machine guns."

He said he'd see what he could do.

I said he should bring them to my office at six tomorrow afternoon.

He said okay and vanished into the shadows.

When I got home, I put my ride away and I stopped by the fruitas guy for some carrot juice. He told me I had company in my place again.

I didn't ask who because he would have told me if he knew. So I just stood there, thinking it over while I finished my carrot juice because I hate having my juice drinking interrupted. I also wanted to see if they'd send anyone after me. They did not, so we must have all night for whatever it was they wanted. I tossed my empty cup and went up to my place.

"Hi Rush, who's your friend?" I asked as two guys frisked me. They left my body suit and boots on, but that was it.

"My name," the guy rasped. "Is Kevin."

He had a hatchet face and no lips. I found this fascinating and repulsive. He also had my copy of

Borowski's *This Way For the Gas, Ladies and Gentlemen* and I wished these guys would stay the fuck out of my bookcase. I hadn't read it yet, and didn't want anyone pawing it, breaking the spine, or setting it on fire.

"I like your new look, Nellie," Rush simpered. "Any luck tonight?"

"Maybe."

"We would have come down and helped you look, but you didn't take the PDA I gave you," he said, pouting. "No way to trace you."

Lazy bastards. "I couldn't wear another thing, Rush, or my spine would have telescoped from the weight of it all," I said. "What's your interest here, Kevin?"

"Fyodor Chandler," he said, stroking the spine of my book.

"He's dead."

"He's in Lincoln Heights with an army of linguists and other such overeducated types," Kevin said quietly. "Find Millie, you find him."

"What makes you think I can find either of them?" I asked.

"You've been gone for hours, Nellie, you must have found something," Rush said. He sounded cranky, but he was looking nervously at Kevin, like he was afraid of him. That made Kevin very interesting.

"Lincoln Heights is a big place," I said, watching Kevin's face. I wondered if his voice was fucked up from a blow or poison.

The corners of his lipless mouth turned up in what on anyone else might be a bemused smile. On him it was just ghastly. "Tell me, Miss Gail," he said, oh so casually. "What's your opinion of Hermann Goering?"

I love this question. "I think he picked the wrong

side when he had the choice," I said, and decided to trot out a hypothesis I'd had no one to bounce off. "Yes, picked the wrong side. The same as the late General Powell did. Tell me something, Kevin, was Powell really a suicide? He didn't seem like that kind of guy."

"I wouldn't know, Miss Gail, I'm not in that department." He looked bored.

"And what department of what are you in?" I asked.

"Logistics and operations for the Internal Intelligence Agency. I'm picking up where Glenn and his people left off."

"You know Glenn offered me a million for Millie," I said. "Is that still a deal?"

"Yes and no," he said. "I'm after Fyodor Chandler. Give him to me and I'll give you your million and a job in the IIA."

I tried not to show how much this interested me. "What kind of a job?"

"Whatever kind you'd like," he said. "Something you'd be good at, I'm sure. You see, Miss Gail, we in the IIA frown upon wasted talent. And you scored very high in areas in which we can always use another pair of hands."

I mentioned a few other things I'd like, many of the same things I'd asked for earlier in the evening, and Kevin found all of them possible, including the new weapons I wanted. He had Rush send a guy down to get an assortment for me to choose from.

I picked out two lightweight machine guns, a reloading riot gun, a poison-dart derringer, a switchblade, a stiletto, and a crossbow with exploding tips on the bolts. I've always wanted a cross-bow. I told them to meet me at County Hospital the next night at nine. I'd at least have Millie for them.

"And Chandler?" Kevin asked, smiling his creepy smile again, holding my book out to me.

"If dead men walk," I said, smiling my own creepy smile and tucking my book under my arm. "Perhaps."

"Miss Gail, while I have you," he said, still smiling. "What do you consider the main failing of the Third Reich?"

"That their reach exceeded their grasp."

We smiled a little longer and then they left. Not a moment too soon. Smiling wears me out. I also had a lot to think about.

I am a historian of genocide, and because of it, everyone assumes I know a lot about the Third Reich. I know as much as I needed to know to understand how they committed genocide, but not why. I understood the how of all the genocides I'd studied, from Buchenwald, to Eastern Turkey, to Rwanda, to Siberia, to Nanking, to the Great Plains of our own Manifest Destiny, but to this day I don't understand why people kill on that level. I understand why individuals kill each other, but organized, systematic killing puzzles me. Why take all the fun and spontaneity out of it? It was also a waste of time and resources. Especially when, with the slightest effort, the despised can be co-opted into their own destruction, à la voluntarily getting the Ebola pox inoculation and voting Republican.

Everyone I'd met lately from the United States of the Bush Family seemed to think the Bushes were the new Nazis. I thought not. They were in a class of their own: they were decayers more than destroyers. One needed ideology to be a Nazi, and the Bush Family only had a smash-and-grab mentality, no matter how much gloss they tried to put on it. The Bush Family and their minions poisoned everything they could not exploit. It was wasteful, but effective, very effective, and it might be effective longer than Max wanted to believe.

I don't mind being on the wrong side of history as long as I'm alive to be on any side of anything. But at that moment, I was tired, and just wanted to be lulled to sleep with Borowski's account of Auschwitz. I don't get nightmares. I don't need them.

I went to work the next morning. My late boss' secretary complimented me on my new look and handed me his phone messages to return. I made short work of them. If it was this easy being the boss, I should have tried it years ago.

After lunch, the COO of Universal Insurance called to ask why the building was being transferred into my name. I said I won it gambling and we proceeded to work out a rent deal. He seemed pleased; I think I should have charged more but it was only a year deal so I could raise it then. If I'm still alive.

I briefly wondered which organization had transferred the building to me and why they did it that day instead of the next. It would not matter by tomorrow, since we could all be dead by then. And the building was only mine as long as I could keep it. There was no rule of law here, so ownership was a very fluid idea in LA. However, it you had enough fire-power, you could firm it up a little.

At six I went downstairs to the parking garage. I didn't see Paulo, but I didn't expect to see Paulo there that evening. I was looking for another man altogether and there he was, right on time. Reliable, dependable, tall, dark, handsome... and thoughtful!

The DWP guy had won my heart forever. He'd

given my mission some thought and brought me a BMW all-terrain combat motorcycle. I'd always wanted one, but who can afford the gas? It had a full tank, which would get me through the evening and then some, I hoped.

He also had weapons for me: Two lightweight flex machine guns. Nearly flat, they molded to my back and swung out under my jacket, just like they should. One gun shot needles coated with a fast acting poison and the other exploding plastic bullets. They were honeys and I'd always wanted a pair just like them.

I smiled up at the bearer of such swell gifts. He handed me a half a dozen magazines for each gun and the keys to the motorcycle.

"Don't cross us up, Nellie," he said quietly.

In a better world he would have clamped his lips on mine for luck. But we do not live in a better world; we live in a crappy, fucked up world, so he just left.

I went upstairs to watch some IB before I changed into my work clothes and headed for County Hospital.

It was quiet as usual when I got to the rendezvous. I cut the engine and rolled my new ride into the rubble and parked it near the ammo room I was in last night. I waited. It crossed my mind that this would be a good place for an ambush, but I thought I knew who I was dealing with.

A haggard blond girl moved silently out of the shadows. She looked starved and stressed, but grim and determined, and was carrying a trussed up toddler.

"Why is there duct tape on her mouth?" I asked. "I thought she couldn't speak."

"She makes noise," the blond told me. She dumped the toddler on the floor, but kept hold of the strap handle on the kid's back. "I'm Sara Lee."

"Why did they send you?"

"I asked for it," she said, adjusting the machine gun on her back (mine were cooler). "I started this, I'll finish it."

"You're very brave," I said. 'And extra stupid,' I thought.

We jumped slightly when the DWP guy stepped from the shadows. Sara was shaking, but I was too polite to mention it. "I assume the DSL is gone," I said.

"Before dawn, as planned," he said. "Their ships docked in Mexico hours ago." He went into the now mostly empty ammo room and came out with a rocket launcher. It looked good on him.

So Fyodor was safe. I couldn't get too worked up about it; I had quite a night ahead of me yet.

I heard them first. But that was because I knew to listen for the low hum of a window air conditioner. Sara and the DWP guy tensed up at the sound of gasoline engines, big ones, and tires crunching over the rubble outside.

"Well, it was swell, guys," I said, and picked up Millie like an overnight bag.

Rush was standing in a knot of men several yards from the entrance of the rubble. They were flanked by a dozen black Humvees, and six black helicopters hung overhead. There was enough machine noise to repel the scavengers, but also to cover the approach of anyone else. He looked glad to see me, or maybe it was Millie he was smiling at. I stopped halfway between him and the rubble tunnel.

"Good work, Nellie!" Rush said, and laughed his creepy laugh. "Hand her over."

"This is quite a crowd to pick up one little girl, Rush," I said, not moving.

"We're here for Fyodor, too," he said, glancing nervously over at Kevin, who was sitting in a Humvee.

"He's not here," I said.

"Then you're dead," Kevin said, picking up a machine gun and getting out of the vehicle.

"Give me the girl!" Rush yelled, stepping in front of Kevin.

"How about Sara Lee?" I said. I was swinging Millie gently with my right arm. My strong right arm.

"Fuck her!" Kevin yelled, pushing Rush aside.

"FUCK YOU!" Sara screamed behind me and started firing.

"Here's the girl!" I yelled and flung her with all my might into Kevin's chest.

I hit the ground. I heard more than saw reinforcements firing into the Ulluminati and IIA guys. Between weapon blasts, there were war cries of "HOLLENBECK!", "DWP!", "CDL!", and a few "VIVA LOS ANGELES!"—I had no idea who that might be. I, on the other hand, was crawling under Sara Lee's covering fire and back into the rubble tunnel. The last I saw of her, she was shoving another magazine into her gun, but I don't know what happened to her after that.

I ran back to my BMW. The DWP guy was still there meditating on his rocket launcher. "You gotta blast me a hole through them," I told him. I started my ride and rolled along behind him. He got to the tunnel mouth and fired into the center of the Humvees. One of them exploded.

That was all the break I needed. Just as I roared past the DWP guy, I heard Kevin yell, "I WANT HER ALIVE!". 'He can dream on,' I thought, as I powered it down to what was left of Zonal and north to Griffin. I heard the Humvees coming after me. They could try, but the fucked-up roads would slow them down. The helicopters were another kind of problem. I had a machine gun out and was firing at the one nearest me. But it was useless at that range. I ran the bike close to collapsing buildings, under power lines, wherever I could to slow down the Humvees and keep the helicopters at bay. It was working until I hit an open stretch at Five Points.

I gunned the bike up Pasadena Avenue to the 110 Freeway. There hadn't always been a way onto the freeway on Pasadena, but I roared down the collapsed overpass. The freeway was a mess of rubble and downed trees. My BMW combat motorcycle was up to it, but the Humvees were having a bad time. However, they were shooting at me and this was annoying. One of them got alongside me and I fired poison needles into the passenger side window. It swerved and crashed. I was more concerned with the helicopters. I managed to lure one into some power lines. Another one got its rotor too close to the old Gold Line tracks and crashed. Nearly on top of me, but I guess the freeway gods were with me that night. I still had copters overhead and Humvees behind. There was one less Humvee, however, when one of them overturned on a boulder of pavement.

I swung off the road and into the arroyo. It was dark, but my Infra-RayBans let me see what I needed to see. I shot past a park and then another one and into what had once been a golf course. There was a lot of clunking noise as I raced past the rocket launchers, bazookas, and anti-aircraft guns; all compliments of my big brother, Larry. They blasted the remaining helicopters out of the sky and the Humvees into tiny, bloody bits.

It was just as I had planned last night with Max. I

didn't need to see it. I couldn't be bothered to look back. I knew what was happening. Carnage looks the same wherever and whenever.

However, I was hungry. I can never eat before these missions. I decided to cruise on over to Glendale and grab a bite before I went home.

I like these all-night kabob places. It seems nuts to be open like that, but I figured these Glendale Armenians must know what they're doing. They're the penultimate survivors and probably had more fire-power behind the counter than I'd seen in my life. I'd also heard they had the floors wired to electrocute anyone on the wrong side of the counter. Way smart, if you ask me.

If the kid at the register didn't know me, he'd probably have flipped the switch when I strolled in. I was blood- and mud-spattered and my hair was a complete mess.

"Evening, Miss Gail."

"Heya, kid. Falafel sandwich and a side of hummus to go." I nodded to the old guy reading an Armenian newspaper behind the counter. Glendale kept three dailies going: one in Western Armenian, one in Eastern Armenian, and an English/Western Armenian one. I noticed the bilingual one where the kid had been sitting.

When my falafel and hummus were bagged and paid for, I asked the kid behind the counter if he could translate for me. Then I asked the old man if he saw any similarities between the United States as it is now and the Armenian Genocide and also the Third Reich. This is what the kid translated to me:

"Of course, you idiot, bad ideas, fear, murder, and greed are the same always and everywhere, dumb shit."

I exercised my limited Western Armenian vocabulary. "Sh-nora-ha-ga-lu-chune", I said and split.

There was nothing in the LA Times zine about it the next day or ever. There's nothing in the LA Times zine but IB schedules and want ads, so I don't even know why I look at the front page. Because nothing usually happens in Lincoln Heights, or at least no one lives to tell the tale, it's as if nothing east of Interstate 5 even exists. Fine with me, since the message was not for publication; it was a private communication.

The Ulluminati probably wouldn't be back—they were small potatoes anyway—and the IIA would think twice before they tangled with the DWP again. For the moment the IIA would be scrambling to hold things together back east, if they could. I have no idea who survived last night. For all I know, we could have a gibbering toddler on the Presidential throne next week to replace the gibbering idiot we have now.

I didn't really care. I was alive, I owned the building, and I had moved my meager belongings into one of the more comfortable office suites on the third floor. I would ask the fruitas guy and the Limo Brothers if they wanted to rent the empty commercial space at street level. There was no place nearby to get carrot juice and this needed to be remedied.

Somebody had paid a million in the new currency into my bank account. I had no idea who to thank, but thought I'd spend part of it on some new clothes and books I'd been eyeing in the kiosks.

I figured my old Company job was really kaput, and the IIA was too fucked up even for me to consider working for, if they were nutty enough to ask me. The rest of the US could fall apart and based on rumor and what slipped through on the internet, it was rapidly falling apart. This did not interest me because a) I didn't care, b) there was nothing I could do about it anyway, and c) the DWP, CDL and Hollenbeck PD were doing a fine job of defending the city-state of Los Angeles from the barbarian invaders. I could foresee a peaceful and prosperous stretch ahead for the City of Angels, particularly in the area of trade relations with Mexico. There might even be a little infrastructure development in LA from our southern neighbor. And God knew we could use it.

As for me, I had plans for a kinder, gentler life for a while. Money in the bank, the building in my name, a doable day job, no worries on the horizon, the sun in the morning and the moon at night.

But the best part was the sign on the door:

"Nellie Gail Investigations, DWP Security Consultant"

I love LA.

The End of History at Sunset and Vine

"Laguna Woods has been dead a long time," I said over the mylar card with the Company's seal embossed on it. "Who are you?"

On the other side of my desk, the dye-job blonde with pneumatic tits smiled compassionately at me. "I've had this name for three years, Miss Gail," she said. "You know how the Company operates; someday there'll be another Nellie Gail, too."

'Not soon,' I thought, but I'm neither clairvoyant nor immortal. "What is it you want, Miss 'Woods'," I said. I was getting tired of looking at her. She had a Company job, or whatever was left of the Rumsfeld Stasi part of the CIA called the Company since his fatal car accident in a parked car, and she was wearing a cooler ti-tandex catsuit than I owned. She also had a nice fur coat slung over her shoulders in spite of the fact it was July in Los Angeles. I can only handle so much envy in one afternoon.

"Do call me Laguna," she cooed. "The Company would like to hire you to protect Chelsea Clinton when she arrives in Los Angeles." Laguna squared her shoulders (it looked painful) and got serious (which was painful for me). "I'm here to, ah, help you in any way I can."

I've been solo for a long time; I don't need help. And even if I did need help, I didn't need this twitchel's help. While I was pretending to think about what she'd just said, I took a long look at her. She was younger than she looked under all the paint and hairspray, maybe ten years younger than me. I decided to find out. "Who'd you vote for in the last election?" I asked.

She didn't blink. "I was six; too young to vote. Now about Miss Clinton..."

Hm, younger than I thought; I hate young people. "Honey, this is the first I've heard that Chelsea Clinton is coming to LA," I snapped. This was a lie; I'd had a bounty hunter named Abilene in my office earlier that day trying to hire me to kill Clinton when she arrived. He said he was working for the 700 Club. It was possible; the fundie Christians were more than willing to put aside their Christianity when it came to Clinton-hating.

"Is zat so? I suppose Abilene only wanted a tour of the stars' homes," Laguna snapped back.

This was getting way too snappish for me. I should have known that the Company, in its usual thoroughness, would have cased the joint before they sent an operative in. Even if it was one as expendable-looking as the new and unimproved Laguna Woods. "Miss Clinton would be a crazy woman to come here," I said flatly.

"If she was coming to lead the revolution..."

I lifted a hand to stop her. "Oh, please, if there was going to be a revolution, it would need brawn, not brains. Nothing against Miss Clinton, but if there was going to be a revolution, it would be fought for principles, not personalities."

"As a historian, don't you believe that history is made by individuals?" Laguna asked. This sounded almost intelligent and indicated she'd done her homework on me, which, while flattering, was a little unnerving.

"As a historian who never finished her degree because the Company recruited her," I said slowly, "I would say that history is made by individuals in pursuit of ideas. Good ideas or bad ideas, it's still abstractions that keep us going, one way or the other." And survival, I added to myself.

"As a historian who refers to herself in the third person, you seem not to believe in the coming revolution," Laguna said coolly.

"Laguna, why would a revolution start here in this broken down city-state of LA? If there were forces, they'd have their back to the sea, a desert or two to cross, and logist... supply problems for days," I said. "And what the hell do you know that I don't?"

"Just that Chelsea Clinton is coming to town, Nellie. I've transferred two hundred and fifty million into your Department of Water and Power bank account as a retainer." Laguna stood up and adjusted her fur coat. The ti-tandex strained across her pumped-up bust, but held like the good fabric it is. "I'm sure you'll do the right thing when you have no alternative." She batted her eyes at me; I was unmoved by it. "And I'll be around to see that you do. Have a pleasant day." She swept out.

I had to give her grudging credit since she was here either on her own or with minimal back-up. On the other hand, this might be the Company's way of terminating an operative they no longer cared about. Suicide missions, whether you know you're on one or not, are still suicide missions. I think I liked the old, redheaded Laguna Woods better, bitch though she was.

She'd died trying to ambush several Dissident Superior League linguists in an operation that went very wrong six or so years ago. She thought they were DSL economists, who are as dangerous as linguists, but are more cunning than vicious. That Laguna Woods was tough as a boot and about as smart. This new one seemed more sly than tough, and smart, very smart, and that made her annoying, very annoying.

But I was already annoyed. First thing this morning a guy named Abilene (that's all the name he had on his card) rolls in and asks me to kill Chelsea Clinton when she gets to town. As if I have nothing better to do than kill Chelsea Clinton if she happens to drop by Los Angeles. Figuring he was nuts, and there was no way Chelsea Clinton was coming to LA, I said, "sure," and assumed that was the last I'd see of him. But when he deposited five hundred million into my DWP bank account, that made him well-funded and I was no longer so certain he was nuts. He was also tall, dark, and handsome, like someone else I knew and happened to have a date with that very night.

Six months ago, in the course of investigating the DSL in LA, a DWP guy saved my life at least twice. It had taken this long to find out his name was Ed. It would probably take another six months to find out if he had a last name. I'd gotten Dr. Max of the old Live Nude Economics show and Fyodor Chandler and his gang of linguists out of LA and down to Mexico with as much carnage to the other side and as little fuss for the DWP as possible. In the aftermath of the Federal invasion and the inevitable LA Rebellion, and what passed for a half-assed, uncompleted due-to-poor-planning-and-the-over-extended military occupation, the DWP had taken over management of what was left of

LA. Since the DWP is where most of the power is nowadays, I made sure they very much appreciated my actions on their behalf earlier in the year. In gratitude, the DWP gave me this building on Sunset and a retainer to do security consulting for them. It's been quiet in LA, and as I still have my PI license, I've been taking private jobs for locals—mostly research or missing persons; silly little jobs that don't require much ammo—as they came along, just to kill time.

But today already two high-powered out-of-towners were asking for muscle (mine) and for very different ends, if not reasons. I never ask about peoples' reasons; I just assume they don't have any I'd care about. I did know why they wanted my services: Chelsea Clinton is coming to LA to lead the revolution. One person wants her dead, the other wants her kept alive; I've no idea what their motives are for wanting either of those things and couldn't care less. Although I would probably kill them and keep their money, just because anyone stupid enough to pay me up front is, well, too stupid to live. Especially when they seemed to be operating more or less alone, which is how it looked with Laguna Woods and Abilene.

However, this was not uppermost in my mind that afternoon. That afternoon, I was trying to figure out what I was going to wear on my date with Ed. My wardrobe was very basic: Ti-tandex catsuits, mini skirts, halter tops, a titanium-guarded leather jacket, steel-toed Capezio boots, ski mask, Infra-RayBans, a titanium Colt, a Mauser, and a Beretta were what I usually wore when I was working. I hadn't had a date in so long, I'd forgotten where to buy slinky dresses.

As usual, the Limo Brothers Burger Stand and Recycling downstairs turned one up for me at an outrageous price. They and Arlo, the fruitas guy, had come over to the new building, MY building, when the DWP gave it to me, so they owe me, but they're not above making a profit while they're being grateful. But it was a very cool dress and they even included a pair of ti-tantights and a bangle bracelet.

So, with my wardrobe and client base issues resolved, I could think about the other thing that was bothering me: A Klan of the Koffee Kats coffee clip joint had opened at the west end of my block a few weeks ago. Several days after that, a Starbucks opened directly across the street. This meant that things in LA were either getting better or worse, but it for sure created an overpriced coffee vortex on my turf and possibly was causing a seventh seal to open somewhere. Or something. I didn't know. All I knew was that there was nothing I could do about it without more C4 plastic explosives than I was willing to use at this moment. The DWP was cracking down on C4 sales; I was hoarding what was left of my meager cache.

And if I can't get C4 at any price, I'm fucking not going to pay fifteen hundred for a fucking latte! I pounded my fist on my desk. It hurt. I figured I'd better call it a day. I needed a large carrot juice and a view from the street. I went down to Arlo's on Sunset.

"Afternoon, Miss Gail, what'll it be?" the fruitas guy asked when I plunked myself down at one of his little sidewalk tables.

"Hi, Arlo. Large carrot juice," I said. "How's business?" I asked when he brought my juice. "Those coffee motherfuckers cutting in on your action?"

"Not yet, Miss Gail. I'm not sure how they stay in business. They have huge staffs and no customers," he said. "And the barristas at Starbucks are hard to understand; they talk funny."

We peered down Sunset, but nothing happened. A natural gas and solar-powered Metro Transport Authority fortress bus—far too noisy and far too invulnerable (I know this, I fought one to a standstill once and I still hate the fuckers)—went by, making normal conversation impossible. I hate those buses, with their machine gun turrets, armor plating, and who knows whatever other weaponry I couldn't see, not to mention the pair of heavily armed guards in partially-shielded platforms on each side of the rear engine. I hate the MTA; they make all passengers check their weapons before they pass the turnstile, thus making an impossible external assault the only possible way to hijack one. And even if you could, there's nowhere to hide from the wrath of the MTA; it was unthinkable, even for me, however tempting it might be.

"They talk funny?" I asked when my public transportation nemesis had passed by.

"They have weird accents. They talk like that skunk on the IB."

They talk like Pepe le Pew? "Oh yeah? Are you sure they don't talk like Speedy Gonzalez or Foghorn Leghorn?" I asked, hoping it was neither, because either would be really really bad news for LA and probably me, too. I wouldn't like an infiltration into my neighborhood from Mexico, as it is now being run by Drs. Krugman and Saches on Soros' and Gates' money. Nor would I like the Southern Christianists, a truly scary lot, crashing my party either. I have enough problems with the scavengers, the MTA, and the little cretins that think they can take me on because I'm a skirt, the fools.

"No, like that skunk," Arlo said firmly, but politely.

"What about the Klan of the Koffee Kats people?" I asked.

"They talk okay, but they wear funny shoes."

"Funny shoes?"

"Sandals with socks," Arlo said, and asked me if I wanted anything else. I wanted my life to stay what passes for quiet nowadays, but there wasn't much he could do about that. After I said no, he presented me with last week's tab. I have got to start juicing my own carrots. But I paid it. Arlo was prompt with his rent and, unlike the Limo Brothers, didn't haggle, so I wasn't going to haggle over my fruitas tab. And I had the Laguna money and the Abilene money, so I wasn't exactly hurting for cash just then.

Except for the fact that my country had been under martial law for the past twelve years, was a complete shambles, had been looted and pillaged by the Bush Family and their bravos, due to which all the brains and integrity were in exile in Mexico, that everything around greater LA was a wasteland from the rebellion against the failed Federal Occupation, we had a theoretical Governor appointed by our mysterious, sequestered president-for-life, and the only thing keeping it all together here in LA was the DWP's razor thin control of water, power, and the infrastructure that kept those two things flowing—no, I wasn't hurting at all.

As a student of history, I knew things could be worse, but I also knew they could be better. Unlike Laguna and her age group, I could remember when we could vote, protest, plan for the future, go to grad school... Oh fuck it, fuck the past; I can barely handle the present.

So, in this crappy present I had to live in, I went

up to my little room on the third floor. I wanted to read a few chapters of *Bury Me Standing* before my date. My specialty in college, before the Company discovered and developed my talents for mayhem, had been the history of genocide. I was weak in the area of the Third Reich's genocide against the European Gypsies, what the Gypsies call "The Devouring." To me, devouring has the purpose of feeding something. As far as I could tell, the 1.5 million Gypsies rounded up and murdered in the camps were murdered for as little reason as anyone else who died in them. It was all such a waste of time and resources, but what else is an agenda based on irrational hatreds and the power to act on them but wasteful? Evil? Well, I'd have to believe in good to believe in evil and I only believe in what facts I can get corroboration for. But I do know waste, futility, and the void when I see it.

I could understand the mechanics of how genocides occurred and were carried out, but I was fuzzy why they happened. Or what purpose they served; certainly not as a warning—no genocide was ever discouraged because the one before it hadn't worked out very well. Hadn't worked out very well for the perpetrators; genocide never works out well for the victims, which is, of course, the point of genocide, however wasteful.

I was beginning to wonder if the Ebola pox vaccination program could be considered genocide. The effect and intention were not to kill, but merely render large segments of the population, those who could be terrorized into the series of "inoculations," harmless and docile through brain damage. It had kind of worked; dissent was crushed, but so was the viable workforce and much of the military and potential recruits for the military.   Also, the Internet had tipped off anyone paying attention that there was no Ebola pox, and that caused hundreds of thousands to go underground and flee to Mexico.   George Soros and Bill Gates (when he wasn't on the run in the tropics) had pumped billions into Mexico, effectively buying it for the exiled US nationals there.   They brought in Jeffery Saches, the economist, to run the place, and were lucky Paul Krugman got out of the US just ahead of a bullet. Between that pair of docs, Mexico was humming along, holding free and fair elections, trading with everyone except the US, making all the coolest clothes, electronics, vehicles, weapons, and, rumor had it, planning an invasion to restore democracy to the United States. This all sounded great to me, as long as they kept it out of LA; we have enough problems without revolutionary zeal.

Or Chelsea Clinton. Fuck. I checked my email; nothing from Laguna, Abilene or anyone else who might have a dog in this fight. Actually, I had no email—I'm unpopular—which was fine with me.

I sat in my armchair by the window and read until the light was gone. I got dolled up to the best of my ability and went downstairs to meet Ed at Arlo's.

He was punctual; I like that in a man.

"Would you like to go for coffee?" he asked, jerking his chin at the caffeine dens down the street.

I said I preferred to support small local business and ordered two large carrot juices. I also thought, but did not say, that I thought coffee was too expensive, and because I hadn't had any in several years, I had no idea what it would do to my nervous system if I had some that night. As sexy as I was finding Ed, I wanted my nervous system in top form later on.

But it was nice of him to offer. He seemed like a nice guy. I had to wonder what he was doing with the DWP, so I asked, "How long you been with the DWP?"

"Fifteen years," he said. "It was my first job after high school. It's been a pretty good one. Long hours though."

"And dangerous?" I smiled at him.

"Sometimes," he said. "But there's a lot at stake. If I wanted to be safe, I'd be in Canada or Mexico."

"Why aren't you?"

"I'm a native Californian. I don't like what happened to my State. I'm doing what I can to fix it."

Well, I'm a native Californian, too, and I think that our State got what it deserved, but I decided a first date was not the place to air that opinion. "Well, you and the DWP are doing a great job," I said. I meant it, too. "Why is that?"

"Why are we doing a great job? We're the DWP, Nellie." He smiled something between a leer and a clerk wishing one a nice day.

"Why do it at all?" I asked. "Why not let it rot?"

"There was a vacuum; we filled it," he said. "It was better than walking away."

"And it was the one chance for the DWP to grab everyone's money," I said. "No offense," I added.

"Well, do you really mind your DWP bank account? Do you really miss compound interest that much?"

"No, where else would I put my money?"

We smiled over our juice. There was something inexplicably comforting about having no control over my money. In my previous data entry job, I'd seen other people run their DWP accounts out of money and get scolding emails, but they got more money. They had to pay it back, but they got it. If you worked your job and kept your mouth shut under the benevolent dictatorship of the DWP it was very hard to slip between the cracks. I didn't care; I had what I needed and in my line of work, you never know when the next bullet will...

"What?" I hadn't heard his question.

"Why let it rot?" he asked.

"Because the pre-Occupation property owners of California were cheap and greedy fuckers who wouldn't pay their fair share in property taxes to keep the place going for everyone. Fools. Of everyone, property owners had the most to lose," I said. "I mean, did they really think State income taxes and fees were going to pay for police, fire, sanitation, you name it? No wonder we devolved into lawlessness and chaos that not even Federal troops could contain. The DWP, the MTA and AT&T are just helping people who'd rather not pay a car tax than have a decent society hobble along. I mean, what's left of them; California has lost about half its population."

"Nellie," he said waving at the dark street. "Do you call this a 'decent society'? We are prolonging the agony, as a lesson to others, until things can get back to normal."

"Normal?"

"Back pre-December 12, 2000," he said. "That normal."

"You're an optimist, Ed." I had to wait for a fucking MTA fortress bus to go by. "Let's go to my place, optimist."

We left without paying the check; Arlo knew I was good for it. I don't like people in my personal space, so I led him to my office on the second floor. We were barely across the threshold before he was all over me like a cheap suit. I love cheap suits. I wrangled him to the desk and let him bend me over it. While he was busy pulling up my skirt, I was reaching for the condoms I hoped were in the middle desk drawer. We hadn't stopped to turn on the lights, so I was fumbling as fast as I could. We both let out strangled screams when Dr. Max, formerly of "Dr. Max's Live Nude Economics" IB show, turned on the desk lamp.

"Help you find something, Nellie?" Max drawled in that annoying, pedantic way of his. "Hi, Ed."

"Max... get OUT," I spat through clenched teeth. I'd find out what he was doing there later.

"Hi, Alison!" My brother, Larry, linguist and former PhD candidate, better known as Fyodor Chandler, the dangerous leader of the DSL, chirped up from behind Max.

I gave up; I could feel Ed behind me giving up, too. We might have survived Max, but not my brother.

"Hi, Larry," I said, wrestling my skirt down. "What the fuck are you doing in my office?"

"Waiting for you," Max said.

"Why?"

"We want you to protect Chelsea Clinton when she gets to town."

After much yelling, mainly by me at Max, he finally left once I agreed to meet him at Starbucks the next day at 11 AM. Ed, who was annoyingly intrigued by the idea of Miss Clinton's visit, left after laying a big wet kiss on me and agreeing to meet again the next evening at Arlo's. I didn't want him to leave, but the mood was ruined and Larry needed a place to stay. Say what you will about me, I am a good sister when called upon. Hadn't I risked my life to get him and his DSL linguists out of town and to the safety of Mexico merely six months ago? And it showed; he looked great—tanned, relaxed, sane. What a difference not living under the rubble of County Hospital makes in a man.

"What are you doing here?" I asked as I led him to my little rooms on the third floor.

"What Max said. We want you to protect Chelsea Clinton when she gets here to lead the revolution," he said.

"Oh, c'mon, Larry," I snapped, but stopped because he had a weirder than usual look on his face. "What's wrong?"

"I'm not used to being called Larry," he said.

"Well, okay, Fyodor," I said (see what a great sister I am?). "You better call me Nellie, I haven't been Alison in a long time."

"Yeah, well, we became those names the Company gave us, didn't we?" he asked bitterly.

"Did we, Fyod? Then we fucked up somewhere or we'd still have Company jobs or be dead, no?"

"Hm."

"How's Paulo?" I asked.

"We broke up. I've decided to give women another try. Know any you could introduce me to?"

"Not off the top of my head," I said, taking one of the Limo Brother's brainier daughters right off the list. Julia was a lovely girl, who thought she might be a vegetarian, and she would be much more confused if she got involved with my brother, who thought he might be Paul Revere or something. "No, no one comes to mind. But it's been a long day; I need sleep, you need sleep. I might kill Max tomorrow."

"You need sleep, Nell," Fyodor said, putting his arms around me. "And you get another date tomorrow; another chance, and I promise to be elsewhere, honest."

I have the best brother, but I still made him sleep in the tattered Barcalounger for which the Limo Brothers had shamelessly overcharged me.

I rolled into Starbucks the next morning at eleven, as promised. It was not as horrible as I thought it would be. There were good-sized tables and chairs, no couches, no dim lighting, and no background music. In fact, it looked very much like the mini-market that had been there in a previous incarnation. Just a big, empty space with no aisles of overpriced chips, toothpaste and cigarettes for the insomniacs, street people, and locals who just needed a gallon of milk at 3AM. The freezer cases along the walls had their glass shattered and doors removed long ago. The linoleum was torn up here and there, there were pieces of plywood over the worst places, but this matched the boarded up plate glass windows fronting on the street. Aside from the scratched-up plastic tables and chairs, the only redecorating I could see were a few espresso machines and a drape veiling the back third of the store. The whole place looked hastily assembled, temporary and unashamed about being either. Someone had spray painted "Starbucks" above the coffee bar. It was a jaunty little tag and therefore extra pathetic in this dive.

But I have no use for décor. And there was Max, already at a table with a coffee, a clipboard and Fyodor Chandler; they were both waving me over.

However, one of the barristas headed me off. His name tag read 'Jacques Cousteau'. That sounded familiar, but fishy. I decided to test Arlo's premise: "Bonjour, je voudrais un eau minérale sans gaz, s'il vous plaît."

"Mais bien sûr, mademoiselle!"

So they were French, or Francophone, if they

could understand my crappy French. I headed over to join Max and my brother.

"How the fuck did you get into my office last night anyway?" I asked Max, as I pulled a relatively clean plastic chair under my ass.

"The DWP gave me a key when I got to town," he said.

"They just gave you a key?" I asked and he nodded. "You're a very dangerous man, Max."

"Oh, hardly dangerous, Nell." He smiled suavely (it was a gruesome sight). "But I can be charming and compelling when necessary. And the DWP has an interest in Chelsea Clinton's upcoming visit."

"What's their angle?" I asked.

"They don't want their town torn apart," he said seriously. "They're willing to work very hard with us on that."

"I see." I watched an MTA fortress bus go by. The floor vibrated; I fucking hate that almost as much as I hate those buses. "I still think it's bullshit. Why would an icon like Miss Clinton come here?"

"To rally the troops, Nellie. Morale," Max said, with a touch of drama. "She's our Joan of Arc. She's going to save the United States."

I looked at Fyodor; he gave me one of those rabid, fanatical, wide-eyed looks linguists get when they believe in something. I mean really believe in something, like the significance of the palatization of the letter "T". He gave me that look, the look that usually meant he was about to do an hour non-stop on aspiration, epenthesized vowels, and laryngeal structure. I love my brother, but I would do almost anything to avoid another one of those hours. "Okay, Max," I sighed. "What must I do?"

"Sign here." He shoved the clipboard under my nose.

My mineral water sans gaz arrived, so I took a few sips to stall while I skimmed the typewritten sheet. We all looked up when Laguna came in. She must like Starbucks coffee and be able to afford it on her Company expense account. Max and Fyodor stared; even I must admit Laguna is an eyeful. I ignored her; this wasn't a business meeting or better not be because that would mean Max had really gone over the edge.

"Don't forget to initial beside the sanity clause," Max said. "Very important, that sanity clause." He chuckled and sipped his espresso.

I wondered if he'd had too much espresso. "The sanity clause?" I asked Fyodor, who just rolled his eyes.

"Oh, don't worry about that, Nellie, there is no Santy Claus." Laguna swept up to our table. "May I join you?"

I said no, but Fyodor pulled out a chair for her. She and Max locked eyes.

"I see someone was properly briefed for her assignment," Max said, low and dangerous.

"So, what a pleasure it is to meet the famous Dr. Max of Dr. Max's Live Nude Economics, the greatest IB show ever!" she said. Her lips were smiling but her eyes were glaring a hole in him. "I always feel so much smarter after I watch that show."

"Yes, too bad your people ran me out of the country and I had to give it up," Max said coolly.

"Can't you broadcast from Mexico City?" she asked, sweetly, but still slicing him up with her eyes. "Such a civilized, prosperous place since Messrs. Soros and Gates decided to invest in it. I mean, with Dr. Krugman and Dr. Saches in charge, you have so much economist talent, you ought to be able to do something constructive with it."

We all laughed, I mean, even nowadays, when something is funny, we still can laugh. Laguna dropped her hostility since even she must have realized it wasn't getting her anywhere.

"My dear Laguna, how sweet of you to think of us," Max said with a sigh. "But we economists are far too busy these days for art and culture. Perhaps someday, in a perfect world, my show will be back on the net, the U.S. will have free and fair elections, and espresso will only cost eight hundred in the new currency. Until then, we must toil and toil and toil for a better world for all of us."

"Amen!" Laguna smiled brightly around the table and introduced herself to Fyodor. She was even more impressed with meeting the great logistical genius of the DSL than she'd been meeting Max. "What brings you gentlemen to town?" she asked at last.

"Business," Max said. "Let's cut the bullshit, Laguna; highly reliable sources within the Company tell us we're on the same side for once: saving Chelsea Clinton so she can lead the revolution. I'd rather have you where I can keep an eye on you than off being a loose cannon, so here's the deal. I'm sending Fyodor and Nellie up to Highland Park to talk to a Tax Mystic named Dr. Caterham-7. She's at the old Spiritual Realization Fellowship compound because she used to do their taxes and they took her in after the Rebellion. She's completely insane, but I think she might have a line on when and where Chelsea Clinton is coming in. I think you should go with them, Laguna."

"What's a Tax Mystic, Max?" I asked, when it became obvious no one else was going to.

"Someone who could understand the old IRS rules when there was an IRS," Max said solemnly. "Someone who understands the mysteries of income redistribution leading to equality, peace, and harmony between the classes. Someone who once believed there was enough for everyone, if only the math could be worked out. Dr. Caterham-7 almost had the math worked out and then it all went to hell. Her life had no meaning without the IRS; of course she went insane." Max looked very sad. Fyodor and Laguna were visibly moved by this.

"And we're supposed to ask this crazy tax expert about Chelsea Clinton?" I asked.

"Yes! Here's a map! See you later!" Max sprang up, called for the check and was out the door before it arrived.

Laguna picked up the check on her Company expense card. It was really the least the Company could do for me and Fyodor after they killed our family, derailed our educational careers, and exploited our latent sociopath tendencies. Left on our own, we'd have ended up on tenure track at some obscure state college where, with the possible exception of a killing rampage with an automatic weapon due to extreme boredom and frustration, we would have lived out our lives in a Xanax-fueled academic haze. But we live in a crappy, fucked-up world where no one's dreams come true, except the nightmares, and...

"C'mon, Nellie, shake a tail feather," Fyodor said, cheerfully hauling me to my feet. "What are we using for transport, girls?" He was way too happy about all this.

"My ride's outside," Laguna said. "But I can only take one of you."

Her ride turned out to be a hybrid Triumph Speedmaster. Goddamn, the Company really spoils its people. It was just a shame to waste a nice ride like that on a thing like Laguna. But I merely said it was 'very nice' and got my own ride, an Electrocatti made in Mexico, and off we went. Since her hybrid had more power, Laguna got to haul Fyodor across town.

I was not completely unencumbered. I stopped by Casa Gail to put on my ti-tandex bodysuit, get more guns, a small carrot juice, and Julia, one of the Limo Brothers' daughters. She was carrying my machine gun and the Mauser. I wasn't expecting trouble, but one never knows. I also thought we might need someone to watch the bikes while we communed with the Tax Mystic, and Julia had proven herself to be a good bike guard and a dead-eye shot on more than one occasion. Her father or uncle or elder cousin—I'm not clear on that family structure at all—had haggled over what to charge me and in the end he got the better deal. However, there was a side benefit to having Julia, or any member of the well-connected Limo clan, on board: The way was cleared in advance. No one tried to stop us for "tolls" and we even got a few friendly nods along the way to where Riverside turns into Figueroa on the other side of the viaduct at San Fernando.

In the foothills above Figueroa in Highland Park, there had once been an enclave of wealthy white people who were too grand to live in Highland Park and so called the area Mount Washington. There was also a lovely religious community called the Spiritual Realization Fellowship, founded by Paramahansa Yogananda in the 1920s. Nine years later, Swami Prabhavananda would found the Vedanta Society's lovely center in the Hollywood Hills. However, unlike the Vedanta Society, the SRF center and Mt. Washington surrounding it were wiped out in a bombing run during the Rebellion. The pilot had a few bombs left from a run over Lincoln Heights, which was the real target, and Mt. Washington was the biggest target outside the do-not-bomb area, which was pretty much everything east of the Interstate 5 freeway.

Bombs kill the just and the unjust just as well. All the prayers in the world had not saved the monks and nuns of the SRF. And all the recalls, referendums and Prop 13 could not save the smug homeowners of Mt. Washington either. Location, as any realtor would tell you (when realtors still existed), is everything.

For me, the saddest part was that even though most of Highland Park escaped the worst of the damage, it was still a ghost town. Or a town of ghosts; people lived there, opened their empty shops and restaurants on Figueroa, which had been the main commercial street, and waited for nothing. At dusk they barricaded their businesses up and retreated into their fortified apartments above them. Occasionally one of the younger generation would go on a quest to Mexico City and come back with a truckload of gear, fashion, whatnot, all the wonderful stuff the U.S. no longer had the capacity, desire, or will to make. The best minds and skilled labor had fled when martial law was imposed, most businesses were nationalized and the universities closed. Those who could get out, got out. Many unfortunate professors, union members, engineers, and really anyone who might mount any kind of organized resistance were swept up by the Company and the FBI. Once incarcerated, there was an obligatory interrogation and then a series of Ebola pox vaccinations. After they were rendered harmless (of the harmless-due-to-brain-damaged variety of harmless) they were cut lose to roam and scavenge as best they could. It was not the most elegant solution to dissent, but it was very much in vogue at the time.

But that was more than a decade ago, when I worked for the Company, and the illusion of security still existed.

More recently, and in Los Angeles, on those days when there was something to buy or barter for, Figueroa Street came alive again. The restaurants put a grill on the street and sold the most delicious carne asada (or whatever it was) tacos on earth. The shops hung dusty piñatas from the eaves and the latest pop music from downtown Mexico City blared from speakers in front of the shop windows. It was almost normal. And even if I didn't buy anything, I liked to be there, just to remember what it used to be like. As a historian, I knew things were changed beyond redemption, but the past is as much of a model of what to strive for as a model of what to avoid. I also knew it would take more than history to save us. I didn't care who or what was saved as long as I survived. I guess I'd like Fyodor to survive, but if it was me or him... hm, that was a toughie.

However, there was no reason to go that far down Fig to get where we were going. At San Fernando, I swung us north into Cypress Park, also a quiet as a tomb area, and up into the hills from there. Max's directions turned out to be pretty good. I was hoping we could park closer to Dr. Caterham-7's, ah, office, but, leaving Julia to mind the vehicles, we had a little climb up to the cluster of smashed-up stucco and timber that had once been the SRF center.

It was quiet up there, too quiet. I moved my flex machine gun from my back to my side, though still concealed beneath my jacket. Julia had the exploding plastic bullet machine gun, so I was left with the poison needle one. It was effective at relatively close range; flex guns can't handle much gunpowder projection and so rely on poison or impact explosion for effect. I noticed Laguna tense a little and unstrap the guard on her shoulder holsters. Only Fyodor, unarmed and unalarmed, was cheerful.

"Let's go, girls!" He led us uphill and across an open space.

I could tell Laguna didn't like the open space any better than I did, but there was no other way. I looked back at Julia, who waved and went back to scanning the approaches to her perch. Unlike Fyodor, and even me and Laguna, Julia was cautious, prudent, and would probably outlive us all. And smart, too, because she doesn't listen to Dr. Max, the bastard. Why were we on this errand—his errand!—without him? What kind of idiots–?

We stopped when a guy in clean, but well-worn, orange robes waved us over. He had a shaved head and an AK-47. "Are you looking for Dr. Caterham-7?" he asked. We nodded. "She's expecting you. Please follow me."

"The DWP must keep the water and power going even up here," Laguna murmured beside me.

Having seen lights in bombed-out Lincoln Heights, I was not as impressed as I might have otherwise been. I had also noticed a few solar panels and windmills on the property, so it might not be all DWP power.

However, I was impressed when we were led into what looked like rubble, but turned out to be a fortified structure. I wished I'd had a ball of string, because it was a maze inside and I'd never find my way out on my own.

Brother AK-47, the monk guy, led us deep into the compound and knocked at a metal door that had 'Jane Caterham-7, Ph.D., CPA, MDiv' scrawled on it. He ushered us in and took up a position by the door.

Except for the tidy desk and the tidy woman behind it, the room was a wreck of tax forms, tax code books, exploded file cabinets and overturned chairs. And dust, a thick coating of dust on everything but the desk and the woman. I'm not the greatest housekeeper in the world, but not even I live like this.

Of course Fyodor either didn't notice the condition of the room or just ignored it. "Dr. Caterham-7, I'm Fyodor Chandler. Dr. Max sent us to ask you–"

"I know who you are, young man," she said in a whispery voice we had to strain to hear. She waved a hand at her computer screen. "You haven't filed a tax return since 2003, nor you, Miss Gail. Miss Woods has never filed a tax return."

"I see Max has been in touch–" Fyodor began again.

"An email."

"Yes, well, did he email that we want to know when and where Chelsea Clinton is arriving?" he asked.

(Thus causing me to wonder why this whole errand couldn't have been done online. Max. Grrrrrr!)

"Yes," she said.

"Oh great!" Fyodor looked at his watch. "When and where?"

"No."

"No? No, what?" Fyodor looked puzzled. Laguna looked puzzled. I probably looked pissed off, but there wasn't a mirror in the joint, so I didn't know.

"Yes, Max emailed. No, I don't know when or where Chelsea Clinton is arriving, but I do know why, and I thoroughly disapprove," Dr. Caterham-7 intoned mysteriously.

"But Chelsea Clinton is coming to lead the revolution and save us," Laguna said quietly. "Why do you disapprove?"

Dr. Caterham-7 gave her a pitying look. "My child, the truth of this world is cause and effect, yin and yang, debit and credit—balance in all things. Our country has sinned and we must be punished. Our sin was allowing the Bush family to steal the 2000 presidential election. Our sacrifice was the three thousand on September 11. In our sloth, avarice, and fiscal recklessness, we tossed away the greatest, oldest continuous democracy in world history like it was nothing. God is punishing us for our complacency. Our penance is far from finished, our debt is far from paid, our account is far from cleared. We do not deserve to be rescued from the consequences of our actions."

"But– " Laguna, who'd only been a child in 2001, began.

"All evil must be punished. All sin must be atoned for," Caterham-7 chanted. "All penance requires sacrifice, such as the Six Million of Europe."

Ah ha. Suddenly we were on my turf. I tipped one of the chairs up and planted myself in front of her. "Hey, lady! Whaddya mean about the Six Million?"

"Six Million Jews were sacrificed so God could punish the most evil and anti-Semitic countries of Europe," she said, staring into my eyes.

"Which were?"

"Germany, Poland, and Russia."

Poland and Russia had a long and savage history

of pogram and oppression of their Jews; Germany was a late-comer but a very effective late-comer in genocide. I had to remind myself that this was a crazy woman, suddenly now a very interesting crazy woman who had a crazy idea I didn't want to get crazy enough to even begin to understand. In fact, I wanted to forget it as quickly as possible, before it started making sense. "I see, that's the punishment," I said, fishing. "And the sacrifice was for what?"

"To establish the State of Israel."

Now, as a historian, I'm of the opinion that what was left of European Jewry could have declared Bavaria the Jewish State in 1946 and gotten massive support for it. The trouble the State of Israel has had since 1946 has been with people who hadn't historically killed six million and more, if you count from the Crusades. The Islamic Middle East had no real backlog of Jew-killing guilt to work with; however, they've been getting those numbers up since then. Israel, on the other hand, is giving as good as it's getting, if not more so. I hadn't decided if the Palestinian death toll qualified as a genocide yet because it was still part of a war. I hadn't decided this any more than I'd decided there had been a Polish genocide during World War II. Losing half a population of 40 million is significant, even if anti-Semitic Dr. Caterham-7 didn't think so. The Poles hadn't been the aggressors, either; they just had scary neighbors in 1939. And since the dead weren't with us to defend themselves it was a moot point. But since this was really interesting, if only to me, I decided to find out where Dr. Caterham-7's thinking was on the Israel issue. "So, other than dying themselves while killing Palestinians and their neighbors, what purpose is served by establishing the State of Israel where it is now?" I asked, wondering which insane answer I'd get.

"Oh please, Miss Gail, Israel must defend itself," she said, disgusted with me. "Israel must exist."

"Oh, yeah? Why is that?" I asked.

"So the Messiah can come and God can destroy this evil world."

I love this answer. It means everything that has ever been, is, or will be has no meaning. All the sacrifice, punishment, redemption, art, music, joy, love, puppies, kittens, you name it, mean shit, because we're all shit, and God needs to wipe us off his shoe and start over. Or not start over; how the hell would we know? I love this answer. It makes me so glad I don't believe in God. I was beginning to enjoy this. "Now, let me underst–"

"That is all."

"But–"

"THAT IS ALL."

I looked at Fyodor for guidance. He mouthed, in what can only be described as lip reading for the blind, 'Let's go'. So we did. Brother AK-47 led us out of the room and out of the building. We rode home in silence and, after dropping Julia off, went straight to Starbucks. Even I needed a latté after that experience.

"What'd you find out?" Max asked brightly.

"Osama bin Laden and Adolf Hitler were working for God," I said, staring at him. I heard Laguna groan softly and then brush past us.

Max blinked first and turned to my brother.

"She was fairly useless, Max," Fyodor said. "She had a collection of facts and was trying to force them into her theory. Very bad science, if you ask me. Almost as bad as Phonology. What did you think, Nell?"

"Don't look at me, pal, I'm a historian, I get on

well with facts," I said, heading for the bar at the back. "When I can find some."

I heard Fyodor say, "We got zip, Max, that's what we got," but I was too deep in milk foam by then to care. Next to me, Laguna said she had a headache and went to the bathroom. Max waved me to his table. I sat next to Fyodor, who put his arm around me.

"What now, Max?" I asked.

"We know when and where," he hissed at me. "We meet at six PM tomorrow on the east side of the 6th Street viaduct," he added, and stared hard at me.

"Okay," I said. Mission and 6th, I knew where that was.

"I said, 'the 6th street viaduct'," he repeated with meaning.

"And I said, 'okay'." I was wondering what I was missing here. I glanced over my shoulder at Laguna, trying to get past a knot of plate-bearing barristas. "But, Max–"

"Nellie, you're either on the bus or not on the bus," he growled at me.

His timing was bad because there was an MTA fortress bus going by at just that moment. "I hate buses, Max, hate 'em, hate 'em, hate 'em all," I growled back. "But, we meet tomorrow, eh?"

"Fine. See you then!" Max leapt up and was gone.

Laguna sat with us long enough to pick up the check (again) and get a date that night with Fyodor. In fact, Fyodor grafted his date with Laguna onto my date with Ed, but I was too tired or wired or something to argue about it. I think Laguna really did have a headache because she excused herself and left a few minutes later.

"Fyodor, is there something wrong with Max?" I asked when we were alone.

"No, he just needs some new material."

"What?"

Fyodor sighed. "When he said, 'viaduct', you were supposed to ask 'why a duck?'"

"Wh–?"

"Because it's not a chicken," he said firmly.

"What's not a chicken?" I asked, looking around for one.

"A duck."

"I knew that," I said. "But why–"

"Beca–"

"No, wait!" I smacked the table; the caffeine was kicking in. "Why was I supposed to ask 'why a duck' in the first place?"

Fyodor sighed. "Because Max needs new material."

I love my brother, really I do, but there are times when it's just not worth trying to understand him. There was a fortress bus going by and that annoyed me as usual. I took my coffee and went home to get ready for my date, which was now a double date. I found Abilene lounging around Arlo's with a carrot juice.

"Whoa, Nellie, how's the Chelsea Clinton hunt comin' along?"

"Ah think she's a no-show, pahd-nur, and ya oughta get outta Dodge while ya can," I said, affecting my best drawl, which must have been the caffeine talking.

"I shall keep the faith, missy," he said, winked, and sauntered off.

I thought he was kind of sexy, but that was probably caffeine goggles. I traded what was left of my latté for a small carrot juice. It would, I hoped, take care of the jitters. "Save me a table for four, hey, Arlo?" My mouth was dry; I was having trouble talking at a comprehensible speed. "About 7:30?"

"Sure thing, Miss Gail," he said kindly. "This is good coffee, thanks!"

"That coffee is strong, Arlo, be careful," I said, and went up to my place to drink lots of water. And think about my least favorite subject as little as possible.

I don't believe in God. I can't reconcile the facts of genocide with the idea of a deity that is powerless to prevent it. Or worse, the idea of a deity that allows or even causes such horrors to happen. There is just force, survival, and death in my world. Oh, and insanity—Dr. Caterham-7 had been a good reminder about that. What a lulu, I thought, running a brush over my stubby hair. I was wearing it very short because a crazy man had burned most of it off earlier that year. It was easy to take care of and suited me in a gamine sort of way.

Well, anyway, Ed seemed to like it. I decided not to change out of my bodysuit, because it suited me, too. I did wriggle into my slinky dress and get out my heels for the occasion.

I also checked my titanium Colt, Mauser and Beretta. I hadn't fired a shot since I loaded them that afternoon, but I'm meticulous as well as paranoid. I usually wore the Colt under my jacket, but that night I wore it on my right hip and the smaller guns in shoulder holsters. I dug out a suit jacket that hid all the guns and whose padded shoulders made my waist look smaller than it is. I was all set. I was even in a good mood when Laguna buzzed from downstairs and asked to be let in.

"You ought to get a cell phone, Nellie," she said, primping in the mirror next to me.

"I can't afford one," I said, envying her catsuit and boots. "I can't even afford the wireless charges for a BayaNegra or PDA."

"They're expensive," she said. "The Company pays for mine." She looked uncomfortable.

"The Company invests a lot in their agents," I said, when she didn't go on.

"You're a legend at Langley, Nellie," Laguna finally said, staring at my reflection. "You and Fyodor Chandler, brother and sister geniuses. You were the last really brilliant agents we had..." She cleared her throat and looked away. "I don't know what to talk about with your brother tonight."

I never had a kid sister, and that's probably a good thing. "Oh, you know men, get them talking about themselves and you're all set," I said. "You could ask Fyodor about his research on the palatization of the letter 'T'. He's very hepped on the subject."

She smiled so genuinely I almost felt bad. Almost.

We went down to Arlo's. Ed and Fyod were already there. We settled in over carrot juice and cucumbers, which suited me fine. Eating doesn't interest me much. I've never enjoyed cooking and, even if I had a kitchen, I live alone, so there's no point in lingering over meals. But it was nice to sit with my brother and our "dates". I'd never really had a social life; before the rebellion it was all studying and then working for the Company. No time for love, whatever that is.

And because I have no social skills, it was up to Ed, Fyodor and Laguna to keep the conversation sputtering along. Or try to; the fucking MTA buses were going by with their halogen lights blinding us and their big engines drowning out our words. I hate those buses and I was beginning to contemplate some revenge.

I was beginning to get bored, too. But luck was with me; Laguna must have asked the magic question, because Fyodor was going on about aspiration, laryngeal, and supralaryngeal specifications, and had that ecstatic linguist look on him. When Laguna's eyes glazed over, I figured it was safe for me and Ed to blow.

I leaned over Ed's shoulder. "Let's go," I whispered.

"Where?"

"Up in the hills. Let's go hunting."

Fyodor and Laguna hardly noticed when we left.

We rode up into the Hollywood hills on his DWP issue Harley. I wish I could afford a gas powered chopper, but I must live within my means. And I only consult for the DWP, so when I asked for company transportation, they were very sorry, but no. It's a good thing I'm good natured or I might have taken umbrage at that.

I like the Hollywood Hills. I used to hunt farther west, in Beverly Hills and Brentwood, but lately I've been content to kill scavengers closer to home. In some ways I did feel sorry for some of the former residents of Laurel, Nichols and all those other canyons; they had been a pretty liberal, tax-paying, social-services-voting bunch. But, well, when the whip comes down, it comes down on everyone who doesn't get out from under it quick enough. I think many of these people saw their dream of a beautiful life die with the appointment of Schwarzenegger as Governor. Some of them fought in the rebellion, but most just put their homes in order and waited to die.

The hills were a beautiful maze. Unlike Brentwood, there were no walls, so the ravaging hordes of scavengers, soldiers, rebels and assorted Rebellion crazies roared through here in a tsunami of death and destruction. The lovely open-plan homes clinging to hillsides never stood a chance. But beauty, along with truth, honor, freedom, hope, and decency, is among the first casualties of war.

It was still pretty scenic up there among the ruins. The moon was out, and almost everything looks pretty in the moonlight. It was also good for shooting scavengers, some of whom were in fits of moon madness and made an easy target.

Ed drove, I shot. The DWP frowned on senseless killing unless it was in the course of their DWP duties. There were no witnesses, but Ed's a rule-following kind of guy, so he drove and I shot.

We parked the Harley in a clearing and I ran down the last pair of scavengers I'd been hunting. They hid, but I found them. I always find them. My former employers at the company thought I had a sixth sense for causing pain, extracting information, and finding prey. I think I can just smell fear. Either way, they were dead and I was in the mood.

I sauntered back to where Ed was guarding his ride. "Come here often?" I asked in my most sultry voice.

"Only when there's a pretty lady involved."

Well, pick-up lines and come-ons pretty much died in 2008, so these really were the best we could do. But they still did the job; Ed pulled me against his cock, stuck his tongue down my throat and his hand up my dress.

I don't need much more message than that. Even through the advanced, blow-repellant fabric of my bodysuit, I could feel how hard he was, sliding his cock against my slick ti-tandex covered clitoris. Frottage would have to do, since I wouldn't be able to get out of it until we got back to my place. Or his place. Or just somewhere less exposed. This didn't stop me from reaching into his pants for a better feel of him; warm, pulsing, and the head slick with pre-cum. I was getting close, but I'm hot-blooded that way. From his moaning, I could tell Ed was close, too. So the last thing I wanted was my goddamn client, Abilene, to cruise up on a Polaris Victory. A very quiet one, too; must have been a hybrid or all electric.

"You two are nuts and reckless," he drawled, and fired at a scavenger behind us.

There wasn't just one either. Ed and I disengaged. While he fumbled with his fly, I was shooting at what seemed to be a whole lot more scavengers than I had thought were around.

In the ensuing melee I got separated from Ed. From what I could see, which wasn't much, he was doing a pretty good job defending his ride. Abilene was shooting the scavengers attacking me and Ed and trying not to hit us, but very soon was fighting them off himself. Low on ammo after hunting, I drew my knife and did some hand-to-hand killing. I've never been good at hand-to-hand combat, so I was shooting again fairly soon. There were too many scavengers between me and the men with motorbikes, but there was an open space in front of me that, if I ran fast enough, would eventually get me down to Hollywood Boulevard, where there were lights, something the scavengers didn't like at all. I figured I was my best chance, as usual, and bolted away from the fray.

I hate to run, but when I have to run, I run very fast. But as fast as I ran away from the scavengers behind me, I was running to the scavengers in front of me. I got out the Colt, which makes lots of noise and does lots of damage, and blasted a path for myself. Over the pounding in my lungs, I heard Ed's ride start up and more shooting. If something didn't happen quick, I'd have to find a place to hide and get my wind back. My chest felt like it was going to explode. I barely heard the bike behind me, but I did hear Abilene yell, 'I got her, get my back!', as he scooped me sidesaddle over the motor cover. As winded as I was, I shot a few more scavengers on the way out of the Hollywood Hills. When we got to the lights, I holstered the Colt and looked over Abilene's shoulder.

"I don't see Ed behind us," I said.

"Who's Ed?" he asked.

"My date."

"Oh. He seemed plenty tough when he got his pants fastened," Abilene drawled. "Want to go back and look for him?"

I thought about this. "No. He's plenty tough."

We rode to my office in silence. Abilene offered me a drink. The perfect end to the perfect evening, except Arlo's was closed, so our choices were Klan of the Koffee Kats or Starbucks. Since I'd been in Starbucks already that day, I said the KKK.

"What were you doing up there?" I asked when we were settled, he with a latte and I with a mineral water ('no bubbles' as they say at the KKK, the barbarians). We were seated in what I recalled were classroom chairs from junior high and at a rickety little table. It seemed the KKK was as hastily assembled as Starbucks, but the floor was less fucked up.

"Spying on you," he said shamelessly. "You're not out looking for Chelsea Clinton and, as your client, I find that worrying. If you're not on my job, I want to know what you're up to."

"Well, you got an eyeful tonight," I said, sipping my water.

He looked me over and admitted that he had. Then he suggested we go to my place and compare guns.

"I don't fuck my clients, Abi," I growled.

Leaning close, he slid his hand up my nearest thigh. "How about you're fired for the next forty-five minutes?"

I could hear my heart pounding again. I could also hear the distinctive sound of shotguns being pumped around us. Abi leaned back, not looking surprised that we were surrounded by shotgun-wielding Klan of the Koffee Kats barristas. And in addition to their shotguns, they were all wearing Birkenstocks... with socks, just like Arlo warned me.

"Keep your hands were we can see them, Nellie," one of the pasty coffee jockeys said nervously.

I put my hands on the table and stared hard at Abilene. "What the fuck is it now, client?"

He didn't answer. He didn't have to: Kevin, logistics specialist for the IIA sat down at our table. That was more than enough answer for me.

"Oh, fuck, Kevin, I was really hoping you were dead."

"Life is full of these little surprises, Miss Gail," he said in the same soft rasp that made me wonder if his voice was fucked up or if he just liked to whisper because it made him scary. "They keep life from becoming dull and routine."

I hate surprises, but I didn't disagree. "How are things in the IIA?"

"I'm no longer with the IIA," Kevin said. "Their

goals and mine have diverged irrevocably." He told Abilene to take my guns and put them on the table. I like my guns very much, so looking at them on the table wasn't a hardship. I had a knife in my belt, but it wouldn't do me much good against shotguns. After my guns were out of my reach, Kevin told the barristas to sit down but keep their guns handy.

"I see," I said. "What brings you to LA?"

"The same as Max, Fyodor, Laguna, and Abilene: Chelsea Clinton."

I looked hard at Abilene. "And how do you know Kevin?"

Abilene just looked at Kevin and shrugged. Kevin scares me so I didn't doubt he scared my client, if he was still my client. The air is dead around Kevin; he carries a death-like silence with him and the most frightening thing is that his rapidly graying black hair is perfectly groomed and smooth as a bird's breast. In his inhuman tidiness, Kevin looked like a conservative bank executive transported into hell, but too strung out on Prozac to notice. Except for his dead air and killer's eyes—eyes that always seem to be watching something die—he could have been on the cover of Fortune, Forbes, or GQ, when there were such things.

"Abilene and I have conjoined our interests because we have a common goal, Miss Gail; our clients want Chelsea Clinton's head on a stick," Kevin said softly. "We now also have a common problem: The Militias of Christ are about to invade Southern California because they want to kill Chelsea Clinton as well. However, in the course of killing her, they'll ravage this city. Not that I have any fondness for Los Angeles, but, as you know, I hate waste. I would also hate for those particular extremists to get a foothold on the West Coast, especially in a city that is currently operationally poised for a return to greatness."

"We are?" I asked.

"If you survive, yes," Kevin said. "Los Angeles almost has a working infrastructure and the proximity to Mexico makes it a prime trade partner for the best in goods and technology. Some of those goods are simply passing through LA and ending up in other parts of the US and Canada. Losing LA to the Christianists would be a terrible blow to commerce and the possible recovery of this country."

"Recovery of this country by and for whom, Kevin?" I asked, I was starting to smell a rat or a bush.

"Does it really matter?" he asked.

"Yes, it really does," I said. "Abilene is working for the 700 Club; I can see how they'd want Chelsea Clinton dead so the US can be a 'Christian' nation and take out anyone who isn't a 700-Club-approved Christian, but I can't even imagine whom you're working for."

"My clients simply want a better world for everyone," Kevin sighed. "On their terms, of course. But things must bottom out before we can begin to rebuild. Circumstances must get worse before they can get better in this great nation of ours."

I live in post-Rebellion/Occupation Los Angeles, I had no idea how things could get much worse. But I was having a flashback to the 2000 election. I stared hard at a the barrista's Birkenstocks sitting catty-corner from me. The two ideas clicked together like a magazine into a gun butt. "Oh my God, Kevin," I said trying to keep the horror out of my voice. "You're working for the Greens." What a come-down for a guy like Kevin. .

"And the Progressives," he said. "The Greens

could never afford me on their own."

But knowing Kevin even as little as I did, which was more than I wanted to, I figured there was another angle in the works somewhere. "Of course, I'm sure there's lots of folks in D.C. who'd like her dead, too. Especially since the CIA and IIA assassins have had Clinton and her mom and dad on the run in the tropics for the past ten years. Since Chelsea Clinton is coming to town, I guess those agencies' killers have lost their touch."

"Since you've been contacted by Laguna Woods on behalf of the Company, you must realized that the CIA has changed its position, at least on Chelsea Clinton," Kevin said. "President and Senator Clinton have proved harder targets than expected, but we've always underestimated them. However, it can only be a matter of time before they're liquidated."

"I bet you said that about Bill Gates when you had him on the run in the tropics," I said, jabbing where I thought it would hurt.

"Allowing Gates to get safely to Mexico City was a Langley miscalculation, Miss Gail," he said. "And I was never in that department at the IIA."

"Yes, Planning and Logistics was your bailiwick, as I recall," I said, further recalling that his department oversaw the murder and mayhem, but I guess oversight is not the same as being "in" something.

"At any rate, Miss Gail, all that hardly matters," he said smoothly. "It came as no surprise to me that after your amazing luck at County Hospital earlier this year, I was able to rise above my termination from the IIA and surpass my previous accomplishments. I find I like working for myself, I now understand your freelance mentality, I no longer feel constrained by the goals of others, I am thriving on this freedom, I can do anything. Anything at all."

"Can you juggle?" I asked.

He ignored me and lowered his voice even more. "However, you must realize that Chelsea Clinton's death will mean many things to many people. It will impress certain people in my old circles," he said. "And this can only be good. And what is good for me can only be good for you, Miss Gail. I'm sure when I am returned to a responsible position in the IIA, there will certainly be your choice of positions for you. And then there is your brother's welfare to consider. My sources keep track of his every move in Mexico City. He walks in certain parks at certain times every day; you could set your clock by him. So far we've just been interested in his movements, but it would only take one bullet to end our interest."

I could believe Fyodor would walk in certain parks at certain times every day. He was a creature of habit except when he knew his life was in danger. I would have to speak to him about this foolish unguarded park rambling of his. And Max, too, the bastard, why wasn't he keeping an eye on– "What?" I'd not caught what Kevin was saying.

"I said, Max is keeping you occupied, isn't he? That little trip to Jane Caterham-7, it was a total waste of time, wasn't it?" Kevin asked.

"If you know, why ask?"

"Of course I know," Kevin said, looking at his watch. "Dr. Caterham-7 is one of the most brilliant minds this country ever produced. And when her field collapsed, she went mad as a hatter. She lives in her own little world now, but if income tax is ever resurrected, she'll be the first and foremost person involved."

"And what are the chances of income tax replacing the income looting we now have?" I asked, looking at my guns because I was getting bored.

"About the same as democracy replacing the dictatorship we now have: Nil," he said.

I shrugged. "What is it you want from me?"

"I want you to kill Chelsea Clinton for the greater good, for me and for Abilene. The last thing this country needs is a revolution," he said. "I'll move ten million in the new currency into your account. She arrives tomorrow; I'll expect to see you with proof that she is dead soon after that."

"You have a lot of faith in me, Kevin," I said. "Why is that?"

"Because you're the only one who ever beat me, Miss Gail," he said, sounding even deader than usual. "I have unlimited confidence in you." He called for three empty coffee glasses and proved to me that he could juggle.

I can't juggle so this impressed the hell out of me. Then he left, which made me happy. Abilene suggested we pick up where we left off and I suggested he buzz off. "I don't fuck my clients," I reminded him. "And now that Kevin is in the picture, you're a client squared."

One of the barristas asked if we wanted anything else because they wanted to close. I said no, picked up my guns and went home. Alone.

I would have liked to have been alone at home, but Fyodor was fucking Laguna in my office or vice versa. I was too polite to look. I wanted to talk to him, though, so I put aside my manners and asked him through the crack in the door what he did for exercise in

Mexico City. He grunted that he walked in the park.

Well, I never doubted Kevin, but it's always good to get confirmation. I checked my email; there was a message from Ed asking if I was okay. I figured I'd answer that one when I knew if I was okay. I now seemed to have four clients and four is a very unlucky number. I'd have to sleep on it. If I could.

The next morning I spent some time surfing up video files of Chelsea Clinton. It's important to know how a target moves, if only to estimate how they might move under fire. It was a shame. She seemed like a nice lady, too bad history was against her. And when history is against you, you're doomed. Well, maybe it wasn't history, but forces that shape history had decided she was doomed, so she was doomed. Killing her would piss off Max and Fyodor, and probably Laguna (Laguna I would probably have to kill even before Chelsea Clinton), but Max and Fyodor would forgive me eventually, because, well, she was dead and no use crying over spilt milk. I might even be able to make it look like an accident. That was worth thinking about.

I spent some time looking up what specs I could find on MTA Fortress buses. They infuriated me and, since I had four clients, one or more of which ought to be able to protect me from the wrath of the MTA, I planned to get some useful revenge that very afternoon. Or die trying.

I got dressed for success: Ti-tandex body suit, mini skirt, tool belt, holsters, guns, flat machine guns—one with exploding bullets and the other with poison needles—a blouse to hide some of the guns, ass-kicking Capezio boots, and a backpack with my meager supply of C4 and detonators. I figured I wouldn't need much C4; just enough to blow a few locks off.

Fyodor wasn't around that morning. I figured he must have gone back to wherever Laguna was holed up for more nookie. He showed up in the afternoon to ask me what I was doing until the rendezvous. I said I thought I'd hijack an MTA Fortress bus and meet him on the other side of the river. He laughed; told me to go for it and said he'd see me later, gator. I have the best brother, really I do.

I dropped by Arlo's for a quick carrot juice and to wait for Julia. I'd already decided on my route, so I had Julia drop me off at the corner of Sunset and Serrano. She wished me luck, whatever I was doing, and I watched her ride out of sight on my Electrocatti.

Sliding behind a burned out SUV, I watched the street for a few minutes. It was deserted as usual; that was exactly why I picked the place. East of what was left of the 101 freeway, certain sections of Sunset were still pretty torn up, so the buses slowed down. There was no bus stop, so there were no pedestrians milling around. In fact, at this particular location, there were no intact buildings and it was a very dangerous place, scavenger-wise, after dark. The buses didn't run much after dark, and they certainly didn't head east when the sun was down.

From my hiding place, I could hear a bus chugging toward me. I knew I'd have to move fast because I wouldn't have the element of surprise for long. I drew my Mauser.

As the bus passed, I shot the passenger-side rear outrider and clambered up his dead body to the top of the bus. The passengers inside were screaming blue murder. The front machine gunner took a few shots, but couldn't get his gun low enough to hit me where I was crouched on the side of the bus. The glass on his gun turret wasn't bullet proof and he didn't duck quickly enough, so that solved one of my problems. The driver-side outrider took a few shots at me, but the rear gunner was between us. In the process of shooting at me, he shot the rear gunner, which solved another problem.

In the midst of all this gunplay, the damn bus driver was swerving all over the place, trying to shake me off. He was also trying to scrape me off and crashing into buildings to do so. I, on the other hand, was hanging on the back of the bus with both hands. This worked fine, except the outrider climbed on top of the bus and was pointing his gun at me. Then the top of his head exploded and he fell off the bus.

Looking over my shoulder, I didn't recognize the motorcyclist because of the helmet, but I did recognize the pumped-up tits, sleek black catsuit and the hybrid Triumph as belonging to Laguna Woods. The bitch gave me thumbs up; like I need anything from her.

I was too busy to shoot her so I climbed on top of the bus. The driver was still driving like crazy, but no one was shooting at me. I decided to save some C4 and shot the lock off the rear gunner's hatch latch. I opened the hatch and shot the passenger trying to come out of it at me. And then another and another after that. I couldn't tell if they were trying to kill me or just trying to get off the bus. The other passengers were trying shove the bodies out of the way, but they and the dead gunner were jammed tight.

Laguna, bless her little fucking heart, was shooting into the rear of the bus. If it was to clear a space for me, it seemed to be working. I shoved the bodies out of the way and hung upside down and fired both machine guns into the screaming, moiling mass of what was left of the passengers. Pretty soon they were no longer screaming or moiling, they were just dead.

I put on my gloves as the poison in the needles would be active for another five minutes and I didn't want kill myself when I was so close to success. Now that I was in the bus, the driver was barreling straight down Sunset, blowing his horn that sounded like a cross between a foghorn and the scream rabbits make when they climax. I hate that noise more than anything and I was going to kill the fucker if only because of that. I used a glob of C4 on the steel door of the driver cage and blew the lock off. The driver was shooting at me and trying to drive and, consequently, not doing either very well.

And here was my dilemma: I needed to wrest control of the bus from him and then kill him, because if I killed him first, we'd crash. Goddam Laguna decided to get helpful again and was shooting at the driver from the driver side. This distracted him enough that I could jerk the door open, shoot him in the head and grab control of the bus. It was a little awkward because I was sitting on his lap and what was left of his head was bouncing against my back. I got the bus under enough control that I could unhook his seatbelt and shove him out of the way.

Success! Victory! I had conquered an MTA fortress bus all by myself! I was so elated, I almost failed to notice Laguna banging on the front passenger door. I waved her away; she was spoiling my moment. Then I heard the big, gas SUV engines that were chasing us. Laguna was banging on the door, making so much noise, I wondered if she had on titan-chainmail gloves. Well, fuck her, I wasn't letting her in. There was so much shooting going on outside, I'd get hit if I opened the door. A few seconds later she swerved away. I heard a crash and bump and figured she'd been hit. I mentally ticked her off the list as one less person to kill.

I hadn't figured she'd climb up the side of the bus and come in through the gunner's turret, but she did. In the passenger area monitor I saw her stomping up the aisle toward me. I might have shot her then, but she had her very big gun out and the business end was pointed in my direction. I looked over my shoulder as she stomped her way through the carnage. "WHAT THE FUCK IS IT NOW, LAGUNA?"

"Weren't you going to open that door, asshole?" she yelled.

I shrugged. "I couldn't figure out how." I sort of lied. I hadn't even looked for the door open button.

"It's this button!" Laguna stabbed a broken acrylic nail at the console and the front door opened.

Opened right into a machine gun mounted on an MTA SUV Assault Vehicle. We screamed. Laguna fired and I swerved the bus into the SUV, which crashed very nicely.

"How did you know that?" I asked my uninvited, heavily armed passenger.

"I saw the schematics of the inside," she said, reloading. She punched a few more buttons and there was some clanking in the back of the bus. "I have a higher security clearance than you do." She smirked at me. I hate that. "Oh, and don't shoot me in the back; I'm about to help you get rid of that pesky helicopter."

"What heli–?" Oh, fuck! "There's two!" I yelled.

"I see them, Nellie, just drive!"

I heard some clanking around the bus, but was too busy driving to really notice. Laguna went into the back of the bus and came back with a belt-loading riot gun and an Uzi. "Where'd you get those?" I asked.

"There's an arsenal back there," she said, handing me the Uzi.

I hadn't known that. "Oh yeah? How'd you know?"

"Like I said, I have a higher security clearance than you do," she said. "I looked it up on the net."

Laguna climbed up into the front machine gun turret and fired at the SUVs until they retreated. The helicopters were still a problem, but she kept them at bay with machine gun fire.

At Alvarado, I turned right to go south. The helicopters seemed to be backed off and there were no SUVs around. I found that odd, until I heard Laguna scream and then I saw it: A roadblock at Alvarado and Wilshire. Not just any roadblock—this road block was three fortress buses head on.

Laguna was next to me, punching up screens and windows like a madwoman. There was an IM flashing on the CRT sunk in the dashboard and, since I was only driving the bus, I clicked on it:

MTA: "Surrender Nellie Gail"

"Laguna..."

"Just keep driving!" she yelled over the clunking in the front of the bus. "Hope I did this right," she growled. "Every missile system is different."

"Missile?" I had hardly said it when she fired three missiles and blew a huge hole in the buses in front of us. I barely had time to wonder why they hadn't fired on us—maybe they were going take us alive and kill us slowly—because I was too busy turning left and heading east a block above Wilshire, on Sixth Street. I was glad; it would have been a real mess driving through all the rubble, bodies, fire, and chaos one block south.

I still had a pack of SUVs, a helicopter or two, and

the least-damaged of the roadblock buses to shake off on the ride through downtown. Sixth Street was less torn up than the streets north of it, but still a maze of rubble. However, my bus bashed itself a path through it all quite nicely. That it was also bashing a path for everything behind us was a problem, mainly for Laguna, firing from the machine gun turret. I was shooting at the occasional SUV that got past her, which was far too often.

The Sixth Street bridge across the river was just ahead. Good thing, because Laguna was low on ammo. I roared across the bridge toward what looked like a small army. I was damn glad to see the DWP logos on the vehicles. Home free! And the MTA hadn't crossed the bridge with us. Cowards! Ha!

Fyodor grabbed me up in his arms the minute I stepped off the bus. "Oh my God, Nellie!" he shouted. "You did it! You hijacked a bus!"

"YES!"

"All by yourself!"

"YES!"

"My sister hijacked a bus all by herself!" he yelled, twirling me around. "MY SISTER RULES! SHE RULES!!! YEARGH! YEARGH! YEARGH!"

Laguna was standing next to Max, looking pissed off, but I couldn't hear what they were saying over Fyodor's screaming. I only have one brother and he's plenty for anyone. I was tired, so Fyodor continued his war dance by himself. I leaned against the bus and waved at Ed, who was making his way over.

"So, you lived," he said.

"I did."

"And hijacked a bus."

"I did."

"Why?"

"Because it was there," I snapped. I remembered how pissed off I was at him. I couldn't remember why I was pissed, but that I was, so I walked over to Max and Laguna.

"Hi, Nell," he said. "Nice bus."

"Yup."

"Hijacked it all by yourself, did you?"

"Yup."

Laguna, the bitch, rolled her eyes so hard, I thought I heard them rattling around in her empty head.

"Were you following me, Laguna?" I asked in an undertone.

"Of course. I'm on the job making sure you're on the job."

'Bitch,' I thought. "Where do you fit in all this again?" I asked, mainly because she was still standing there.

"I just work for the same idiots you used to," she said. "They think Chelsea Clinton is coming to LA to lead the rebellion, and they have their money on her."

'What a bunch of idiots,' I thought.

A reedy guy in a suit came up to us, cleared his throat and introduce himself as Mr. Fontana of the DWP. "The MTA would like a word with you, Miss Gail," he said. He held out a PDA with an IM message: 'Surrender Nellie Gail.'

"Never!" I said.

"Never what, Nell?" Fyodor asked behind me. He looked at the PDA and asked what the MTA would do to me.

"They'll kill her," Fontana said matter-of-factly. "They don't like their defenses breached any more than we do."

"Well, they can't kill her," Fyodor said as if it was

the most obvious thing in the world.

"Well, not yet anyway," Max chimed in.

"Why not?" Fontana asked.

"We need her," Laguna said. "For now."

I wasn't sure I liked being needed by Laguna Woods, but I'd just hijacked an MTA fortress bus all by myself and didn't care what anyone thought of me. Although dying at the hands of the MTA did not appeal to me, I was too deep in my victory high to be very worried. I also had other worries, like Chelsea Clinton, Kevin, Abilene, the Greens, the Progressives, the Militias for Christ, Arlo was talking about raising his prices...

"Okay, let's go talk to them," Max announced into my reverie. "Laguna, you're representing Langley, right?"

"I can, but I was on that bus with Nellie while she was hijacking it all by herself," Laguna purred. God, I hated purring blonds almost as much as MTA fortress buses, maybe more now.

"Be that as it may, your Langley ID carries some weight," Max said. "Are you with us, Mr. Fontana?"

The DWP bureaucrat shrugged. "I've never even heard of anyone hijacking an MTA bus before," he said laconically. "We might be able to get her off the hook on the sheer novelty of it."

I really hate it when people talk about me as if I'm not standing right next to them. I'd let this one pass because I was so serene from my recent success, that nothing could upset me. Much. The only thing that could've improved that afternoon would have been a large carrot juice.

"Okay, then it's the three of us," Max said, while Fontana tapped in an IM message to the army on the other side of the LA river.

"Want me along, Max?" Fyodor asked.

"No," Max said, thoughtfully. "No, you'd better stay here in case they kill us all. You'll need to finish the mission." He looked at me. "I hope you appreciate this, Nell."

I just laughed contemptuously and sneered. I'd been practicing laughing and sneering for this very occasion. I was glad I got to try it out. It must have been good, because Max frowned at me and walked away.

Max's group met the MTA group in the middle of the bridge. I borrowed some field glasses, but all I could see was some arms waving and fists shaking. And some rational talk from Max (he's good at that when he decides to do it); then there were handshakes, and our guys, except for Laguna, came back with one of the MTA guys.

Actually it was a big woman named Ms. Lewis, who would be our driver for the Chelsea Clinton mission. "Very impressive, Miss Gail," she said, towering over me. "I understand we'll be sending the bill to Mr. Soros and Mr. Gates."

I gave her the old laugh and sneer routine. She just rolled her eyes and went to check out the bus. After she saw all the carnage in it, she called for a new bus. In fact, after taking a good look at our "forces," she called for three new buses and two drivers.

When I asked, Max told me he'd sent Laguna back to LA with the MTA people. He said she put up a fight, but ultimately took his word that he'd keep me in line when Chelsea Clinton arrived. I laughed and sneered; all this laughing and sneering was wearing me out. But I was glad Laguna was gone. I don't work well with an audience.

The DWP and MTA keep the 710 freeway in good condition so goods from Mexico can get from the port into the city. We rolled south on its smooth and well-kept surface—it was like riding on glass compared to most of the LA roads now, and got down to San Pedro as the sun was setting. If Max was hoping for anything like stealth, three MTA fortress buses, a dozen DWP SUVs, three DWP defensible cherry-pickers, and daylight wrecked it. Max was unconcerned; Fyodor was his usual happy-go-lucky linguist self and even Ed, whom I figured had some sense, was not worried. I was the only one worried. We were out in the open in daylight with a circus of city services, and if I were on the other side, we'd be dead by now.

However, we made it to the docks and settled down to wait. I figured this was a good a time as any to spill my guts to Max. "Max," I said, planting myself in front of him "Max, Kevin threatened to kill Fyodor if I don't kill Chelsea Clinton for him."

"He did?" Fyodor squeaked.

"I'd heard something like that," Max said, staring dramatically at the horizon.

I strolled around him so I was between him and the horizon. "Max, did you know he's working for the Greens and Progressives and they want Chelsea Clinton dead?"

"They do?" Fyodor was having a tough time in this conversation even though I was talking to Max.

"I'd heard something also like that," Max said, turned his back on me, and stared dramatically at the MTA fortress bus behind us.

"Why do the Greens and Progressives want her dead?" Fyodor asked me.

"Because things in this country have to get worse

before they can get better," I said, walking around Max.

"Worse than this?" Fyodor asked, waving at the rubble of that had been one of the great Pacific ports.

"You'd have to ask them, not me, Fyod," I said. "Max, did you know Abilene is working for the 700 Club and has joined forces with Kevin and his clients to off Chelsea Clinton?"

"I'd heard—"

"Yeah," I said, putting my hands on his shoulders to keep him focused on me and stationary. "But did you know they've joined forces because the Militias of Christ are in it now, and they scare the bejezus out of everyone, including me?"

Max and Fyodor exchanged nervous looks. "You mean the Militias of Christ are here now? In LA?"

"I don't think they're in LA," I said. "They could be out in the desert waiting to strike and having visions of de debbil like St. Anthony. I barely know what's going on in Hollywood, let alone in the wastelands outside the city limits. But it worries me that you didn't know this."

"I suspected it, but I never thought they'd come this far west," Max admitted, getting some of his old poise back. "Chelsea Clinton is quite a draw." He smirked. I found it disgusting.

"Which brings me to my next question," I said, staying in front of him. "Why've you got all your hopes pinned on Chelsea Clinton?"

"She's coming to save us." He sounded like he was quoting.

"Max, I spent years watching your 'Live Nude Economics' show on the internet," I said. "One of your main ideas on that show was that economics, progress, fairness, et cetera, were about ideas, not personalities. I was quite young and this made a big impression on me. Have you changed your tune so much since you got chased out of the US?"

"Yes! Talk me out of it, Nellie!" He looked way too smug and I suspected he was lying, but I had no idea why or about what he was lying.

"I can't talk you out of this crazy idea if you've become that much of a coward and need to hide behind Chelsea Clinton's skirts." I could tell he didn't like that by the way he scowled so I went on. "The US was built on ideas, not perfect ones, but good ones. Good enough to roll with historical forces and still come up swinging. If it was about personalities, Washington would have agreed to be King and Jefferson would have become some kind of Pope."

"Not Franklin for Pope?" Fyodor asked. He loved these historical "what if" conversations.

"Franklin was cooler than all of them put together," I said. "He knew ideas were dangerous when they became dogma yoked to a cult of personality. He'd never have agreed to 'represent' freedom, justice, and so on. Jefferson, I think, would have done it, thinking it would begin and end with him. And he would have been wrong, He also said 'The liberty tree must be watered every twenty years with blood' or words to that effect. He was wrong about that; he wrote the document that kept us from having to kill each other every twenty years and he never realized it. So I think Jefferson could have been blind enough to be Pope of the United States. However, because even he knew it was about ideas and not personality, we got a Supreme Court, separation of church and state, and two other branches of Government. It's an arrangement with enough wiggle room so we can all live in peace. In their time, these were mind-blowing ideas. Freedom, equality–"

"Yeah, for rich white guys." (Fyodor—what a killjoy.)

"Yeah, and there were slaves and women as chattels, and indentured servants and Native Americans. Don't be confused, Fyodor; smart, rich, white guys designed our government, not God, so some of those issues got addressed when they could be addressed."

"Kicking and screaming," he added.

"White guys never want to give up power, that's for sure, brother. But for the time it was conceived, the United States was the most radical, most outrageous, most dangerous experiment on the planet. And it wasn't that most of those old white guys thought they were so much smarter-worthy-better than anyone else; they just knew they wouldn't live forever. But they also knew that ideas live forever, and the ideas of freedom and the mechanisms of justice might, maybe might, keep the country on the side of fairness and the right side of History long after they were gone. And, yeah, it's been more miss than hit, but, as a general rule, Americans have been willing to try to do the right thing once they figure out what the right thing is. And that's what the founders were counting on; that we'd at least try to do the right thing, and by God, for over two hundred years we did try. That is, up until December 12, 2000, when the Supreme Court stopped the recount. In retrospect, we should have been in the streets watering the Liberty Tree with blood and lots of it. But we are a reasonable people most of the time, or try to be, we were willing to give the illegal Bush Administration a chance, and they blew it repeatedly. Our Democracy, as we knew it, might have survived a four year hiatus because the Founders' ideas were still strong in us. But the Founders never counted on their future citizens wimping out."

"How so?" Max asked when I stopped to catch my breath.

"We trusted our government to keep us safe, and either through stupidity or wickedness, they let us down. So what, with the exception of the martyred Congresswoman Barbara Lee, does our Congress do? They hand more power, a King's power, to George W. Bush, the very unelected despot who let us down in the lead-up to September 11, 2001. How incredibly stupid was that? If I believed in God, I might agree with crazy Janey Caterham-7 that we are being punished. Fortunately I only believe in historical forces, guns, money, and the reek of raw power and its eventual decay.

"But I digress, Max, and I hope you'll understand that American history and political science are not my fields. Although the US has had its share of genocide, I've never had to consider it in the larger context of our national character and history. However, since the fall of Los Angeles and my disciplinary leave from the Company, I have had some time to study my new demon. Because I have no future, I must romance the past. Not, mind you, romanticize it, but woo it, court it, and make peace with it, if only for my own peace of mind.

"We've had good leaders and we've had bad ones, but we've always had a core of ideas to govern us through thick and thin. The Bush family thinks they can rule us because they're better than we are. They and their minions believe they can rule through fear and personality. And most of the country has been cowed or drugged or murdered into submission because we've lost our way, Max, we wanted someone to take care of us and we got the worst of all possible worlds. We traded our ideals of freedom and justice and truth for the illusion of security, when the only security we've ever had in the country were those ideals, and the hope that we could make a better future for everyone if we worked hard and played by the rules. So since when are you going to be led by and fight for Chelsea Clinton or any one person? Are you going to set her up as the new boss? Make her the Queen of the United States? We need our ideas back, Max, we're dying without them. There's no point to the United States without those ideas."

"I hadn't realized you were so philosophical, Nellie," he said quietly.

"I'm not, I just prefer ideas to people, that's all." I shrugged. "I feel more comfortable with ideas."

"Why is that?" he asked.

"I've never had an idea try to kill me," I said. "And people are either prey or predators, so I find it hard to like them."

Max thought about this for a moment. "You're more dangerous than I suspected, Nell," he said at last. "I might have to kill you someday."

Fyodor put his arms around me and said if he wanted to take me out, he'd have to go through him.

Now, I love my brother as well as any sister does, but in all honestly, Fyodor Chandler couldn't defend a slice of cheesecake from a fork. So it seemed I was going to have to come clean.

"Max, I'm not going to kill Chelsea Clinton for Kevin or for anyone," I said over Fyodor's shoulder. "I'm not going to kill her because she seems like a decent person and must be very fucking brave to come here for any reason. But you've got to promise me you'll keep Fyodor safe from Kevin and his thugs, and if you do kick down the Bush dictatorship, you'll put the ideas back in place and rebuild the country on them."

"You want all this in exchange for not killing you?" Max asked.

"I thought you were going to kill me 'someday'," I said, stepping back from Fyodor. "I'll probably have died of natural or unnatural causes by 'someday', so I'm not too worried about that. No, this is in exchange for getting Chelsea Clinton wherever you want her; that's all, Max, just that."

"That might be plenty," Max said.

He must have very sharp ears, because he heard the boat before I did. It was dark and we were some distance from the dock. I picked up a rifle with an infrared sight on it. Max raised his revolver to my temple.

"Max..." Fyodor warned softly.

"I'm just looking, Max, no harm in looking..." I said. And looking I was, looking hard. The woman on the dock looked like Chelsea Clinton, but she moved like an ostrich on crack. She jerked along on spike heels with her chest thrust out in a bad imitation of the old runway models.

Now, I had never seen Chelsea Clinton in person, but I'd studied enough internet videos of her to know she didn't move like this prancing puta down there on the dock. I looked at Max over his gun. "Max," I said. "What the fuck is that down there?"

"Chelsea Clinton," he declaimed. "And she has come to lead the revolution."

"Impossible." I shoved the rifle at Fyodor and stomped over to where Mr. Fontana was standing. He was at the end of the little path that lead down to the dock, waiting in breathless expectation for his idol.

"She's here," he said reverently.

"Wanna bet?" I snarled. I don't like surprises; they make me cranky.

Max and Fyodor joined us and there was a hush as the... this... whatever this person was minced up to greet us. One of the buses shined its lights on her and we were treated to a vacuous smile beneath vacant eyes. Since this made her a target in a spotlight, I told them to turn it off.

"Well! Here I am! Who's Dr. Max?" she chirped. There was nothing but horrified silence to answer her.

"He's Max," I said, pointing at him. "And who the fuck are you?"

"Chelsea Clinton."

"Oh, come now," I growled, circling her.

"Hey, an acting job is an acting job even if it does involve plastic surgery," she spat at me. "My agent said this would be good for my career and it's better than doing anal."

We thought this over in silence. I suppose it all made sense on some level. I just couldn't figure out how it made sense for Max. Did he know she was a fake from the gitgo? Was he really expecting Chelsea Clinton to put her ass on the line for the country that mistreated and humiliated her family and still sends assassins after them? Why should she? But would she? Had I on some level been hoping for someone to save me, too? But then the shooting started and I figured I'd better save my own ass and worry about Chelsea Clinton, faux or real, later.

The sniper was a rotten shot. Unless they just meant to pin us down until... Until the helicopters arrived. There were three fast and quiet gunships. The MTA took out one right away and drove off the other two long enough for us to get to the buses. Which was also when the SUVs of Christ showed up to chase us.

I wound up with Max, the faux Chelsea Clinton, Fyodor and Ed in Ms. Lewis' bus. That woman can certainly drive, I'll give her that much. We headed back the way we'd come, north on the 710.

Now, I had mixed emotions about this. The 710 is wide open and we were being chased by two gunboat helicopters and an unknown number of SUVs for Christ. The DWP was doing a good job taking out the SUVs and the MTA buses were keeping the helicopters off us. Still, I don't like running in the open like this, but there was no way for the fortress bus to travel with more cover. That was the downside; the upside was that there was lots of armor on the bus and lots of guns, many of which Ed and I were using.

"Where are we going?" the faux Chelsea Clinton screamed over the noise.

"DreamWorks. To see Spielberg," Max yelled.

She squealed, it sounded happy; anything to keep her from freaking out. Just yet. She didn't have to know Dreamworks moved its operation to France years ago. Good old Max, always the right lie at the right moment.

"Here." I handed him a Colt Anaconda. It weighed a ton and I decided right then and there that I wanted to work for the MTA, if only for the weapons. I'd taken a Colt Trooper for myself.

Bullets slammed into the side of the bus, way too close. Max and I leaned out the windows and fired at what we could see. Apparently the DWP wasn't doing such a great job at keeping the other side off us. One of the MTA buses exploded a little ahead of us. Ms. Lewis swerved us out of trouble, but I had the feeling we weren't out of the woods yet.

The faux Chelsea Clinton was freaking out. Max comforted her: "Keep your head down, dear," he said.

"Yes, just there, and a little to the left."

Well, I was glad someone was having a good time, so I figured I'd better get to work. I climbed into the front machine gun turret and put my 'if it moves, shoot it' theory into practice. Ed liked this idea, and climbed into the other turret.

Shooting at the gunships was a waste of time. The other MTA bus fired a missile that took out one of them. The MTA driver and crew didn't have much time to enjoy that, because a pack of SUVs pulled them down.

It was too dark to see how many Militia for Christ SUVs were out there and what else besides them. It seemed like they had an endless supply of potential martyrs, because Ed and I emptied our machine guns and yet the SUVs kept coming.

"What now, Nell?" Fyodor asked when I dropped from the turret. He'd obviously didn't like the way the logistics looked.

"I–" I didn't get to finish because we all dove to the floor to avoid the hail of bullets coming our way. Max managed to land on top of the faux Chelsea Clinton. He was looking way too serene for a man who was as close to death as we all were. Through all the shooting, I could still hear the ominous thump on the roof of the bus. Well, that's what I'd do; hell, that's what I did. "Oh shit," I said, handing Fyodor the Colt Trooper and a speed-loader. "Shoot at anything," I said, pointing at the windows and machine gun turrets. "That isn't me," I added.

Raiding the ammo locker once more, I took a Skorpion submachine gun and a Jericho 941. Under Fyodor's covering fire I got to the front entrance of the bus. I waved at Ms. Lewis to open the front door. The turnstile speaker crackled and she told me I was crazy. I said, "I know, just open the door, please".

"Well then, hold on a minute," she said. She smashed the bus into the nearest SUVs and then she opened the door for me.

I sprayed the remaining SUVs with machinegun fire. They swerved away from us and crashed.

There was so much shooting going on inside the bus, that the three guys on top of it never saw me climbing up behind them. They had shot up both gun turrets and were trying to get past the shooting from the inside to get inside. I shot those three and two more jumped on from the other side. Ed and Fyodor could have done me a favor and shot at the SUVs on the other side of the bus.

I was pinned down at the front of the bus. One guy was shooting at me while the other was shooting inside the bus. Ed must have shot him, because his head exploded and he fell off the bus. I figure the last guy was fair game, then the last Christianist helicopter shone its huge halogen light on me and suddenly I was fair game.

But Ms. Lewis was a woman who knew her job. She took the helicopter out with a missile. The MTA should really give her a raise; I planned to write a letter telling them. If I lived, that is.

So it was a shootout on the MTA fortress bus. The bus was swerving all over the place, so between shots we were hanging on for dear life. Not that I would admit it out loud, but I could have used Laguna's help just then. I finally got a clear shot at the last man on the bus and took him out. I wasn't sure there weren't more Christianists hanging on the back of the bus, which I knew from experience was possible. I figured I'd better go look. I was half way down the bus when the loudest, largest helicopter I'd ever seen was suddenly directly overhead. It was firing at everything around the bus and descending at an alarming rate. There were huge metal bars, bus-length bars, where the landing skids should have been. It shone a huge light on the top of the bus and the voice of God issued from the PA:

"Passenger, return to your seat."

It was that or be crushed to death. I half fell, half dived through the rear turret.

"Nell! Are you all right?" Fyodor asked, helping me sit up.

"I–" I started, but, our driver, Ms. Lewis was sitting on the floor in front of me. "Who's driving the bus!" I screamed.

"That MTA tow-copter I called has got it on remote," she yelled back over the noise. Whatever else she said was drowned out by the screeching of metal. The huge bars I'd seen on the helicopter were being clamped on each side of the bus. From the bars, thick metal prongs extended and tilted up, clamping onto the roof of the bus.

We passengers were glued to the floor, cowering away from the flying shards of glass and metal. As the helicopter lifted the bus off the tarmac, I, for one, was cowering on the floor hoping the bus was going to stay in one piece.

As usual, Fyodor wouldn't know danger if it bit him on the ass. He climbed on a seat and was looking out the window. "This is awesome!" he yelled. "Nell! Come up here!" He reached down and dragged me up next to him. "Look at this! We're in a flying bus!"

He certainly wasn't wrong; we were in a flying bus and it was awesome.

We flew to the MTA facility in Burbank. Surrounded by MTA fortress buses and whatever other terrifying technology they had out there, I felt safe in my own strangely paranoid way.

But I had a job to finish and finish it I would. Grasping the faux Chelsea Clinton's dyed-up, permmed-up, frizzy mop from behind, I put a nine millimeter into her heart. I waited until she stopped flopping around before I cut off her head and put it in a garbage bag.

"All that for a fake," Ms. Lewis said, shaking her head. "But why kill her?"

"I have to prove I did," I said, figuring this crazy brave bus driver deserved an explanation. "I promised her head to a client. He doesn't have to know it's not Chelsea Clinton. As long as it looks like her, he'll be happy."

"Well, I don't understand what we just did, but I'm not going to argue with the first person in history to hijack a fortress bus." Ms. Lewis sounded tired.

"Ms. Lewis, I'm not sure what we were supposed to do back there," I said, hoisting the garbage bag on my back (heads are heavier than they look). "But if we did nothing else, we repelled a second invasion of Los Angeles."

We shook hands and I asked if I could borrow a bus. She said sure, and got me one. I think I really do want to work for the MTA one day; they have the best equipment I've ever seen. Max and Ed wanted me to wait for them, but I had a bus, and my bus and I wait for no man.

My bus and I rolled into Hollywood miles and miles ahead of everyone else. I can drive these muthahs; there's no doubt about that. In front of the Limo Brothers recycling and burger joint, I yelled for Julia until she came out.

"Miss Gail! You did it! You did it! I knew you'd

do it!"

Such a sweet kid; this totally made my day. "Yeah, well, never a doubt," I said, waving her into the bus. "Take this monster for a quick joy ride, then have your family get rid of it. I'll take my cut of the proceeds in goods and services. You're my agent, Julia, get me the best possible deal you can. I've got business to finish up at the Klan of the Koffee Kats."

She lit up like a Christmas tree. I picked up my garbage bag and watched her roar off into the night. I figured I'd find Kevin or get a message to him at the KKK, so I headed in that direction. I waved at Arlo on my way by his place. The Starbucks guys were hanging out in front of their shop, watching the KKK intently. This would have made me nervous except I only planned to be in there for a New York minute, less if possible.

I found Kevin and, not surprisingly, Abilene. Alarmingly, I also found Laguna. "Nice night, Laguna, what the fuck are you doing here?" I asked, while the KKK stripped my weapons off.

"My fucking job, you bitch," she snarled. "Why didn't you tell me Kevin was in this?"

I shrugged, partly because I shrug well, but also to hide my grudging admiration. Laguna was in the middle of the KKK vortex of political intransigence, all by herself, facing down the bad guys and me. It was brave, it was crazy, it was stupid, and it was probably what I'd do in her place.

I met Kevin's dead eyes. "Here's my end of the deal," I said, handing him the bag with the faux Chelsea Clinton's head in it. "I expect you to keep your end."

Kevin looked in the bag and smiled his creepy smile. "Whatever you say, Miss Gail," he drawled. He showed the contents to Abilene, who nodded grimly and gave me thumbs up. Passing the bag to Laguna, Kevin gave me a bland look and turned to the nearest shotgun toting Starbucker. "Kill them both," he said, gesturing to me and Laguna.

The order was drowned out by Laguna screaming, "Nellie, you cunt! I thought we had a deal!" and lunging for my throat. She had a grip like iron and her arms were longer than mine, so I couldn't hit her in the face. I dragged her down to the floor, hoping to kick her off or slam her into the bar or something.

Well, everybody enjoys a good cat fight, so nobody shot at us. But as we were rolling around like enraged trash, a whole lot of other shooting started. Glass, pieces of furniture, and pieces of flesh were flying. Laguna was too intent on strangling me to notice. My vision filled up with blood from being choked and things were going dark. Flailing around, I found something sharp (I knew it was sharp because it cut my palm). Hauling Laguna down by her catsuit with one hand, I raked her eyes with what turned out to be a broken coffee glass with the other hand.

Howling like a fury, Laguna let go of my throat to claw at her eyes. In a moment of poor judgment, she staggered to her feet and was cut in half by machine gunfire. Her upper body fell on me as I rolled away from the shooting match, trying to get my breath back.

I'm so glad blood beads on ti-tandex. What I really hate is the feeling of blood soaking into my skin. I shoved what was left of Laguna off me and dragged myself into the nearest corner. From there I could see that the gun battle was between the KKK's Green and Progressive and the Starbucks' Francophone barristas. The KKK were using the coffee bar for what cover it was worth. I was a little behind them, wishing for more cover and hoping they didn't see me. They were between me and the back exit. The Starbuckers were outside, badly concealed and getting the worst of it. They were also between me and the front exit. Basically, I was stuck and probably going to die. This seemed unfair in its inevitability and annoyed me very much.

However, I hadn't counted on Julia crashing the MTA Fortress bus into the middle of it all. She drove that monster right into the back wall, conveniently crushing most of the KKK. Most impressive. Her brothers, cousins, whoever the hell they were, poured out of the bus and finished off the KKK in short order.

There was much shooting and screaming in the dark; the bus had knocked out the lights. I figured my best bet was to lie in my corner until things calmed down. It was pretty much all I could do right then anyway. I thought I heard big engines—buses, SUVs, helicopters maybe? It was hard to hear over the shooting and the ringing in my ears. The shooting went away and the screaming was replaced with masculine voices shouting orders. I thought I could hear Julia calling, "Miss Gail! Miss Gail!", but that might have been my imagination. Over all this cacophony one voice was raised to a hysterical note:

"ALISON!!! ALISON!!!"

Poor Larry; I guess it's not easy being my brother. I figured I better pull myself together before he completely lost it.

The lights were flicking back on, enough for Julia to find me, at least. "Miss Gail!" She was next to me, helping me up. She was being useful instead of standing in the middle of the room, screaming my name.

"NELLIE! NELLIE!" That was Ed, somewhere in

the room.

Well, it was nice they were looking for me. I, on the other hand was most interested in finding Max, because I had some urgent questions for him. "Julia, honey, see if you can find me a nice loaded gun, okay?"

"Sure, Miss Gail, are you okay?" The lights were completely back on. I must have been a mess—cuts, bruises coming out and eyes full of broken blood vessels from being choked (I know I was seeing red)—if the stunned look on Julia's face was anything to go by.

"Pretty much."

"Your eyes..." she began, but Larry found me at that moment.

"ALISON!!!" He wrapped me in a bear hug. "Are you okay?"

"Pretty much," I said into his shoulder. "Where's Max?"

"Around here somewhere. I–"

"OH, MON DIEU, C'EST LA TETE DE CHELSEA CLINTON!"

"Tell them to run some DNA on that before they freak out," I said.

"Oh, merci Dieu," one of the Pete's barristas said next to us. "Voila Mademoiselle Gail."

"Yeah, bon soir, who the fuck are you well-armed guys?" I asked.

The barrista looked at Larry, I mean, Fyodor (who nodded), and said, "French Foreign Legion. Jacques Cousteau, je suis ici!" He gave me bow and walked off.

"Fyodor? What the hell–?"

"Oh my God, your poor eyes. What hap–"

"Fuck my eyes, and tell me–"

"We figured we'd need back-up when the opposition arrived," he said, looking guilty. "The Royal

Canadian Mounties, the ones from Quebec, are here, too. We wanted to be able to take them all out at once."

I assumed they were from Quebec to maintain some kind of linguistic purity, but I was too tired to assume much more. "And?" I asked.

"And we hadn't counted on the Christanists piling on," he said. "Thank God, you brought the MTA into it or we might have lost that fight. The DWP is good, but we needed the extra firepower. Oh, speak of the devil, there's Ed. Ed!"

"Nellie! There you are." Ed hugged me.

Julia sidled up to me and handed me a Colt KingCobra. "I found you a gun, Miss Gail," she said.

"Thanks," I said. She must have raided the ammo locker in the bus.

"Hey, Ed! There's an IM from your wife," someone from across the room yelled.

"Wife?" I asked, weighing the gun in my hand.

"But I think there's only one bullet in it," Julia added.

"Um..." Ed said, backing away a little.

"Ed! IM from your wife!"

"I better go see what that's about," he said and bolted.

I opened the cylinder and, yes, in fact, there was only one bullet. Ed was in luck that night, because I needed the bullet for another guy. "Okay, Fyodor, where's Max?" I asked.

"Outside somewhere," Fyodor said, looking nervous. "Nellie, look, what are–?"

"Not to worry, big brother, not to worry," I reassured him. Max was the one who had something to worry about.

Outside, I saw Arlo being led off in handcuffs.

"What's up with that, Fyodor?" I asked.

"He was spying on you," Fyodor said. "Didn't you wonder how everyone knew exactly where you were and what you were doing? It was Arlo."

I had wondered, but now I was wondering where I was going to get carrot juice. And, incredibly, I had more pressing things to wonder about just then. "MAX!"

He turned toward me and I raised my one bullet gun.

"Okay, Max. Too many coincidences to be accidents. Explain."

"It was a diversion, Nellie," he said coolly. "We had to make the other side think the invasion and revolution was happening in LA. The invasion is actually happening from Quebec and the Gulf of Mexico. We'll split the country, contain the east and liberate the west."

Like Churchill wanted to invade Occupied Europe from the Mediterranean, through the Balkans, and Eisenhower overrode him. How different history would read had Churchill, who knew what he was doing, prevailed. "And Chelsea Clinton?" I asked.

"Was never anywhere near it, Nell. You were right: it's not about personalities, it's about the ideas this country was founded on and grew great on. We just want to find our way back to those. We can heal the country on those ideas. We can only die from this or any dictatorship," he said solemnly

"Give me a break, Max. Why bring me in?"

"You put on one helluva a show, Nellie. No one on the other side had a clue we were coming from anywhere but LA, where everything starts," he said with a smirk.

I pointed my gun at his smirk. "You played me."

"Yes, I did. Was it good for you, too?"

134

Well, I didn't off him; my killjoy brother talked me out of it. He went on and on about what a valuable contribution Max was making to freedom, justice, and macroeconomic hygiene. It sounded like a bunch of Fyodor Chandler bullshit, but I was too tired to argue with him that night.

But now that I've gotten some rest, the more I think about it the more the whole Chelsea Clinton Is Coming To Lead the Revolution and Save Us All scam looks like a Fyodor Chandler production. Much as I admire Max, this had more of that almost comprehensible, convoluted, vicious (with an annoying dash of slapstick) cunning plan and execution that linguists so excel at.

I asked Julia and Fyodor to look around for bodies: They found what was left of Laguna, but nothing of Abilene or Kevin. This bothers me enough that I'm more careful these days.

Because I needed a reliable carrot juice source, I turned Arlo's juice and fruitas place over to Julia. Business is booming for her. She even got the Starbuckers-French-Foreign-Legion and Royal-Canadian-Mounties-from-Quebec-Francophone coffee guys to give her—just flat out give her—their coffee scorching equipment and tacky furniture because they wouldn't be needing it anymore. Due to the increase in business, she brought her brother or cousin or whatever, Jim, on as help. I just want to be able to get carrot juice 24/7 without being spied on, that's all.

But I still have my Security Consultant contract with the DWP and picked up a Strategic Assault Tester contact with the MTA, so right now I'm sitting pretty with dough and work I can put my whole personality into and be proud of. I'm steering clear of private jobs for the moment. I hope it's a long time before the next Laguna Woods blows into town. A very long time.

I haven't seen Ed since things cooled down. If he were around, we might be able to finish what we started. If his wife will give him the night off, that is.

So, I guess that's just how it is in this big city.

I love LA.

It's men that annoy me.

The Project for the New American Century at Sunset and Vine

I wasn't sure what to think when the hookers came back to Hollywood. It happened fast, even for this town; one day there weren't any and the next there were three or four on my stretch of Sunset. I thought they were mostly wiped out in the Occupation and then, when the cash system crashed, there was only so much they could barter for sex. They starved, were murdered, or died of disease.

I was too busy with my own post-Occupation survival to worry about anyone else. While I was looking for Fydor Chandler and the renegade linguists of the Dissident Superior League (DSL), and getting put on disciplinary leave from the CIA for a few honest mistakes (they sent me too much C4, damn it, it wasn't my fault Cheney was in the building when it blew up), Los Angeles staggered up to its commercial feet. With an online debit card system in an economy and infrastructure the Department of Water and Power (DWP) ran in conjunction with AT&T and the Metro Transit Authority (MTA) the city ran badly, but, miraculously, the lights were on, the phones worked, most of the heavily rationed water supply was potable, and the buses kept order on their routes. We Angelenos, what was left of us, had enough to survive on, but hardly flourish, let alone afford hookers.

Gradually things got better for me. In the course of saving the city from the Ulluminati and the Militias for Christ, the DWP and the MTA took me on as a security consultant. As part of my fee, I also got the building on Sunset near Vine that I had worked in as a data entry clerk. I moved my scene from East Hollywood; the Limo Brothers Burgers and Recycling, and Arlo, the late fruitas guy who kept me in carrot juice, came with me because I offered them low rent and protection.

I was offering a lot of protection these days; somehow this part of Hollywood had become my turf. Through no effort on my part beyond defending my home and carrot juice supply, I'd become a sort of Warlord, and my several square miles were some of the safest in the city. This, I supposed, was the main reason the hookers were operating here. Julia Limo, who'd taken over for the late Arlo as my carrot juice connection, thought they brought down the tone of the neighborhood. She was able to overlook the streets the MTA's fortress buses chewed up, the decaying buildings, the thrashed sidewalks and trash-strewn gutters beyond the neatly-kept storefront café she defended with her brother Jim and an impressive cache of automatic weapons. Julia was able to overlook all that as long as she could look down her nose at the women, girls really, who sold their bodies to survive, whereas she and Jim didn't flinch at killing a customer who ran out on a bill for a small orange juice. Survival was all the hookers and everyone under twenty knew of the ugly world they inherited from the Bush family and their mafias.

Unfortunately I'm old enough to remember before the Rebellion and Federal Occupation. When I was a would-be historian and my brother, Larry, was a Berkeley linguist. Before we were shanghaied into the Company, and became operatives Fydor Chandler and Nellie Gail. I could even remember a little of the Clinton administration, but that seems like a dream now. I read about it, but it's like reading about a paradise we lost to greed, hatred and fear, and being too lazy or stupid to fight back until the fight was already lost.

Anyway, the hookers were back singly and in skittish pairs shortly after their arrival some tacky beige scrip calling itself currency started circulating around town. I was still using my debit accounts for everything, but I noticed Julia was grudgingly accepting scrip in her café. She said it made her nervous because it didn't feel real, but she'd used it to buy some produce, so it must be okay. I asked her why she couldn't use her debit account, and she said the produce guy in question was only taking barter or scrip.

Not being an economist, I didn't know if the (re)-emergence of an underground economy was good or bad. The only economist I knew well enough to ask was liberating the southern U.S. from the Christianist Republicans with Fydor Chandler and the DSL. Before I met my idol, he used to have a show on the Internet Broadcast called "Dr. Max's Live Nude Economics!" I loved that show; I always felt so smart watching it. Well, of course it went off the air, but only because the Bush permanent administration chased Max into Mexico, which had been bought by Soros and Gates, and was being run extremely well by Dr. Krugman and Dr. Sachs. Max had a lot to be bitter about, but he never had time for it, so he was cheerfully busy wreaking havoc wherever he went. I hadn't seen him in a year and a half and I was glad.

It gets really fucking cold in LA in January. So I had to wonder why the little girl in the alley by my building was half naked. Then I wondered why the skinny young Asian guy slapping her with a stack of beige scrip was screaming at her. In Esperanto, I think, or maybe Ebonics. Young people today, I just can't understand them, even when they stick to languages I know.

It had been a long and frustrating day of ambushing MTA buses to test their new security features, so I was not in a great mood. Furthermore, I hadn't pointlessly killed anyone that day and short daylight gives me Seasonal Affective Disorder if I don't pointlessly kill someone every day. I didn't know if this would fix my SAD, but I stuck my gun in the pimp's face.

"I think she could tell you why she's a stupid fucking ho better if you stopped hitting her in the face."

"Miss Gail..." he sputtered, backing away. He let go of the girl and she dropped to her knees between us. "Please..."

I pulled the trigger and then, according to my deeply ingrained Company training, walked over to put one in his heart. "Happy to oblige, asshole."

I'd kept an eye on the girl while I was doing all this, so I stepped out of her way when she scrambled over to the stiff. I didn't know what I was expecting—tears, rage, screaming—but all she did was roll him for scrip, jewelry, and whatnot; it all went into what was left of his hat. I caught her by the arm as she was about to run and dragged her into Julia's juice bar.

"We don't let hookers in here, Miss Gail," Julia called from behind the bar.

"Then bring us two carrot juices and she's a

customer," I said. "Jim around?"

Julia's brother Jim stuck his head out of the kitchen. "Yes, Miss Gail?"

"Got a recycler in the ally," I said. I nodded as he thanked me on his way out. "Julia, bring me a damp towel with the juice."

I turned the girl's head up to the light. Her nose and lip were bleeding and she'd be bruised up tomorrow. There was a hank of hair missing near her temple, but I couldn't tell if that was recent or not. She was young, maybe fourteen or fifteen, but her eyes were hard and wary. She kept jerking her head away from me as I cleaned her up.

"Hey, luchune, quiero? Quiero?" she spat at me, clutching her dead pimp's loot laden hat.

"I quiero you to sit still."

She did for three seconds. "What you want, lady? Two girl action?"

"No."

"Then what?"

I held up two fingers. "How many fingers?"

"Dos."

"Yes. Take your juice and get out." She grabbed her glass and skittered back into the night on her high heeled sandals.

'Luchune?' I thought, wondering why a street kid was using the suffix for Armenian abstract nouns like a verbal shrug. Not only was society breaking apart in the U.S., so was language. Or maybe language was just doing the best it could under the current circumstances. I'm not a socio-linguist so I wouldn't know. I noticed some blood on one of Julia's surgically clean café tables and wiped it with the towel.

"Here," I handed the towel and my debit card

over the counter. Then Julia, member of the Limo Brothers Recycling and master recycler in her own right, wrinkled her nose at the towel and tossed it into the trash. She charged me for two carrot juices and the towel.

It had been a long day, I was too tired to argue about it, and if I could be bothered, I'd buy a fucking juicer and make my own carrot juice. So I just went up to my third floor lair, checked my email, and fell into bed. Killing the pimp had lightened my mood, so I slept well that night.

Two mornings later I was drinking carrot juice and eating the pathetic mango I'd been able to wring out of Julia for an exorbitant amount. She was having mango supply problems, she said. I'd originally asked for cucumber salad, but she was having cucumber supply problems, too. Or it was too early for her to have made any salads. So I was stuck with a puny, pulpy mango. I would have just stuck to carrot juice like usual, but I had a meeting with some suits from the Metropolitan Transit Authority that morning and I needed more calories to think on.

As much as I enjoyed my security consultant job with the MTA, I was rapidly putting myself out of business. Every bus I ambushed, hijacked, blew up, or up-ended simply made it harder to do so the next time. Thanks to me, MTA fortress buses were nearly assault-proof, or at least Nellie Gail assault-proof.

The MTA had never asked for a meeting at my office before. Characteristically, I assumed the worst and prepared for it: they were coming to fire me, try to kill me, or renegotiate my contract in some other unacceptable way. There had been a few stray words about "training drivers," and this was out of the question. Well, if I lived, I still had my Department of Water and Power security consultant contract. They always had new facilities that needed to be secured and neighborhoods that needed to be pacified so they could keep the lights on and the water running.

My new status as a Warlord made this easier than it had been. I just had to show up with the DWP crews and stand around looking Warlordidential. Entire blocks were pacified, if not mellowed out, for weeks afterwards.

"And the fuckers are early," I snarled to myself when the downstairs door buzzed. I leaned over my half-finished unloved mango and clicked on the surveillance camera. But it wasn't suits, it was the little girl from the alley, from... when? The night before last? I'd totally forgotten about her. At least I thought it was her; she looked different in the daylight, but who does not?

I should have told her to fuck off, but curiosity got the better of me. I buzzed her in. She passed the metal detectors and Tres MicroREM scan without a blip. I put my Mauser in my lap and buzzed her into the second floor hallway that leads to my office.

She marched right into my office and up to my desk. Like last night, she was underdressed for the weather. The jeans were okay, but the tank top was thin and tight; her nipples stood out in high relief. Not that I was staring at her tits, except to notice she wasn't wearing a bra and didn't need one. Ah, youth!

Dismissing her chest, I stared at her face. It was my experience that if a visitor was going to lunge over the desk for my throat or tits, something usually crossed their face seconds before they did. Those seconds were enough for me to shoot them. But she just stood there, staring back at me. She was as young as she was last night, somewhere in her mid-teens. She had the same hard look, but the fear was gone. I knew this look; I saw it in every mirror I passed. Except I didn't have that look until I was in my late twenties and everything I ever cared about was gone. But that was where the resemblance ended. She had lank mousy brown hair, washed out green eyes, a round face, with a few fading bruises and few new ones, and she was built like a fire-plug.

She tossed a bundle of grubby-looking scrip on my desk. "I told a trick you'd kill him if he didn't pay me," she said, jutting her chin out. "This is your cut."

I wondered what she charged; it couldn't have been much, that pile of scrip wouldn't keep me in carrot juice for more than a day. But I decided to overlook that. "I'm not your pimp," I said. "Don't take my name in vain, kid."

She shrugged. "They know you killed Ming," she said. "They think it was for his ho's."

"Ming was the guy in the alley?" I asked, mainly to remind myself. He'd been several kills ago.

She nodded. "He was patho-loco, but he'd off a trick what didn't pay. Everybody paid. I said your name, and he paid."

It crossed my mind that killing her would solve the problem my reputation might have in the near future, but rescuing her from a beating only to end up killing her seemed patho-loco even to me. I sighed heavily. "I don't want that," I said, pushing at the scrip with a pencil.

"It's yours."

"I don't want it."

"But it's yours."

"But I don't want it."

"But it's yours."

I considered shoving it down her throat, but it looked like too much effort. And I was running out of time to argue. "Look, this is your money, I'm just going to keep it for you." Keeping one hand on my Mauser, I reached for an envelope. Canada and Mexico were making paper goods again and competition was making them affordable. I had a nice assortment of stationery, which was useless without a postal service, but still nice. I tossed a pen and an envelope across the desk at her. "Write your name on there and I'll keep it in my safe for you," I said. I don't have a safe, but my desk locks. She didn't move but mumbled something. "What? Look at me when you're talking to me, gal."

"I can't write," she spat. "I read un poco, but not writing."

I clasped the Mauser between my thighs and reached for the envelope and pen. "What's your name?"

"Wilshire."

"Like the street?"

She nodded and watched me like a hawk as I wrote her name in block letters on the envelope. "Can you...?"

I looked up. She was scared again. I relaxed my hands on the desktop and waited.

"Can you do that on something else?" she whispered. She was poised for flight and trembling.

It took a second for the penny to drop, but drop it did. Moving very slowly so as not to spook her, I tore two sheets off an amarilla abogado pad and wrote her name in block letters, using three lines for each letter. The first stroke of the "W" slanted down all three lines, the next went up and touched the middle line before shooting back down to the bottom line and then whipped all the way up to the top line. I marked the body of the "i" clearly between the middle and bottom lines and the dot hovered perfectly between the top and middle lines. I held my head so I could watch her in my peripheral vision. She was rigid with concentration, barely breathing, as if any movement might stop me.

I'd broken a light sweat by the time I finished the "e." "Here," I said, pushing the paper at her. "Take the pen, too." She gathered them up and held them like treasure. "Now blow. I've got an appointment."

She looked at me really hard and grunted, "Comsa," and left. I buzzed her out of the building.

'Comsa?' I thought. 'Not 'shnor-aha-ga-lu-chune' or 'gracias,' but 'comsa'?' I ran my mind east along the street she was named after, slowing at Normandie and stopping at Vermont, or what was left of it. 'Korean?' My Korean sucked, but I did know how to be polite in stores and restaurants. Com-sa-mi-da, thank you in Korean, but not really the word, just the meaning. I pulled my amarilla abogado pad toward me and in my half-assed phonetic shorthand jotted down all the weird words I could remember her saying. Someday I might run into a socio-linguist and I could get swanky about the new slang in the City of Angels.

The front door buzzed and it was my suits. Two middle-aged guys in suits, in fact. I'd only been expecting Mr. Compton, the security liaison, and one of his endless rotation of wide-eyed interns who didn't last very long. Or perhaps they were promoted to other departments. The inner workings of the MTA were a mystery. But today Mr. Compton had a grown man in a suit with him. They both looked like they had some

146

miles on them, especially under the clothes-defying Tres MicroREM scanner. The guy with Compton had some meat and muscle to go with the fat on his bones. Only the powerful could afford to be fat these days. That meant high, and I mean stratosphere high ranking MTA, DWP, or even... AT&T. I'd never seen an AT&T employee; they never got this far down the food chain.

Whatever he was, the new guy had too many electronics on him. I pushed the button that slid the armored drawer out on the landing and flipped on the intercom. "Unload, gentlemen." I switched on the camera over the drawer as they dumped cell phones, pagers, BayaNegras, PDAs, and a slim white contraption with an earpiece plugged into it into the drawer. "Excuse me, what is that white thing?" I asked.

Mr. Compton glanced at his pal and got a nod. "It's an iPod, Miss Gail," Compton said.

'Ah yes,' I thought. 'I remember those.' But I kept my mouth shut and buzzed them in.

Compton introduced me to Mr. Kern, who was representing AT&T on this visit. Kern didn't speak; he just nodded politely at me.

"What can I do for you, gentlemen?" I asked when they had their overfed asses settled into my intentionally uncomfortable chairs.

"Mr. Kern contacted the MTA in connection with a matter we believe you've, ah, had some experience with, Miss Gail," Compton said, looking very uncomfortable.

"Which is?" I asked, staring at Kern, who was staring at me.

Compton cleared his throat. "Interrogation."

"Of whom?"

"Um, I'm not entirely sure," Compton said,

looking nervously at Kern. "As you know, we've been having more eastern border attacks lately. They're not organized or professional guerrilla attacks—those we can handle—they're more like little bands of stragglers who look harmless and then one of them knifes a security guard and the rest slip into our territory. I understand AT&T has been, ah, collecting the more interesting ones lately, and they were wondering if you could ask a few questions. So..."

"Just 'ask a few questions,' huh?" I directed this at Kern. "I'm sure AT&T's been asking plenty of questions."

Compton cleared his throat again, but if AT&T was going to ask me to torture detainees, the AT&T guy was going to have to *ask*. "Is Mr. Kern a mute or a mime?"

"Neither, Miss Gail, I just find talking a waste of time." Kern had a low rough voice that was not a pleasure to listen to.

I bit back a sharp remark about wasting my time and merely folded my hands in front of me. I smiled in what I hoped was a pleasantly menacing fashion, while looking encouragingly at him.

"We've been asking questions, but we're not getting many answers and we've lost several promising detainees," he continued.

"Lost?" I asked.

"They died during interrogation."

"What methods are you using?"

"Low tech. Sleep deprivation, stress positions, high volume noise, extreme cold and heat. We've tried needles under the finger and toe nails, careful beatings, electrodes on erectile tissue, water boarding–"

I cut him off. "And you lost your subjects in

water boarding, didn't you?"

"Yes, how did you know?" he asked.

"Because it's the one chance for suicide," I said. "Where are these people coming from?"

"Hard to say."

"But they're religious fanatics, aren't they?"

"Yes."

"So inhaling filthy water for Jesus is the best thing they can do," I said. "The next best thing is enduring their torture, like Jesus endured His. So, that's why you're not getting anywhere."

"That seems to be the case," Kern agreed.

"Or they simply don't know anything," I said. "As Mr. Compton said, these are not commando units or mercenaries; they might just be trying to get out of harm's way."

Kern gave me a long appraising look, and seemed to come to a decision. "We believe they are part of a larger force massing on the Nevada border."

I looked at Compton. "Stragglers?" He nodded, so I looked at Kern.

Kern folded his hands in his lap and did something with his mouth that almost looked like a smile. "Miss Gail, I understand you're a historian of sorts," he said.

"Of sorts, yes," I said, wondering what this was about.

"Then you might have read about the Children's Crusade, I don't know the number or the year," he said.

"It was in 1212, and there was no Papal Bull issued for it, so it didn't have a number," I said. "Many of the children died on the way to the Mediterranean, and then what was left of them were offered free passage to the Holy Land 'for God' once they got there. The story goes that seven ships departed: two were shipwrecked, and the other five went to Africa, where the little crusaders were sold into slavery. However, this very strange crusade did inspire the Fifth Crusade in 1218, also a disaster, and cranked up the Crusader mania again."

"Yes, the Children's Crusade was a disaster," Kern said, nodding approvingly at me. "But if it had been better orchestrated, it could have served as a major diversion for the real show, whatever that might have been."

"They were religiously insane teenagers," I said. "How can that be orchestrated?"

"That was then," he said. "Religion in America has become more, oh, let's say, directable."

"I see," I said. "And this directed religion we have now is being used to mask something else, that's what you're saying, Mr. Kern, isn't it? There's a bigger show than what you've seen so far."

"Yes," he said. "Our thinking is that this is a Crusade against the infidels of the West Coast, but directed by pros."

"Who?"

"That's what we want you to help us find out," he said. "We'd like you to have a try at this one last detainee we hope will yield the location of the main invasion group, if not the leadership."

I looked at Compton and then back at Kern. I only had one more question: "What does it pay?"

We haggled a bit, payment contingent upon results, as usual, but the fee was three times what MTA paid me to successfully ambush a bus. I phoned down to Julia's for a carrot juice for me, and orange juices for Mr. Compton and Mr. Kern. It was my treat. I got my guns, purse and ti-tandex jacket and went down to the waiting armored car, flanked by machine gun trucks and motorcycle outriders, that Mr. Kern was chauffeured around in. He must be pretty far up the food chain to have this kind of escort.

Mr. Compton excused himself, saying he had other pressing business. He got into his own heavily-armored vehicle, which had a fortress bus escort, impressive in its own right.

We were driven way far out into the San Fernando Valley. I didn't annoy Kern with small talk on the way to what I think used to be called Calabasas. It was still pretty much wasteland. The DWP had only recently been able to re-establish lights and water after the hard fighting here ten years ago. We drove into a secure building complex, mostly warehouses with a few office buildings and some rubble neatly piled up next to them. The place looked deserted; it was supposed to look that way to the casual observer, but it was teeming with activity in the warehouse structure we debarked in.

On the mezzanine, I was introduced to Mr. Augora, the technician on the project. He was very pleased to meet me.

"Your reputation gives us much hope, Miss Gail," he said.

I smiled politely. "What's the subject?" I asked, getting right down to it.

"Caucasian female, between twenty-five and thirty-five," Augora said. "Won't tell us her name, so she's Prisoner 365."

"What have you done to her?" I asked.

"Well, we started with sleep deprivation and stress positions," he said consulting a chart. "Then some electric shocks. We tried water boarding, but she spooked us by almost drowning. We had to use the paddles to revive her.

"Any of this on video?"

"Yes, but..." Augora trailed off and looked at Kern.

"Yes, but we don't think we'll get anything from her," Kern said. "We do have her children in custody. Or the children she had with her when she was picked up."

"And you want me to torture her children in front of her."

They nodded.

"Let me see a few minutes of video," I said.

Prisoner 365 was a scrawny dull looking woman. I couldn't tell if the dullness was natural or the product of the vaccination program. Under the electric shocks, she was a normal subject: stoic at first and then screaming in pain later. Calling on Jesus to save her and eventually passing out. After she was revived it was the same. She either didn't know anything or she just wasn't going to tell. This was not toughness on her part, but the incredible resolve some subjects have... unto death.

"Can you show me her kids without them seeing me?" I asked.

After some fumbling, they found the camera in the kids' cells. The boy looked about seven or eight; the girl around ten. They both had the vacant, vaccinated look. Or maybe they were just bored in their separate cells.

"What have you got for me to work with?"

Augora gestured at a tray of what looked like dental instruments and household tools. "No drugs?" I asked.

"We wouldn't know what we were doing with

drugs," Augora admitted. "Frankly, I'm an electrical engineer, or I was an electrical engineer. This is all new to me."

Amateurs. Oh well. "I won't be needing any of this," I said, waving the sharp objects away.

"What do you need?" Kern asked.

I gave him a hard look. "A clipboard."

I cooled my heels on the other side of the interview room's two-way mirror while they fetched Prisoner 365 into it. I watched her sit there at the white table in the empty room for a while. She was as dull there as she was in the video. AT&T finally found a clipboard for me and I rolled on in with Augora in tow. Mr. Kern would be watching from the room I'd just left.

"Aaaah, let's see," I said, consulting my clipboard. "Mrs., uh, Mrs. 365, I guess is what we're calling you for this interview. I'm Gail Nelson from Los Angeles Child Protective Services." I stuck out my hand; she just stared at it. I sat to her right and Augora sat next to me. "I'm here about the children you were brought in with. You see, we can't allow them to stay here and we'd like to know if there's next of kin we can give custody of them to. Ah, here they are now."

The kids, Prisoners 366 and 367, rushed up to 365, who tried to push them away. Then she gave in and hugged them fiercely. I figured they were her kids, but I'm not an expert on these things. And not being a parent, I've also never understood why parents put their children in so much danger.

"So, as I was saying," I continued over the hug-fest. "We'll need to place them and we prefer to place with family, if possible."

The 365 family simply stared at me like I'd just landed from the moon. They were as pale as death, but it was only prison pallor. I had plans for it.

I turned to Augora. "Excuse me, but when was the last time these children were outside."

He said, "Never."

"How unhealthy," I said, all business. "Do you have a yard they could walk in?"

He said, "Yes."

"Then I suggest you let them out for an hour or so," I said, rising. "My business can wait at least that long."

Augora called in two security personnel and they escorted the 365 family into a fenced yard. 365 cringed then stretched under the weak winter sun. The kids stuck close, but, being kids, eventually started to hop around the yard. It almost looked normal, except for the chain-link fence and the machine-gun-toting, uniform-wearing guards.

365 strolled around the yard, occasionally having a huddle with either 366 or 367 or both. Watching her, I decided she was closer to the boy than the girl, so he was the one we'd use second. The girl looked a little brighter and tougher; she'd be my Plan A operator.

Back in the interview room, I said, "Ah! Much better! Put a little color in your cheeks. Now, Mrs. 365, where can we take these children?"

No answer. I tried for about 30 minutes. "Well, I see this is not going to happen today," I said. "We'll let you sleep on it and try again tomorrow."

Augora had the guards take them back to their cells. I took myself and my clipboard back to the room Kern was watching from.

"Well?" he asked.

"We use the girl," I said. I looked up at Augora coming in. "Did your people plant the transmitters in their clothes?"

"Yes, ma'am, and we're assembling a tracking team," he said. "Hope this works, Miss Gail, it's a damn clever plan."

"If it doesn't," I said. "I'll be back to work on the boy for you."

Kern claimed he had work to do and left while Augora arranged my ride home.

It wasn't a bad ride. I got to sit in the back of an armored Cadillac Coupe de Ville while a duo of motorcycles and a machine gun truck rode along to protect the AT&T property, and, by extension, me. The Caddy was a vegetable oil/petroleum hybrid, so it was fast. Since the DWP and some refugee ex-Red Stater wildcat oilmen got a few of the offshore oil derricks pumping again and gasoline prices were down around $20,000.00/liter, we were seeing more, and more powerful, petro hybrids. Hell, even I could afford to gas up the hybrid BMW and Triumph motorcycles I'd inherited over the past few years.

But I wasn't thinking about this on that ride home. I was allowing myself to be relieved that I hadn't tortured a child. I'd never done it, but as part of my training, I had studied it.

When my brother Larry and I were first recruited, even before we became Fydor and Nellie, we were trained in terror by a guy named Milton Keynes. He made us call him Uncle Milty, even in bed, which was as sick then as it sounds now. I never asked Fydor, but I think he nailed us both. I know he fucked me on a number of occasions. It was never a pleasure with Uncle Milty, sex with him was all control (his) and obedience (mine). The only relief was when it was over. But that wasn't the worst thing about him.

Fydor summed it up once, before he disappeared for a few years. He said that Uncle Milty had no "resonance." When he was torturing a subject, Milty was "in tune" with the ebb and flow of pain and relief, but nothing penetrated beyond his intellect. In later years, I discovered that poor torturers hate or love their work and this destroys them. I myself felt a certain pride of accomplishment in breaking a subject, but only if it yielded real information. But Milty... it was odd; he was so detached from everything, even when he came, he was nowhere near his body or his pleasure and certainly nowhere near mine.

So watching him torture a seven-year-old boy should have been a soul-killing horror, but I was so numb by then, it was merely interesting. The subject was given increasing electric shocks for three hours. It took three hours not because the subject was holding out, but because it took that long for Milty to work through the immature labyrinth of logic and memory to get the information he was after. Eventually he got it and the subject was returned to custody. I don't know what happened to it. Milty later said to us observers that working with children under twelve was difficult; it was necessary to break them, but one was always skirting the edge of destroying them before they yielded the information. They required more patience than subjects over twelve who might be susceptible to pain, fear and humiliation, which gave the operator another lever to push. Under twelve years of age, there was only pain and fear. And hope, which is always the greatest tool in any successful interrogator's tool box.

Hope. Hope that the pain will end, hope that when they next wake it will all have been a nightmare, hope for freedom, hope for... for anything, but their current reality. That child had looked to a monster for mercy and Milty the Merciless had given him none, but just tiny spaces where he could hope for relief. It was a delicate dance of pain/despair; relief/hope Milty led him, and led him right up the abyss, and shook him over it until in one last hysterical rush, the child's mind spit out what we wanted. It was an address, if I recall correctly, many people died at that address that very night.

I wasn't sure I still had a light enough touch to torture a kid. That and I'd never done it before, let alone done it in front of the child's mother. Would they give each other hope? Or courage to endure? Could I use either of those to break the kid, without shattering him before I had what I, or rather AT&T, was after? Perhaps we'd make mom watch through a two-way mirror in a sound proof room. Ah well, no point in thinking about this too much. I was hopeful my ruse would work and the girl would lead them to whatever they were after.

There was no way for Mrs. 365 to do her children any good in this situation. If she told them the location of their base, we'd torture it out of them or torture them until she told us. Don't tell them, and she still wouldn't talk, we'd torture them until... until it would be useless to continue to do so. I hoped I'd avoided all that, for all of us; the AT&T techs didn't look like they had the stomachs for watching me work on a kid, either.

Back in the bad old days, I was, unfortunately, reunited with Uncle Milty during the Los Angeles rebellion and occupation. They sent us to interrogate prisoners at Dodger Stadium. Uncle Milty did some of his best work there; so did I, but I also watched my hometown being destroyed. And, though I hid it, it hurt a little. By then I didn't "resonate" any more than Milty, so I was surprised to feel anything for this fucked up

City of Angels.

During the Occupation I stayed close to the stadium. Milton Keynes was restless in the warm weather, and when he got bored with his version of sex, he wandered farther and farther into the city. One night he never returned. A search patrol came back empty handed; it was assumed he was dead.

I had a different theory; I believed the city consumed him, changed him so he just wanted to be in it peacefully. Los Angeles is a strange place: you can struggle against it, hate it, and ultimately be crushed by it, or you can make peace with the dissonant, fragmented city that seems to have no center, but actually has one every few miles. If you learn to see it. I think Milty saw it, and wanted to stay with it. There is a story in Bradbury's "The Martian Chronicles" where new settlers on Mars turn into Martians from exposure to the Martian elements. I think that's what happened to Milty: he became an Angelino. Gracious, stoic, patient, wry, and capable of rolling with any punch—this is how the people of Los Angeles, the ones who can cut it, survive the myriad riots, fires, floods, earthquakes, and long hot summers year after year. We have nerves of steel because we need them, and we love them, too.

So Milty disappeared into my town while I cowered in the stadium, afraid of the pain of connecting with the bombed streets and the starving citizens. We were occupied once before by Marines, after the Rodney King rebellion, Bush I brought combat Marines up from Camp Pendleton to "keep the peace," but really to show us that he could. Those of us not cowed by this act thought Bush I was overplaying his hand by sending the Marines, our own Marines, to occupy the city after the riots had burned themselves out, with no help from the gutless LAPD. But the message was clear: annoy the Bush family, and your own soldiers paid for by your own tax money will kill you.

At the time I thought that was a little hysterical; I could not possibly have predicted the destruction and occupation of my city by Federal troops. And when it happened, it wounded me. A small wound no one could see, but a wound that bled steadily for years, and so bled a lot. I was sent back East eventually and was even more detached in my work. And I worked steadily until I blew up the right building at the wrong time because the Company sent me too much C4. I love plastic explosives, so I'll lavishly use whatever I'm sent.

I was put on disciplinary leave from the CIA. I always felt slightly sorry for the CIA having to take the responsibility and blame for me, Fydor and our fellow sociopaths when we only worked for Rumsfeld's Stasi part of the CIA called the Company. I think even he disowned us shortly before his mysterious and fatal car accident in a parked car. Very mysterious, but very effective.

So I came home to LA and have never tortured anything since. I have killed a lot of people, but I'm very quick and efficient at that. Successful torture requires a certain kind of patience and people skills, and I was in short supply of both. I could ambush buses for the MTA and breach fortifications for the DWP 'til the cows came home, but deep down, I wanted people to stay away from me. And I from them.

"It's in the next block, driver," I said as he slowed on Sunset, east of Vine. "Yes, just here, thank you."

I was glad to be home and have the afternoon off. I was reading *Gunfighter Nation* about the myth of the frontier in the 20th century. I was having trouble getting into it because, even though I agreed with Slotkin's thesis, as a historian of genocide, history has few heroes for me.

For most people the West, including Los Angeles, starts with the Frontier. But Los Angeles is older than that, even older than the Missions. Maybe even older than the Gabrieleno Indians who lived in this basin before the Missions assimilated them with even easier food and shelter. Our city wells up from the Gabrieleno myth of Wyot, the first man, murdered by Frog, who was talked into it by Coyote, and this brought death into the world, where there had been no death before. Los Angeles, as we know it, is built on a firm foundation of raw deals. We might not like it, but we know how to make it work for us.

I got home and found a testy note from Julia taped to my door. According to her, the hookers were back looking for me and bringing down the tone of the neighborhood. They'd gone so far as to actually buy orange juice in her establishment and drink it there while waiting for me.

Julia and her attitude were starting to annoy me. However, I was disinclined to kill her, not because I'm ever disinclined to kill anyone, but because I didn't want to piss off the huge, lethal and highly useful Limo family. We had a good relationship, the Limos and I; they'd done me a few good turns for a high price and I'd sent quite a bit of business their way over the years. But they might forget all that if I killed one of their daughters, especially Julia, to whom they pointed with some pride as a restaurateur, conveniently forgetting I was the one who originally set her up.

My snit lasted as far as the first landing and was forgotten by the time I was settled behind my desk with

Gunfighter Nation. The genocide against Native Americans was approved of by Theodore Roosevelt, the man who wanted to preserve the wilderness for white people, and only white people, preferably white male people. When one group decides another group is less than human is when the killing begins in earnest. The process of that decision has always been interesting to me. Much was written about the sanctity of the Frontier when the railroads had already destroyed it. Therefore, much had to be written to prop up the murder and pillage still in progress. The same props would later be used in the slaughter of the Chinese who built the railroads. The White Man must prevail... especially when he's wrong. Ah well.

Slotkin's writing bored me, so I was less annoyed than I might have been when the downstairs door buzzed. 'Never a moment of peace...' I thought, adjusting the monitor. There was either something wrong with the monitor, I was seeing double, or Wilshire was standing on my doorstep with a girl who looked exactly like her. And not wearing much more clothing on this chilly January afternoon. I buzzed them in; the Wilshire look-alike was carrying a shiv, which she left in the weapons tray before I let them into my office. "We're seeing a lot of you today, Wilshire," I said.

She smiled and looked at the other girl, who said, "I'm Wilshire. This is my sister, Alvarado."

I looked from one to the other and could not tell them apart. "Wilshire and Alvarado," I said. "That's quite an intersection."

"We were born there," Alvarado said. She had a softer voice than Wilshire and smiled more. I wondered if that was usual or just for this situation. Wilshire was wearing the same scowl that I'd seen soften into wary curiosity once or twice.

"What can I do for you two?" I asked. They were kind of interesting to me, but being interested in people wears me out these days.

Alvarado cringed a little, but Wilshire dove right in. "Alvarado has some money for you to keep for her," she said. "It's your cut, but you don't want it, so—"

"Girls, I am not a bank," I said firmly.

"What's a bank?" Wilshire asked.

"A place to keep money," I said to cover my... what? Shame? Sorrow? Anger? That they'd been born into a world without anything as normal as a bank? What did I care? They were alive, they survived by selling sex, they were not much more than children, it was all their bad luck. And yet I was furious about... because... of something. I let out a long breath I didn't realize I'd been holding. "Okay." I found another envelope. "Can you write your name, Alvarado?"

She shook her head and, as intently as her sister had earlier in the day, watched me write her name on the envelope. Without being asked, I wrote her name on the same pad, tore out two pages and gave her a pen to go with it. Nellie Gail Banking and Office Supply, that's me. I stuffed her wilted pile of scrip into the envelope and tossed it on the credenza next to my desk. I was beginning to hate the sight of that frowsy, crumpled scrip; I could only associate it with these hookers and it made me sad and angry in ways I chose not to think too hard about. "Anything else?" I asked sharply.

"No, no, gracias luchune," they chirped on their way out. "Comsa luchune. Bye-bye."

I bit back the words "Be careful" and merely buzzed them out of the building. "What the fuck is wrong with me today?" I said out loud. At least the day was ending and after dark I could work off a little of my frustration hunting scavengers in the hills.

Of course when I got back, they were huddled in my doorway and it was raining. Wilshire, I suppose because it sounded like her, informed me that it was safer to stick close to my building. As an afterthought, she mentioned that it was cold, too.

I was freezing my ass off in my thermal ti-tandex catsuit and jacket; I couldn't imagine how they felt in their little tank tops and jeans. I must have gone insane, but I offered to let them sleep on the fourth floor.

I had my office on the second floor and lived on the third floor of my eight-story building and rented the rest of it to the Universal Life Insurance Company. But there was some space that wasn't rented on the fourth floor. I used it to store old office furniture and other junk. They got right to work making a bed out of some broken furniture. This caused me to cave a little, and I got them some blankets, a couple of homeless couch cushions, dried fruit and bottled water out of my supplies. I told them I was locking them in. I could tell one of them, probably Wilshire, didn't like it, but she just scowled a little more as I closed the door.

Downstairs, I periodically found myself listening for noise from the fourth floor that wasn't there. Wilshirado, as I'd already come to think of them, were very quiet. Or they were just dead tired and sound asleep in a safe-ish, warm-ish, somewhat comfortable place. I imagined they didn't get that very often. This made me irrationally angry and sad and something I couldn't figure out, so I immediately stopped trying to figure it out.

I let them out the next morning. They could have climbed out the window and gone down what was left of the fire escape if, for some reason, I had not let them out, but that was not necessary. They said "gracias luchune" on their way out.

That day I successfully blew up a bus and unsuccessfully stormed a power plant. Wilshire and Alvarado were on my doorstep again that night. I let them stay on the fourth floor again. The blankets they'd left neatly folded were still up there anyway.

The next day I spent the day carefully explaining with small words and in writing to the numbskulls at the MTA why I was able to blow up their fortress bus. It seems to hurt their feelings when I, or anyone, can get past their bus defense systems. They need to get over that. This is exactly why they hire someone like me to punch holes in their impenetrable buses.

I was in the house most of the day, but made a point of going to Julia's to get juice when I thought Wilshirado might be on my doorstep. I made several trips, and finally Julia said she'd phone me if they showed up. They never showed up that night. This bothered me; and then it bothered me that it bothered me.

I spent the next day chasing DWP trucks that were driven by their advanced defensive driving teams. Not bad; I only caught nine of the ten trucks with my paint gun. I prefer live ammo, but the DWP was trying to economize.

Of course the minute I wasn't busy, Wilshirado's whereabouts were on my mind. To try to get my mind off it, I went scavenger hunting in Pico Union. Nothing focuses the mind like being in a kill-or-be-killed situation and on unfamiliar turf. And I needed some release after my day of wimpy paint guns. But I was bothered all over again when Wilshirado weren't on the doorstep when I got home, and more relieved than I wanted to admit when Julia telephoned to tell me they were there now, and she'd put their hot cocos on my tab. A font of humanity, that Julia Limo, I must say.

On my way downstairs, I boiled my problem down to two solutions; one was I could kill them and be done with it. The other was... oh fuck it.

If only for my own peace of mind, I caved. I went downstairs and brought them in and told them they could stay on the fourth floor until the weather warmed up as long as they used the back door and didn't annoy the paying tenants. I dug up a set of keys, a space heater, and laid down the law:

"No tricks anywhere near here," I said handing them keys, bottled water and a space heater. "Don't annoy Julia, she doesn't like you very much. Stay away from the other people in the building. Piss me off and I'll kill you."

"Yes, Miss Gail. Good night, Miss Gail. Comsa luchune, Miss Gail!"

I went downstairs and washed the blood off my boots and jacket. Dead tired, I fell into bed. I was asleep when I hit the pillow.

Wilshirado were good, or at least smart enough to obey the rules and not annoy me or anyone else around me. They asked if they could cook, and I said they'd have to use my jerry-rigged kitchen on the third floor. They did and they insisted I have some of their food. They were pretty good cooks, so I set up an account with the Limo Brothers for food and they did their shopping there. They also, very stealthily, moved into a vacant space on the fourth floor, which was, even I had to admit, more comfortable than the storage closet. I didn't really mind; all my guns were in the room I slept in and it had a steel-reinforced door with the toughest Mexican locks money and muscle could buy. We kept our distance from each other, too, until they asked me to teach them to write.

I'd been a student most of my life, so the urge to learn was strong in me. But the urge to teach was there, too, although it was so buried it almost didn't sound like me when I said, "If I can find the right book, I'll teach you."

I think Wilshire started to ask "Why do you..." but Alvarado made her shut up. I still couldn't tell them apart just by looking at them, but they spoke and behaved differently enough that I could tell. For example, Alvarado had better manners and more sense than her hothead sister. On the other hand, without Wilshire's fire, they'd probably be dead by now. She'd certainly taken a big risk barging in on me.

And it had paid off for all of us: I liked their cooking and I'd stopped waking up when they dragged themselves in after a night turning tricks. Their profession didn't bother me; it was that they did it at night that bothered me. Night was dangerous in Los Angeles, especially when I was out in it. I was fairly sure they weren't turning tricks in my hunting grounds up in the Hollywood Hills: nothing but scavengers up there anyway.

Of course now that they had my roof over their heads and access to my Limo Brothers account, they could stay home a few more evenings. Free time is a luxury and if they wanted to spend it learning to write, I would teach them. If I could.

After not finding what I wanted on the Internets. I sent an email to Madeline the Librarian, asking if she could dig up a writing primer or whatever it was to teach writing from scratch. Mad was a clever little woman who had a well-guarded bunker full of books over on Hollywood near Highland, on the extreme edge of my so-called Warlord turf. Maybe a little out of it; she'd annexed herself to me when she moved in from Malibu after the last big fire scared her enough to get the fuck out of that wilderness. Those fires were scary when we had a Fire Department; they're doubly so without one. There was also more food in Hollywood, so she could keep her student muscle fed on more than learning. She'd done some research on me and then made me an offer I couldn't refuse: all the books I wanted to borrow or buy and decent history conversation because she had a doctorate from Stanford in Chinese history. She once said she might read twenty hours a day for the rest of her life and only make a tiny dent in the literature. There was a mountain of books in her field and a score of years after she'd been hooded, she was still in the foothills.

I didn't envy her her area of research; mine was much more manageable and less intimidating. I once asked her about genocides in China. She said there was no such thing in China. Large numbers of people died there all the time and it was hardly noticed because the deaths never made a dent in the population. She thought she might possibly make an exception for Tibet during the Cultural Revolution. But, after doing a little research, she rejected the idea the next time I saw her. "Not enough killing and only a small, very focused population," she said. "Only killed those in religion who objected to their monasteries being blown up. Doesn't qualify."

I could not disagree, but I thought it was a shame that there was no word for murdering a culture or religion.

She said there was a word for it. "The nice word is 'imperialism,' but the reality is still just brute force."

Mad fired back an email that she would look into a writing primer for me. Could I come by the following afternoon or the next day? I wrote that I'd shoot for tomorrow afternoon, but there was no answer. She was probably running her mind over the miles of bookcases in her place. I never knew where she got them, but she was constantly bartering (sometimes raiding) to add to her collection, so maybe she started out small and ended up big. That's how it is with books: you move in with one box and move out with thirty.

Anyway, I'd done my part; I went to eat corn chowder with Wilshirado with a clear conscience. They squinted curiously at me, but didn't ask any questions. They served the chowder with tortillas and white rice, but I didn't ask any questions. They served everything with some kind of rice, but the tortillas puzzled me as I had no idea what they were for.

Later that night I got an email from Augora of AT&T asking for a nine AM meeting with me at my office. He said he would be bringing a Mr. Harve de Grace with him. Harve de Grace could be nothing but a Stasi or CIA name, albeit one I'd never heard before, and this made me a little nervous and curious. However, the last AT&T job paid remarkably well, so I emailed back that nine AM was fine with me.

They were prompt. Augora was the same tall glass of water as I recalled, exuding the same thoughtful competence, if distaste, for whatever he was doing.

The other guy, de Grace, was short, dark and scrawny. He had a friendly, but bookish look to him, which made me wonder what kind of desperate barrel Rummy's successor was scraping the bottom of to keep the Stasi staffed back East.

Introductions were made and we got right down to it. Or at least Augora did while de Grace and I sized each other up.

"As you might have realized, Miss Gail," Augora began. "AT&T doesn't like being in the torture business. However since the breakdown of other forms of government, we feel there is a void that must be filled. And we feel we need to protect the areas and people in our service area. Therefore we must do, and ask you to do for us, what is in the best interest of that."

'Since the end of democracy on December 12, 2000, we've just moved from one form of dictatorship to another,' I thought, but Augora was going on again.

"As you also know, we don't know jack about torturing information out of people," he said bluntly. "We've subcontracted that to Mr. de Grace and he's been doing a fine job for us. However, he's asked to consult with you on a particular case, and I shall turn this over to him now."

"A pleasure to meet you, Miss Gail," de Grace said smoothly. "You're something of a legend at the Company and when I was told of your brilliant play with the mother and child, I felt you were the one person who could help us. I'm so glad to find you still alive."

"Me, too," I said. "What's up?"

"AT&T and the other institutions in Los Angeles have made this one of the more stable and pleasant places to live in these chaotic times," de Grace told me. "I don't know if you've been in any of the Christopias in the Southern U.S., but they are hardly as well run or, well, enjoyable."

"Enjoyable?"

"Well, I found the restrictions on certain

behaviors unpleasant."

"What behaviors?" I asked, wondering if he was gay

"I'm not anti-religious, Miss Gail, but I prefer to believe in some kind of future here on earth, not solely in heaven," he said.

"How decadently sybaritic of you, Mr. de Grace," I said. "Having a little trouble breaking one of the hyper-religionists?"

"They have nothing to tell us, Miss Gail," he said. "In the raid you were so instrumental in obtaining the intelligence for, some of the leadership was captured." He paused; I waited. "We feel that this is not some random migration of displaced citizens trying to get out of harm's way, but a more organized flight west to the Pacific."

"They'd be mad to try to go through LA," I said, dismissively.

"But I suspect these are people with connections to call ships to any deserted stretch of coastline," de Grace said.

"Who?" I asked.

"Maybe what's left of the Cheney family, maybe the remnants of the NeoCon mafia, maybe..."

"Maybe the Bush family and their mafia?" I asked, when he trailed off for good. He nodded. "How bad are things east of the Rockies, Mr. de Grace?"

"Complete chaos," he said. "The Mexican and Canadian forces are sweeping everything before them. They've split the country along the Mississippi river and are spreading east and west faster than anyone could imagine. There's no resistance, Miss Gail; prior to the invasion, our own people had either killed or vaccinated anyone with any fight in them out of existence. No one could have foreseen–"

"Could have foreseen that the Bush family was ultimately going to lose and they'd need sane foot soldiers." I cut him off. "Most of the Red Staters running for the Pacific are idiots, except for a few of their leaders. That's what you think you've got out there in the Valley at AT&T's warehouse, isn't it? One of their leaders."

"Not the very top leadership, Miss Gail, but I'm sure he has more information than the others," de Grace said. "No, and that's why I asked to bring you in. He's going to be tough to break, and I have less experience than you do."

"And we need this information, Miss Gail, and need it badly," Augora said.

I'd almost forgotten Augora was in the room, but didn't jump as badly as de Grace did. Where did Rummy's people get this kid from anyway?

"I have one more question for Mr. de Grace, if I may." They nodded. "What are you doing on the West Coast?"

"The Company no longer exists, Miss Gail," he said. "I was swept in with the rest of the refugees."

"And where were you before that?"

He sighed. "My first mission was looking for nukes in the Midwest."

"Nukes?" I'd totally forgotten about those. "Find any?" I asked.

"Yes and no; we found missiles, but no warheads," he said. "We think the DSL nuclear scientists or Canada took them. Or both; you know the DSL, Mexico and Canada are working together now. What's left of the Military is in such disarray, anyone could have taken them, but we think anyone else would have used them by now."

"How interesting. And after that?" I asked.

"I was trying to rally the militias in the Northwest," he said.

"And you couldn't rally them against the freaks and perverts of Los Angeles?"

"I think I could have," de Grace said thoughtfully. "Except there's nothing left to work with up there. Too much vaccination, AIDS, malnutrition, and the break-down of the medical system have wiped them out."

'So much for self-reliance and rugged individualism,' I thought. De Grace looked shaken by these memories; I can't say I blamed him. Life outside Los Angeles was too nightmarish for me to even consider thinking about. "Tell me about this subject you want my advice on."

"We'd like more than your advice," Augora said, handing me a file and a portable DVD player.

I opened the file and looked at the photo first: white male, overweight, somewhere around fifty years old, arrogant, bordering on mean-looking. There were few details because he wasn't talking. The location of his confiscation... I looked up at Augora. "'Confiscation?'" I asked.

"We're the phone company, Miss Gail," he said patiently. "We don't arrest or imprison people."

'No,' I thought, 'That's what the State used to do.' I flipped on the portable DVD and watched a few minutes of the intake interrogation. "What did you do with him, Mr. de Grace?" I asked.

"Just questions, Miss Gail, we wanted to wait for you for the..." he cleared his throat. "For the heavy lifting, so to speak."

I watched more DVD; Mr. X was not cooperating, he was refusing to talk, but not saying they had the wrong guy, just that it was an outrage that he was being held. Bluff and blustery, he had the AT&T questioner on the ropes and de Grace's questions were brushed off as well.

If de Grace was really a Company man, he should have been able to handle this. Unless he was brand new and poorly trained, like he said, which I was beginning to wonder about. "How long did you question him?" I asked.

"Several hours over the three days we've had him," Augora said. "We were very glad when Mr. de Grace offered us his services. We were over our heads. At least he was able to separate the ones who didn't know anything from the ones who might know something."

"How did you two find each other?" I asked de Grace.

"I found the AT&T brass, Miss Gail, everyone knows who's running LA," he smirked a little at his own cleverness.

Just to be polite, I smirked back. "So, you, ah, confiscated this Mr. X guy in Oxnard, is it?" I asked, flipping through the pages. "Who else was there?"

"I'd have to look at the database, but there were several hundred people confiscated in the raid," Augora said. "Mostly women and children, but a few men like Mr. X."

"Any equipment? Weapons? Vehicles?" I asked.

"Not much," Augora said. "Again, I'd have to check the records, but I believe there was very little equipment or other things at the location. We looked at the computer we confiscated, but there was nothing but a few emails."

"Then what makes you think this is the guy?" I asked.

"He had a cell phone and a top of the line PDA," de Grace said when Augora deferred to him. "And he was making more sense than anyone around him."

"You mean he wasn't religiously insane." de Grace nodded and remained silent. "Okay," I said, turning to Augora. "What's AT&T's deal this time?"

We haggled a little, just for the sake of form, and got the deal authorized via email before we left. I sent Augora and de Grace downstairs to wait for me while I slipped into my working clothes. I strapped on my Mauser, Titanium Colt, and Beretta, brass knuckles, and slid a sheathed stiletto into my right boot, as well as one into the cleverly sewn sheath at the back of the neck of my ti-tandex catsuit. I was ready for anything as I slid into the armored limo beside de Grace.

Half way there, de Grace asked me if I'd known the previous Harve de Grace.

"No, I'm afraid not," I said. "I never worked with any of the East coast names, they mainly worked the Caribbean and the southeastern U.S. I was always in D.C. or on the West Coast." I couldn't tell if he was relieved or disappointed. "Did you ever know a Company blond named Laguna Woods?" I asked.

He said no, she must have been before his time.

"How long have you been with the Company, Mr. de Grace?" I asked.

"Less than two years," he admitted. "And a very chaotic two years at that."

It must have been indeed because unless the Company no longer existed, there would have been a new Laguna Woods five minutes after the other one's termination was confirmed. But I just smiled and acted nice, making small talk about militias, terrorists, torture, and subjects like that. Augora cringed politely next to us and kept quiet. Civilians will never understand the joys of scaring the hell out of the innocent as well as the not-so-innocent. However, in the course of talking to me, de Grace confirmed what I had begun to think: that he was either not Company or such a greenhorn, he didn't know up from down. No one in the Company talks so freely with an outsider present. We never even talked this freely to each other, and once he got talking, he kept talking.

Listening to de Grace and watching Augora also dispelled any fears that I was walking into a trap. Unless it was a trap for all of us, which made me glad I had as many guns on me as I did.

We made good time out to the AT&T compound and ended up in the same observation and interrogation suite. On the other side of the glass, Mr. X was brought in and left there to think it over. He looked comfortable; annoyed, but not alarmed. Mr. X was old, old people are hard to work on because they have nothing to lose.

"He's been in there before," I said flatly, not bothering to turn my head for Augora's nod. "We'll do this somewhere else, what have you got?"

Augora rattled off a few locations; I stopped him when he got to a conference room. Mr. X had probably been in a lot of conference rooms; this would up the humiliation factor.

"I'll need whatever you're using for electric shocks," I said, shedding my jacket. I couldn't tell if de Grace cast an appreciative glace at my tits or my Titanium Colt. "I will need a PC with a spreadsheet program, and some pages of numbers for data entry–"

Augora squeaked up, "Wha–?"

"And I will need a stopwatch."

AT&T is fast and efficient when they want to be; twenty minutes later I strolled into an equipped to spec conference room. At one end of the table some video equipment was set up, at the other end was a battery with electrodes, a stopwatch, a PC, a typing easel, and a rather nervous looking Mr. X, or Prisoner 12584.

'Ah, to work,' I thought, settling into the chair on his right. "So, Mr.... Mr... " I made a show of consulting his chart. "Well, we don't know your name, so let me just call you Mr. 12584. My name is Nellie Gail, I'm going to be the last person to ask you questions."

"The last? Will I be let go?" he asked, or rather demanded.

"Depends."

"On what?"

"On the answers." I consulted his chart and ran though the battery of questions:

Why are you in the Los Angeles area? Who are your contacts here? Where is your funding coming from? Who sent you here? What is your mission here? Who else is coming to Los Angeles? And variations on these questions. As I expected, he brushed them off so I ran through them pretty quickly.

"Okay then, we will move to the next stage," I said. I picked the restraints on the credenza; nothing fancy, they were like the straps one puts around luggage or packages to carry them. They were just as effective for restraining humans as they were for parcels. Mr. 12584's eyes widened and, with an outraged snort, he started to rise when I approached. de Grace and Augora held him still while I tightened a strap around the chair back and across his chest and upper arms and another one around his calves and the chair legs. "You see, Mr. 12584, we need these questions answered and we have more than one way of asking them."

The wires leading from the small battery had alligator clips on the ends. I have always been of the gradualist school of thought, so instead of hooking them up to 12584's genitals or nipples, I simply laid them on his thighs, near his knees. He was old, too, and I wasn't sure how much he could take, so I would start with educational pain and work my way up to effective pain.

"This hurts, Mr. 12584, it's supposed to hurt," I said, settling back in my seat. "So, before I hurt you, let me ask you again: What is your name and why are you and the people you were with here on the west coast?"

"That's no concern of yours."

I set the meter at 25 volts and looked up at Augora, my hand hovering of the switch. "Do you have this set for one pulse or does it run current until the switch is flipped off?" I asked.

"The latter," he said.

"Ah!" I gave the switch a quick on and off, and made a few notes on 12584's clenching and grunting. In my experience, subjects that try to maintain a level of dignity under torture are the easiest to break. The ones that scream and flail from the gitgo tend to wear everyone out quite quickly. It seems like they're breaking, but in fact they're stalling and sometimes they simply don't break. I didn't feel that was going to be the case with 12584 here. "So, that hurt, eh? And that's just the beginning," I said, staring blandly into his angry, but determined face. Determined to do what, I had no idea. The ones that got that look were eventually, but painfully, convinced that I had all the cards.

I ran through the questions over and over,

increasing the duration of the shock, but not the voltage. When I smelled his pants burning, I moved the wires farther up his thighs. After this, I gradually increased the setting to 40 volts. Five hours later we got his name—Matt Black—and where he was from—Enterprise, Kansas.

As focused as I was on Black, I was keeping half an eye on de Grace. He looked uncomfortable with what I was putting Black through, and yet strangely relieved by the paucity of answers I was getting. I thought this was interesting; either de Grace knew what Black knew and didn't want that information out, or de Grace needed me to determine that Black didn't know what de Grace knew. Whichever way it was, I was now interested in more than the guy tied up in front of me.

Around midnight, I stood and stretched. "I need a break," I said. "How about you, Mr. Black?"

He glared at me. Sweaty and red-faced, but asked to use the bathroom. I thought it over and granted permission.

I caught up with Augora in a quiet corner. "I'm going to need your help later on," I said.

He looked dubious, or maybe he was just tired, but told me to name it. I expressed my doubts about de Grace. It turned out that Augora was wondering a few things, too. Like, where did this guy so conveniently come from out of the blue?

"Let's find out," I said, and outlined my plan. Augora went off to find the equipment we'd need.

Back in the conference room, I turned on the PC and pulled up a blank spreadsheet. "Let's do something different, Mr. Black," I said cheerfully. "I'm going to give you a chance to work your voltage level down. With data entry."

I strapped his legs and chest to the chair, leaving his right arm free. Just to break up the burn pattern, I moved the wires down to his ankles. Pulling the keyboard in front of him, and adjusting the computer print outs on the typing easel, I continued, "Here are some accounts," I said, waving my hand before the rows of numbers. "If you correctly enter these amounts so they cross-foot and answer my question, I won't shock you. However, if you correctly enter these amounts so they cross-foot, but refuse to answer my question, I will lower the voltage on the shock by five points. So, depending on your data entry skills, you might earn zero shocks and your secrets remain your own. Now, there is a small hitch; if you incorrectly enter the data, I shock you. And I'm going to time you, so if you correctly enter the data, then I'll shave five seconds off your time, and if you go over your time, I will shock you. How does that sound?"

"Complicated and stupid, like all of this," Black said, trying to sound tough.

"Oh, come now, Mr. Black, I'm giving you a sporting chance, here," I said. "Would you rather just answer more questions?"

"No."

"Okay then, let's go."

He balked, frowning, but a few jolts got him moving.

He was pretty good. He couldn't do 10-key by touch, but he had a good visual memory, so he was fast-ish, but not very accurate.

"Well, doesn't cross-foot, what a shame," I said. "But if you tell me what you're doing here on the west coast, I won't shock you, how would that be?"

Black just stared at me. I extended my arm very

very slowly to the controls, hovered my hand over the switch, flipped it on then off, and ignored Black's anguished sputtering. "Let's try it again, shall we?" I said, resetting the stopwatch.

He did better the next time, the columns cross-footed in 2 minutes and 10 seconds. I asked my question; he was silent. "Okay, I'll keep my end of the bargain." I turned the setting down to 35 volts and hesitated. "You know, if you tell me what you're doing here on the west coast, I won't shock you." Silence. "I mean, 35 volts hurts less than 40 volts, but they both hurt a lot more than no shock at all. Just letting you know." Silence. I shocked him.

Black was very red faced and breathing raggedly, so I let him sit for a while. I asked Augora to hold his free arm while I gave him some water. "You're not a young man, Mr. Black, but not even young men hold up well under this procedure," I said. "Why not come clean? What have you got to lose?"

He just stared at me like I was some kind of giant cockroach talking to him. One gets used to it in this line of work.

"Maybe it's the question that's the problem," I said, when he'd correctly entered the data in under 2 minutes. "Let's try these questions: What is your mission here? Why did you come here?"

Silence. I lowered the setting to 30 volts and asked again. Silence. I shocked him. I smelled the flesh on his ankles burning, so I pulled the wires away. "This is stupid, Mr. Black," I said, when he'd stopped shaking enough to hear me. "The shocks are bad enough, but you also have burn marks on you that are going to hurt for days." I turned to Augora. "Do you have any Bactine or Neosporin?"

180

"I'll go look," he said, and left the room. He came back with a spray bottle of Bactine.

I put it on the table where Black could see it. "If you answer my questions, I'll spray this on your burns."

Silence. I had a pale and exhausted-looking de Grace hold his free arm while I wrapped the wires around his left foot. I waved the stopwatch at him. "You have to beat the spreadsheet in one minute and fifty seconds. Go!"

He finished but it didn't crossfoot. "Well, I can overlook this if you tell me why you're here and what your mission is here."

Silence. I shocked him, and he made more noise than usual. Pain is cumulative in some people. We ran the spreadsheet again, he was fatigued so he blew it again and again until he was finally begging for mercy, always a good sign (for me).

"If you would just tell me–"

"I CAN'T!"

"Why not?"

"I can't betray my people."

"What people? The ones already locked up here?" I asked, slapping him across the face. "I'm tired, Mr. Black, we've been at this for too long, I just want to know what the fuck you're doing in LA." I reached for the stopwatch.

"I... I'm trying to get my people out..."

"How?"

"A rumor..."

"About?"

"Ships... thousands of ships... come to rescue the believers..."

de Grace tensed across the table, but I'm the only one who noticed because I'd been looking for it.

"Whose ships?"

"I don't know."

"Are you sure?" I asked. He nodded. "Are you really sure?" I said, shocking him.

"I DON'T KNOW! I DON'T KNOW! I DON'T KNOW!"

"Really?" Shock.

"I DON'T KNOW!"

"Really?" Shock. Shock.

"I DON'T... KNOOOOOOOOOOOOW..."

This sounded true to me. And the fact that the panicky look left de Grace's face confirmed my opinion.

I gave Augora the high sign. I shoved Black away from the table so he banged into the credenza; de Grace was distracted and didn't see Augora behind him with a set of restraints. I had my Titanium Colt on him by then, so he sat still while Augora wrapped the strap around his chest and another around his legs.

"What the hell are you doing?!" de Grace screamed in panic.

Oh yes, this was going to be a cakewalk. "I'm getting a few answers for my client, AT&T," I said, shoving his chair against the wall behind him. "What's behind this wall, Mr. Augora?"

"Nothing."

"Good." I took aim and blasted a hole beside de Grace's head. "Who do you work for, kid?"

"I told you!"

"I don't believe you." I shot the wall on the other side of his head. "Who are the ships coming for?" I was yelling because the shots were deafening even me.

"I can't!"

"Oh, c'mon, asshole! Who are the ships coming for?" I shot along his left side. I glanced at Black; his mouth hung open in shock and he was breathing hard.

Colts make a lot of noise, that was part of their effect. Augora was at the door, telling people those gun shots were nothing, just ignore them and get back to work. I didn't envy his job. Or the janitors; the wall was a mess.

"Okay, new question: who sent you here?"

"I told you, I came from the northwest b-b-because–"

I shot the right side of the wall. "No, de Grace, who really sent you here? Rove?"

"No, I–"

"Hughes?"

"No, I told you, it–"

I shot in front of his feet, kicking up carpet and padding. I spun the chambers in my gun and strolled up to him. "That's five, de Grace, I have one bullet left in here. Ever play Russian Roulette? It's an interesting game; you hold a gun with one bullet in the chamber to your head and maybe when you pull the trigger it will be an empty chamber and so you give the gun to the next player. Maybe you'll blow your head off. But this is a variation, because I'm pulling the trigger, and maybe I'll blow your knee off or maybe I'll blow off an elbow. There's a lot of body I can shoot before I kill you. Or maim you beyond hope." I watched him pant and sweat for a moment. "Who are you working for?"

"I can't tell you."

"Why not?"

"They'll kill me."

"Not if I kill you first." I turned my back and, in the few steps I took away from him, palmed the one bullet in my gun. "So, who are the ships coming for?" I asked turning.

"I can't tell you."

I spun the chamber and aimed at his right knee. Click.

He flinched hard, his whole body tensed for the impact that never came.

"Who are those ships coming for?"

"Please, Miss Gail..."

I spun the chamber and aimed at his left knee. Click.

He made choking noises and peed his pants.

"Whoever it is and whatever your mission is, they've given you up, de Grace," I said, spinning the chamber. "Who are you working for?"

"AT&T."

I aimed at his left arm. Click.

He started to cry.

"Don't fuck with me, de Grace." I walked over and slapped him twice. "What are you doing in LA?"

"They sent me..."

Slap. "Who sent you?"

"...Bush family..."

"To do what?"

"Make a path..."

"To what?" I leaned over to hear him better.

"To the coast..." He heaved a sigh. "The Carlyle Group ships are coming for them... and for the gold."

"The what?"

"The Bush family gold... it used to be Hitler's gold, but Prescott Bush took it into safe keeping..."

I stood upright so violently I almost overbalanced. Hitler's gold! Of all the fucking– Mr. Kern and two techs were standing next to a very nervous-looking Augora. "So, Mr. Kern, I understand de Grace works for you," I said. "Is that true?"

184

"Yes, Miss Gail, it is." He told the techs to take Mr. Black back to his cell. We were silent while they did so. No one moved to untie de Grace. "We, ah, contracted with Mr. de Grace to determine the level of threat in the rumors we'd been hearing," Kern resumed. "We did not realize that he was part of that threat. Until now, Miss Gail, thank you so much for your very perceptive assistance. We will of course be adding a bonus to your compensation for the past 24 hours." He headed for the door.

"It was more like 32," I said, following him. "What rumors?"

"Oh, silly rumors about thousands of ships coming to rescue the faithful from these sinful shores, riches beyond compare that would be loaded into them, angels at the helm," he said, waving his hands dismissively, leading me and Augora down the hall and out of the building. "You know, the usual Rapture nonsense."

"Yes, and the usual Bush family trouble," I said. "AT&T is not in the torture business, and yet you've been trying very hard to find something out. What is it?"

"That would be confidential."

"I work for you," I said. "I can only guess that you're after the gold or the ships, but not why. As someone who's done you a tremendous service today, I'm asking."

He sighed heavily. "We need that gold."

I didn't believe in Hitler's gold, but I still wanted to know... "Why? For what?"

"We need it to support the new currency we introduced."

"That scrip on the street?"

"Yes."

"Why the hell–?"

"We're not going back to the United States, Miss Gail. Southern California is too dynamic and has too many forward thinking ideas to shackle itself to that decay."

"Like reintroducing an exploitive black economy with scrip when the paperless exploitive white economy was working just fine? They had a saying in the old United States: if it ain't broke, don't fix it."

He laughed politely and excused himself due to press of work.

I looked at Augora to see how he was taking all this; his face was completely neutral and then he snapped out of it a little.

"I'll get you transport–"

"No, thanks, I'll take the bus." I snapped a speed-loader into my Colt and fired it twice in the air to get the MTA driver's attention. Recognizing me, by sight or reputation, he tossed everyone else off the bus and drove me home. Later that day, I got a nasty email from MTA management about misusing my authority and disrupting the bus service. They docked the fare and two hours of the driver's and gunners' time out of my account, the bastards.

I got home to a frantic Wilshirado, many shouts of "luchune," which sounded like scolding. "If you girls are going to tell me off, you better get some more words," I growled.

"Donde the fuck have you been?" Wilshire snarled; it had to be her, Alvarado doesn't snarl so well.

We stared at each other for a while. "That's not as interesting as where I'm going," I said coldly.

"Donde?" she asked coldly.

"To get your writing books. Quiero come with

me?"

Wilshire said yes, but Alvarado said she'd stay to start dinner. Alvarado often let Wilshire have the spotlight, such as it was. I guess that made her a good sister. I wouldn't know, I only have an elder brother, and he's a big spotlight hog if there ever was one.

After phoning Madeline to let her know we were coming, I handed Wilshire an empty backpack and we rode off down Sunset on the Electrocatti.

Only a small part of Mad's library was above ground. We were expected, so one of her heavily-armed Chinese History and Culture students was watching for us. He directed me to park the cycle in a secure parking spot and even plugged it into a wall recharger. That Mad; the soul of hospitality.

We passed through several steel doors, and down the same amount of stair wells. I think. I lost track, I'm always a little disoriented in Mad's library, so I didn't know if we were under Hollywood Boulevard or Orange or some other side street or even close to Highland. We traversed a small portion of what seemed like miles of overflowing bookcases. I once asked Mad where she got her books. She said they came to her to die, which is why she had so many. We finally ended up in her cluttered but comfy office.

"Ah, there you are." She rose to shake hands with me and be introduced to Wilshire, who was sullen with nervousness. She got that way in unfamiliar situations.

"If you'd like to look around, Mongo can show you the library," Mad offered. "What would you like to look at?"

Wilshire looked at me. I looked at Mad. "Do you have something with drawings or photos of LA before the Bush Urban Pacification plan? Say, the area around Macarthur Park?"

Mad smiled and told Mongo to take her to section 71B.

We settled down over a pair of té verde's. I asked her where she got such luxuries.

"Trade with China is up," she said. "But it's who you know and how well you can haggle in how many dialects that determines who gets this stuff."

"Not just to the highest bidder?"

"Oh someday it will be that normal again," she said, shoving a few books aside. "But for now, there are some things money can't buy." She ripped a page of the LA Times in half and wrapped a small mound of tea in it.

I'm more of a carrot juice person, but I accepted it with thanks. I do like green tea now and then, and I could always barter it to Julia for something.

"You've read Jared Diamond, I suppose?" Mad asked, swerving at a topic in her usual fashion.

"Of course," I said. "I only went to a state university, but we did wear shoes, use electricity, and read one of the most important historians of our era."

"Oh hush, Nellie, I'm not insulting you," she said. "That might be fatal." She paused to let me laugh. "I just meant to limn his idea that without dissent there is no progress. He cites China as stagnating in that way."

"I don't disagree," I said. "It's what the U.S. did to itself on and after September 12, 2001 when the Patriot Act passed, and passing the same kind of insane legislation again and again with our so-called Lawmakers' majority consent. They paved the road for this dictatorship to roll on."

"Some even yelled 'Let's roll!' didn't they?" she asked. "I miss my country, too, Nellie. It's good to talk to someone who remembers what it was and what it might have been."

"Yeah, well." I figured I'd better lighten up or we'd be sniveling in our té verdes. "But China survived, such as it is."

"Yes, they had a bad hundred and fifty years but now they're back!" She laughed. "The deal is, though, China has enough people to loses tens of millions and survive. Our country didn't and doesn't, and, as we know from Jesusland, most of our country would rather break than bend to the wind of progress, science, art, and all that yummy kind of stuff."

"Bend to the wind of progress," I said. "Very poetic of you, Mad, but I'd say it would depend on the wind for me to decide to bend."

"You sound unlike you, Nell."

I considered confiding in her, but decided against it. She might be after Hitler's non-existent gold too, once she knew about it. "I think I have a new kind of flu."

"What flu?"

"Maybe hope," I said vaguely, "that there might be a future to hope for."

"A dangerous, often fatal condition."

"Yeah, and I've no idea where I picked it up."

"You have built something here," Mad said thoughtfully. "Or, at least, made it safe enough for others to build, Madame Warlord."

"I just exist, Mad, whatever connotations people attach to that fact are their business."

Mad shrugged and moved a stack of floppy books in front of me. "Who are you teaching to write? That girl, ah, what's her name? Olympic?"

"Wilshire," I said. "And her sister Alvarado."

"Why?"

"They were born there."

"No, why are you teaching them to write," Mad said between chuckles.

"They asked me," I said. "Why do you still teach Chinese to those student thugs you've collected?"

"So it won't be lost. So I won't forget myself," she said softly. "And it binds us together."

"Yeah, it's strange, I just wanted to be a scholar, but when I have taught, I really loved it," I said, a little too candidly, but Mad just nodded, and didn't look shocked. "I'll take these," I said, gathering up the writing primers. One of them was Mr. Wood's Lotta Letters, from which I'd learned how to make my letters. "What do I owe you?"

She named a ridiculous sum, I haggled her down thirty percent, and I punched my debit card into the banking terminal on her desktop. She tossed in a few pads of Canadian recycled paper; she must have gone nuts or gotten hope or something terrible like that.

We collected Wilshire, who was staring at a picture book with a very relaxed-looking Mongo. Well, nothing wrong with getting a little commerce where you can.

She held up the book to show me a picture of pre-Rebellion and Occupation Sunset and Vine. "Looks different," she said.

Mongo cleared his throat and said something in Chinese to Mad. Mad held out her hand for the book Wilshire was holding, examined it and gave it back, with an urbane little bow.

"We have another copy of that," she said. "Mongo would like to give it to you, as a present. He says you'd like to show it to your sister. I hope you and she will enjoy it."

Wilshire clutched the book to her chest and whispered, "luchune, luchune." Mad looked a question at me.

"Street slang for thank you," I said. "But she really means it." We exchanged rather world-weary smiles and I said good evening. Mad had Mongo show us out. She very rarely left her labyrinth; her pallor told me she hadn't seen the sun in months. Well, it was safer where she was; or at least seemed that way.

After dinner, after the plates were cleared, I sat between Wilshirado and we worked on the letters "A," "B," and "C," and the syllables "BA," and "CA." And then they went into the night to do whatever they did there. I was already settled into bed reading *Gunfighter Nation* when I realized I hadn't killed anyone that day or the one before. The strange part was that I hadn't missed it.

I got a good night of sleep, but other than that my serenity didn't last very long.

Twelve hours later, I was enjoying a peaceful, under-occupied morning, watching the well-dressed tall handsome Asian man on my front door monitor ring the bell and wait. And wait, until he checked a PDA, and he rang again.

Wilshire stomped into my office. I knew it was Wilshire because Alvarado doesn't stomp around. "Luchune! Someone at the door!" She pointed at the very monitor I, myself, was looking at.

"I see him," I said, and did nothing to let him in or communicate with him. I have nothing against Asians; I was just feeling spooky after my encounter with AT&T yesterday. In the clear morning light, it occurred to me that AT&T might not believe I didn't believe in the Hitler-Bush family gold and they might try to do something about it. This guy didn't look like an AT&T killer, but, then again, I'm not sure what an AT&T hit man looks like.

"You gonna let him in!?" Wilshire can be a pest sometimes.

"Maybe. Where's your sister?"

"Shopping."

"Guys like that make me nervous," I said, watching the monitor. "I only have guns, they have five thousand years of continuous civilization behind them. My guns are no match for that."

Wilshire gave a low growl of frustration because I was being cryptic, but otherwise stayed still. By now she knew better than to make any vigorous moves when I'm distracted. A few days ago, after one of her violent shrugs in my peripheral vision, I'd pulled my gun and nearly shot her. It was reflex, but in my business death is only a reflex away.

The Asian guy rang again, looked left and right, and then reached for the lock.

I hit the intercom. "I wouldn't."

He stepped back. I heard, "Miss Gail?" before I snapped off the intercom.

"Why not?" Wilshire asked.

"Because I can run current through the door."

"Like a shocky?"

I nodded. We both leaned forward when Alvarado walked up to the Asian guy. They spoke briefly, and Alvarado rang the bell.

"Donde button for current?" Wilshire asked, encroaching on my personal space. I shoved her back and gave her a dirty look. She laughed; I didn't. I was watching Alvarado bang on the door.

"Fuck," I said, snapping the intercom on.

"Alvarado, stop banging on the door." She did. "Who are you and what do you want?"

"My name is Chung Wah, I'd—"

"You know the corner of Hollywood and Orange?" I cut him off. Chinese: ha! I knew an expert who could handle this guy. She also had more muscle around her than I did at that particular moment.

"Yes, I—"

"Go there and tell the lady there what you want and she'll tell me," I said.

"What the—?"

"Not kidding, do it or forget it."

"How will I know her?"

"She speaks Chinese," I said, rapidly losing interest in the conversation.

"What kind? Mandarin? Cantonese? Chinglish?"

"You look smart, work it out."

"Why?" he asked.

"You want me to get a message, work it out."

"No, I meant why must I do this?"

"Because..." I had to think fast. "Because when asked what he thought the effects of the French Revolution were, Zhou Enlai said it's too soon to tell. Therefore, my area of history is too small for me to speak directly to you. Good-bye."

After he left, I buzzed Alvarado in. She looked scared, but calmed down when I asked what was for lunch. Croquettes of something, and they were good, too.

Mad called an hour later. "A very elegant Chinese gentleman thinks you're nuts, but the message is that Gloria Molina wants to see you."

"Santa Molina? She's dead, died in the siege of Plaza de la Raza. Where's the séance?"

"He didn't say, but he did leave a card and invite you to dine in Chinatown. I'll send it up with a runner," she said pleasantly.

"Much obliged, Mad, much obliged."

"I've heard the food is excellent at his restaurant," she added.

"Oh, yeah?"

"It's called the 'Meng-Po-Niang,'" she said, chuckling. "It's named after Chinese goddess who stands just within the gates of hell and gives each soul a magic potion, so that they would forget their past lives." And then she hung up.

Yes, she hung up before I could ask her who the fuck would name a restaurant that? And when her runner arrived, "Meng-Po-Niang" was indeed embossed on the mylar card. This annoyed me very much because I don't like to associate eating out with going to hell. I want those two concepts to stay far apart.

And he certainly didn't give up either. Every day one of Mad's runners delivered another calligraphically and grammatically perfect note from Mr. Chung Wah asking me for an interview at my office or to dine at the Meng-Po-Niang at my convenience. When hell froze over would be my convenience. It's not that I don't like Chinese food, but I don't have an army to take with me to Chinatown. Chinatown is a better part of town than what's left of Pico Union and certainly better than its neighbor, Lincoln Heights, but it was still far too dangerous for me to go there on my own. But the larger reason was that I didn't want anything to do with anything that had Santa Molina involved with it. I was not a believer in her miracles or her resurrection; to me she was just as dead as anyone else who died in the bombings. However, the cult that grew around her

194

memory made me nervous. Centered in the ruins of Lincoln Heights, it seemed to comprise the remains of the Hollenbeck Police department, who'd fought with the people and ensured their own doom, the survivors of the Lincoln Heights uprising, and some strange cults that came into town from the desert. No one was really sure who or what was going on in Lincoln Heights anymore. The last time I was there, I was nearly killed, but it was just a very short visit to successfully get Fydor Chandler to go to Mexico with Dr. Max. Lincoln Heights had seemed as dead as ever on the surface, with the scavengers seething below it.

Lately I'd been hearing rumors of the desert people being there more often and Hollenbeck police officers were moving supplies around. The DWP had been sniffing around their old power plants down there, but decided to leave them alone. My opinion was they might be okay during the daytime, but they'd need an army to defend them at night. I suggested they wait a few more years as the scavenger population was dying of starvation and disease and, lately, something else. I was hearing rumors that they were being poisoned and shot, as if there was an extermination program going on.

Not that killing scavengers bothered me, I hunted them myself, but there was some kind of organized scavenger eradication effort in progress, which means there was someone organizing it. But why and who I could not possibly imagine.

In the meantime, AT&T had put a truly incredible amount of money into my account for services rendered. I assumed this meant that Prisoner 365's kid had led them to the mother lode of crazy people invading California. To celebrate, I went on a minor spending spree at the Limos, even forced some new clothes, coats, and shoes on Wilshirado as well as decking myself out in new boots and a new jacket. And guns and books, of course, I can never have too many of those.

However, in the course of ordering my books over IM, Mad made me an offer I couldn't refuse. Mr. Chung had invited her to dinner, if she could get me there with her.

NG: No way.

MAD: He's letting me bring three of my men and armed.

NG: I can bring my guns?

MAD: And your bravos.

NG: My what?

MAD: Your muscle, your bodyguards, your gunslingers.

NG: Oh yeah. When?

MAD: Tonight.

NG: I'll think about it.

I don't have any bravos. I suppose I should. I do have the Limos. Julia is always my first choice because she shoots straight and fast. She was busy, so I got her brother Jim, who is almost as good. I decided to take Wilshirado with me, so we'd be a party of four. Four is an unlucky number, but I felt safer that way.

Jim and I were heavily armed when the heavily armed escort came for us. Mad rolled down her bulletproof window. "Well?"

"We're on our own rides, Mad," I said, idling on the BMW motorcycle I'd inherited from a previous job. Jim was next to me on a hybrid Harley. "But you can take Wilshire and Alvarado with you."

Wilshire, sitting behind Jim, growled something I didn't catch, but got off the bike and followed Alvarado into the armored mini-van. The sun was down and we were all on night-vision to make us a more difficult target. Our engines were quiet; Jim and I stayed close to the mini-van and the outriders took care of anything or anyone on the periphery of our procession.

There was some shooting along the way, not by me unfortunately, and when a couple of outriders took off after something, I was hard pressed to stay with the mini-van. It was too early in the evening to get mussed hunting. Annoyed that I had to do this dinner when I'd rather be out killing things, I promised myself a good shooting party after dinner. Aside from my frustrated, but suppressed, homicidal longing, we got to the restaurant without incident. Except for a couple of dusty plastic lobsters in a dimly lit, but certainly bulletproof and probably electrified display case, the place looked more like a fortress than a Chinese restaurant. Until we got inside.

I really like Chinese food, but sometimes I find the décor a little off-putting. The Meng-Po-Niang was the most nauseating swirl of pinks, ruby reds and dull golds I could ever remember experiencing. And sure enough, right inside the entrance, there was a ten-foot statue of an impossibly proportioned Chinese woman with huge blue eyes holding a goblet to all who enter this interior design hell.

Mad was utterly enchanted, Wilshirado gave it several appreciative "Luchunes," and Jim seemed hypnotized, but it might have been the delicious food smells that I couldn't really enjoy at that moment. I was wishing Julia was here; she would have understood my repulsion, if not shared it.

The very handsome-in-person Mr. Chung Wah was immaculately dressed in the most elegant dinner suit I'd seen in a long time. His hair was smooth as a bird's breast and shone like onyx in the moonlight. He was warmly welcoming and completely gracious. Even Wilshirado relaxed a little in all this hospitality. I was feeling somewhat mellow due to the number of guns around me, and then the number of guns in and around the restaurant. As long as Mr. Chung's guns didn't turn on me and my little band, I thought I could have a happy evening. I sipped the carrot juice so thoughtfully prepared for me. If it was drugged, I would have felt something by now. But, no, we sat over our drinks, Mad and Chung chatting about Meng-Po-Niang, the goddess, not the restaurant.

"I believe I'd rather go to a Chinese hell," Mad said over her umbrella drink

"At least you'd speak the language," I slipped in.

"Dr. Ferule's Mandarin is impeccable," Chung said suavely.

I tried not to jump at hearing Mad's last name; in all the time I'd known her, it had never occurred to me that she had one. "So, other than speaking Mandarin for all eternity, what attracts you to this particular hell?"

"The forgetting part," she said. "I think our western idea of hell is that we remember, regret, pine for, mourn our previous lives, and this is the most painful part."

"Yes," I said, thinking I knew something about that kind of hell on earth. "I never understood all those pictures of devils with pitchforks and whips. No one takes a body that can feel pain to hell with them. It's all... some other kind of pain."

"Our hell is a little different from yours, Miss Gail," Chung Wah said in a voice I might, once upon a time, have been able to listen to all night long. "In our hell, it is possible for a soul to atone for its sins and win rebirth. The goddess Meng-Po-Niang only gives the forgetful potion to souls on their way back to an earthly incarnation."

"I think I'd want to remember, so I wouldn't make the same mistake again," I said.

"One must live in the present as well as the past, Miss Gail," he said blandly, if not inscrutably. "The past must not overwhelm the present or the future, nor the dead overwhelm the living." A waiter materialized in the doorway and Mr. Chung nodded graciously at his bow. "Our dinner is ready."

We followed him into the hellish dining salon, where I picked carefully at each dish in front of me. It wasn't so much I was worried about being poisoned, I was too keyed up to really enjoy eating. Chung Wah had not gotten to the point of the visit and the suspense was killing me.

"Are you not enjoying your dinner, Miss Gail?" Mr. Chung asked with real concern.

"I would enjoy it more if we could get to the business part of the evening," I said, ignoring Mad's frown. "I don't mean to be very rude, but is what you want to talk to me about confidential, or can we discuss it here?"

"Yes, we may," he said. "My part of this is just to deliver the message that Gloria Molina in Lincoln Heights wants to see you very much."

"She's dead, Mr. Chung. Have you ever seen her?"

"No, but many reliable people believe in her."

"Who believes in her?" I asked.

"Hollenbeck," he said. "And all those who most need something to believe in."

"Do you believe in her, Mr. Chung?"

"I believe in the idea of her," he said. "With respect, Miss Gail, in this part of LA, we need something more than commerce and force to believe in."

Touché, but it made me laugh a little. "All right, let's pretend for a moment she exists. What does she want from me?"

"I've no idea, I've merely been asked to ask you to meet with her. Please," he added. "Ordinarily I would have refused this request, but it came from a Hollenbeck officer that I have great respect for. That and all the strange rumors of ships arriving for mysterious purposes from the east to pick up ghosts and gold, and all the strange things happening in Lincoln Heights... I don't know what Santa Molina wants from you, Miss Gail, but if it calms this part of the city, it can only be good."

"What's going on in Lincoln Heights?" I asked, hoping to confirm a few rumors.

"My friend in Hollenbeck tells me the scavengers are being killed in droves," he said. "Their bodies are stacked in the riverbed and burned. I don't know by whom because I've only seen the aftermath in the morning."

"In the riverbed?" I asked. No one but a suicidal mad man goes near that riverbed, even in daylight. "Who or what could go there and not be killed by the crazy hordes that live in the riverbed?"

"Those were killed first," Chung said. "Whoever is behind this has tremendous resources, ruthlessness and organizational skills. And an army."

"An army," I mused. "An army massing in Lincoln Heights would not, could not tolerate scavenger attacks. Yes, Mr. Chung, I see what you worried abo–"

There was suddenly a lot of yelling in Chinese.

Mr. Chung stood up. "This way, quickly please, the building is under attack."

"Does this happen often?" Mad asked, grabbing a bottle of plum wine on her way.

"Not quite on this scale," Chung said, leading us through the huge dining room toward the kitchen. "This is a very organized atta–"

Chung's heavily armed waiters exploded from the kitchen ahead of us and the bar behind us simultaneously. We dove for cover and I wished Wilshirado knew how to shoot because the rest of us had our weapons out. We were pinned down in one corner, but Chung's wait staff were holding them off. All we had to do was wait for them to make a hole we could get through.

It hadn't occurred to me there might be a way in, or out, behind us until Wilshirado screamed and started sailing dinner plates over my shoulder. "Fuck!" They had good aim and bought me and Jim the few seconds we needed to open fire at the masked men and women pouring in behind us. Some of Chung's forces turned to lay down covering fire so we could plaster ourselves against the wall and shoot whoever tried to come through. This would work until Chung's men, outnumbered and outgunned, were forced back to where we were. They were even fighting hand to hand not far from us. Of course, the grenade was just overkill, but Chung has incredible staff; and one of the Kung Fu waitresses threw her opponent onto the grenade, and her body on top of him, and saved us. She and the people around her absorbed the rest of the blast and shrapnel.

"Okay, this is fucked!" I yelled, grabbing a sub-machine gun from a corpse. I whipped on my Infra-RayBans and shot out the lights around us, dove into the hole and shot everything that moved in front of me. I glanced at Jim, also in infrared glasses, firing next to me. Love those Limos! We were soon joined by Mr. Chung, Mad and her heavily armed Chinese students. I knew Wilshirado were nearby, throwing chairs and crockery and whatever else they could get their hands on, but I was too busy to notice exactly where.

Clearing a path, we got our little group out of the worst of the fighting. Chung led us out of the building where we could use the armored mini-van as cover, if it was in the clear. It wasn't, but our side was winning that battle and we tipped the balance. Hard to know what was going on behind us, so I stayed focused on what was in front of us. We chased the killers down the alley and onto Broadway, across Broadway and into a ruined shopping area. I had a guy in my sights and ran him down between two buildings and into another alley. I lunged for cover from a poorly aimed shot, and ran after the squealing tires at the end of the alley. I caught a glimpse of a black sedan or coupe with monster tires roaring away down College Street. It was followed by a handful of unmarked trucks and vans.

It was very quiet as I made my way back to what was left of the Meng-Po-Niang. Mr. Chung was organizing his people; directing them to collect what they could carry, and arranging transport. He turned and locked eyes with me.

"I don't know, I really don't." I shrugged and dug out my motorcycle keys. "What now?"

"My people and the Chinatown Defense League will guard the building until morning," he said wearily, picking up a plastic lobster and cradling it. "We'll start repairs at dawn."

"Never say die, huh?"

"Once you establish a business location, it's difficult to move." He looked hard at me. "We didn't have enough firepower to fight them off, whoever they were. Someone or something helped us, and then vanished."

"Santa Molina?" I asked innocently, and jingled my keys at him.

He looked like he wanted to hit me, but bowed instead and went off to arrange transport back to Hollywood for Wilshirado, Mad and her gang.

Jim and I went ahead and got to Julia's without incident. I needed to drink a carrot juice in peace and try to figure out what happened in Chinatown. Somebody with muscle had attacked the Meng-Po-Niang and someone with more muscle had rescued us and I didn't have a clue who either were. I did have a strong suspicion that whoever it was, was after me, and I had a bad feeling it was about the Hitler-Bush gold. So I had much on my mind when I stepped into Julia's, but then it all went out the window.

"Evenin', Miss Gail."

"Abilene," I said slowly. "I can't remember if I'm supposed to kill you or not."

"How about not?" He drawled. "I'm a new man, Nellie, and I've come to lay it all at your feet."

He was as scruffy, dusty, sexy, lazy-voiced, and cool as the last time I'd seen him; I was uncertain I wanted it all laid at my feet. I might want it laid a little higher up. Julia brought me a carrot juice and rolled her eyes. I sat down anyway as I was curious to know where Abilene had gone after the thwarted invasion of Los Angeles by Militias of Christ. I was very interested to know what became of Kevin after the shoot-out in the Klan of the Koffee Kats. I was hoping he was dead, but I had hoped that before. "Where's Kevin?"

"No idea, ma'am. I never saw or heard of him again after that night." Abilene took a pull on his orange juice. "Is he more attractive than me?"

"No, but I want to kill him more than you." I sipped my juice. "Where'd you land after that night?"

"Well, I barely made it out of California," he said grimly. "Y'all got wall to wall crazy people here, but I finally hooked up with some of the Militias for Christ and swung down to Texas with them. They had the food and connections to survive what the hell was going on out there. Southeast of Texas your friends from Mexico were kicking ass all over Jesusland. I would have changed sides if I could've. I'm sure you've heard about the great battles down Memphis way."

"Nope, and don't care," I said. "As long as it stays out of LA county, I couldn't care less what happens to the rest of the country."

"You're wise, Nellie," he said. "It's ugly out there. And I was on the wrong side." He took a deep breath. "You know how stress wears a body down, well it wore more'n my body down. I started to believe all that crazy Rapture crap they go on and on about in Jesusland. Seems like there's nothing to life for those people but everyone else's death and they get to watch from some cloud next to Jesus Himself. In the meantime, they're gonna kill as many unbelievers as they can, as if that will impress whoever or whatever gets to decide how close they get to sit to Jesus."

He tilted his chair forward and put his elbows on the table. "I went to church when I was a little boy," he said quietly. "I never heard about Jesus killing anyone or wanting us to kill each other. Seems like I recall he wanted us to love one another." He sat up. "But maybe

I misremembered it because, boy oh boy, did those Jesusopaths have me going. Sometimes the thought of a little peace and quiet in the clouds really sounded damn fine to me. And one night, after a bad day of gettin' our asses shot off runnin' away from your Mexican pals, I looked around at the faces scrunched up in prayer, I really listened to those crazy words about how we were all gonna end up in heaven or somewhere's together for eternity with the Righteous, the Just, and the Christians and only these particular type of Christians. And I realized right then that I did not want to spend eternity with these crazy mutherfuckers, no way, no how. So, I dispatched them to their Lord and hit the road back to the one person who might make this life interesting enough to enjoy livin' for a while longer." He looked at me with a twinkle.

"Who?"

"You."

I stared at him. Then I glanced at the door when Wilshirado came in. They skirted our table and ordered hot coco from Julia. "Yeah, Abi, that's interesting," I said, rising and walking to the back of the café. "Can we go out the back, Julia?" I asked, herding Wilshirado in that direction. She nodded, and we did.

"Who was that?" Wilshire asked when we got upstairs.

"A bad man trying to convince me he's a good man."

She shrugged and sat down with her sister to practice their letters. They were up to "M," "N," and "O," and the words "can," "man," and "fell." I added "coco" because they were drinking it. They thought that was funny, but I had no idea why.

I left them to their studies and crawled into bed

with Richard Slotkin. He was going on and on about the democratic ideals in the original "Stagecoach." Yeah, right. I was beginning to think the whole book was a waste of time because my chances of ever seeing either version of "Stagecoach" were nonexistent. This annoyed me. I like John Wayne movies because they usually lack moral ambiguity, but shelved my disappointment and went to sleep.

I was very busy the next few days, ambushing MTA buses and besieging DWP installations, so I managed to avoid Abilene. I saw him at Julia's and meandering a little too casually around Sunset, but pretty much ignored him. I did make time to take Wilshirado into the Hollywood Hills and teach them to shoot. Since it looked like they were going to be around for the long haul, two more gun-hands would be useful in the next shoot-out. They were okay with the guns, Wilshire maybe a little better than Alvarado, but they were diligent students and fair shots by the end of the afternoon.

On the way home from a DWP job I stopped by Julia's for a carrot juice. I found Fydor Chandler, Dr. Max, Dr. Jane Caterham-7, and her bodyguard, Brother AK47 in his immaculate saffron robes and AK47, waiting for me over juice there. I threw myself into Fydor's arms; I was truly glad to see him. "Fydor! You live!"

"Absolutely!" He hugged me back. "Hey, who are those ferocious girls in your place? I was taunted to within an inch of my life by them. It was kind of exciting."

"Oh, they're, um... ah, just, some girls," I said stupidly.

"Have you switched teams, Nell?" Max asked me with his trademark leer.

"No, Max, I still like guys," I said. "Although I don't like you very much."

"And what's this I hear about you being a Warlord?" He asked. "Shouldn't that be Warlady?"

"Wouldn't that be completely silly?" I asked back.

"And a whore Madame, I understand," he added, leering again.

"Hardly, Max, the rumors aren't true, and if they were, I'd be a pimp because I don't have the whores working in a house," I said tartly. I looked up a Fydor, who was following the exchange with too much casual disinterest. "Fydor, some whores in town tell their tricks they work for me. They don't work for me, they just say that to scare money out of recalcitrant johns."

Fydor gave me a reassuring one-armed squeeze. "See, Max? What did I tell you?"

"Which whores?" Max asked.

"The ones that wouldn't let you in my place," I said, and quickly said hello to Dr. Caterham-7, whom I liked least of all. "What brings you all here?" I asked the old tax mystic sour-puss.

"You are the end of the line, Miss Gail, as usual," she said, mysteriously. "But God is on our side."

"I'm sure you've let God know in triplicate already. Wouldn't it be better if we were on God's side?"

"It is the same thing," she said wearily.

I might have taken umbrage at her tone if not her words, but Julia wanted the table for a large party, so we adjourned to my place. I got an assortment of sheepish and angry looks from Wilshirado as I introduced them to everyone, but they kept their mouths shut. Even when I said everyone was staying for dinner, they looked dubious, but were silent.

"Yahla, girls," I said, using their word for 'hurry up.'

Fydor took me aside and explained that I was, indeed, the end of the line. "The Combined Armies have got most of the country under control, at least all the parts we care or worry about," he said. "There's some final action here, we think, near LA on the coast."

"You mean the Bush Family is running for it," I said.

"Exactly," he said. "And we need to hole up here and see what shakes out."

I told him everything I knew. I knew he'd share it in ways that would get the most mileage out of it, so I didn't worry about holding anything back. I'd wanted to compare notes with my brother for a long time; he is, was and always will be the smartest guy I know. "But tell me one thing, Fyd; why this coast? Why not run from D.C. or their friends in Miami?"

"They couldn't get out that way because they'd run to Kansas, thinking they could regroup and take back the county from there," he said. "I don't think they realized how much they damaged the country. There were a few dedicated Bush worshippers out in the sticks, but far fewer than the Bush Family thought. Add to that that all the brains are on our side. They were stuck, they just barely got out ahead of our forces, and then we lost their trail. We know there are ships coming, we think they're coming either to what's left of Oxnard or what's left of La Jolla."

"Six of one, half a dozen of the other," I said, and was interrupted by Wilshire snarling that dinner was on the table. I knew it was her by her snarl.

Over the course of dinner, Jane Caterham-7 veered dangerously close to her pet theory that there was a reasonable reason for the Holocaust. As a historian, this sacrifice theory makes me particularly sick.

"Yes, we have lost many in the struggle," she began. "But, as a historian, Miss Gail, you know that death–"

"Stop."

"I assure you, the dead would approve of our actions and–"

"Shhhh."

"Like the sacrifice of the Six Million, this carnage is not in vain, I–"

I was still wearing my shoulder holster so drew my Colt and pointed it at her. "If you say another word, I will blow your head all over that wall."

Caterham-7 froze and Brother AK47 seemed to stop breathing. Now that I think of it, I was the only one breathing normally at that moment.

Then Caterham-7 lowered her eyes, and said, "Of course, Miss Gail."

"Thanks," I said, staring Brother AK47 down. His gun was locked in my arsenal, but I was no good at hand-to-hand and he was a big guy.

Wilshire snarled, "Luchune!" and she and Alavarado cleared the table. I thought they were going to skip the writing lesson, but they brought their books, pens and writing tablets to the table and we got to work. I ignored my audience as they talked softly at the other end of the table, pretending to ignore us, but casting the occasional glace down the table at us making letters and monosyllable words. It was a work night for Wilshirado, so we only studied for an hour. They followed me into the kitchen to help me wash up.

"What was that viej-hag talking about at dinner?" Wilshire demanded.

"A government in Germany called the Nazis killed millions of people they didn't like," I said, not wanting to explain it because no one can really explain it.

"Why?" Alvarado asked.

"Because they could."

"No, why didn't they like them?" she asked.

"Oh. Because they were different or disagreed with them or both." This is one of the few questions I could sort of answer.

"So? That happens all the time, people killing each other. What's so special about this?" Wilshire asked, almost pleasantly. She could be nice when it was just the three of us, which made it harder for me to tell them apart.

"It shouldn't have happened," I said, handing her a dry dish to put away.

"Why not?" And waited for an answer.

"Because we're supposed to be better people than that," I finally said. "The Nazis destroyed a thousand years of progress in just nine or ten years of craziness."

Wilshire shrugged.

"You look sad, Miss Gail," Alvarado said.

I have a long memory and I read a lot about the past. I know what was, and what could have been, and when it doesn't make me angry, it makes me sad. But I wasn't going to try to explain that to kids who lived in 24 hour increments because they had to. So I just said I was tired and talking to our dinner guests wore me out.

"They loco," Wilshire snapped.

I nodded.

"So, where are you girls going tonight?" Fydor asked cheerfully when they were ready to leave. "Can I tag along?"

Wilshirado gave me puzzled looks and shrugged.

210

"No, Fydor, you better stay in tonight," I said, ushering the girls out the back entrance and locking the steel door behind them.

"They're cute, Nell. Twins, huh? You sure you didn't change teams?" he teased.

"Positive."

"I couldn't understand much of what they said to you and each other," he said thoughtfully. "Is that a patois or something else?"

I led him into my office and dug out the list of words I'd noticed them saying. "They're grabbing words from all the languages I know about in Los Angeles, and a few I don't recognize," I said. "But the vocabulary seems very limited; they use the same words over and over, but the meaning is different depending on the inflection. I guess that makes it a patois or a creole."

"Well, well, no, noo," he said, staring at my list. "Based on what you're telling me and what I heard tonight, it's not either of those things..."

"Why not?"

"Because it's not complex enough," he said, in that slow, pedantic voice I found so annoying. "Your girls are just doing a good job corrupting English."

"As if they knew pure English, Fydor," I said, defending Wilshirado against... something. "They've lived on the street most of their lives."

He ignored me. "A creole also wouldn't draw so much from Asian and Middle Eastern languages either. And I don't think it's slang, based on your notes, it's too organized. Is it consistent in other speakers?"

"I've no idea."

"Hm." He thought for a few moments. "Have you documented any other speakers?"

"No."

"Hm. Well, it will be interesting to see what other language mutations crop up when things stabilize," he said, briskly. He was summing up and moving on. "For now, for the sake of this discussion, let's call it a jargon, which was invented by pirates to communicate amongst themselves. Seems fitting somehow."

"Fine." I had no idea why, but I considered 'jargon' a come-down and an insult to Wilshirado, pirates notwithstanding.

"I ran into some odd slang in Jesusland, slang based on the most famous stories in the Bible," he said, ignoring my irritation. "Stories so famous, even I knew them."

"Oh, c'mon, Fydor, we went to Sunday school, long ago."

"Okay, who did Jacob ended up with after the first seven years labor, instead of Rachel, whom he wanted?"

"Leah," I said, surprised I could remember so easily.

"Right! And when you get a bad deal in Jesusland it's a Leah," he said.

I thought about this for a moment. "Oh. My. God."

"Exactly! But I did come across an interesting language in China..."

"Were you in China?" I asked, surprised he'd leave the war in progress.

"No, but I was in a nice big captured library for a while and I did a little reading," he said. "It's called Nushu. It means 'Women's Writing,' because few Chinese women were formally taught to read or write, and they secretly developed it to communicate with each other. It's pretty much extinct because the Chinese educate their girls now. Here's a Nushu saying: 'Beside a well, one does not thirst. Beside a sister, one does not despair.'" He put his arm around me.

I put my arm around him. "Or beside a brother."

"I want you to start calling me Larry again," he said after a while. "I'm done with the past, or that part of it."

I nodded. "Okay, Larry."

"Okay. Why are you teaching them to write?"

"Because they don't know how." I laughed at his frown. "Okay, okay, they asked me to, so I got some books. Writing is hard work."

"Why did they ask you?"

"I don't really know," I admitted. "I don't see what good it will do them. I think they're striving, not just for survival, but for something more, maybe more challenge, more brain stimulation. I don't know. I don't know why they glommed on to me, of all people."

"Because you like teaching," he said. "People who want to learn must sense that in you, Alison."

"Maybe," I said, wincing at my old name. "Hey, keep calling me Nellie, I'm not ready to go back to... to that name."

"Okay, Nell, whenever you're ready," he said, giving me a squeeze. "We're winning, sis, we've won, in fact, and all that's left is to divide up the country into manageable parts, put good administrators in place and plan the elections. Canada and Mexico will take huge chunks, but they've certainly earned them. It won't be the same polarized U.S. we grew up in; we know that doesn't work, and so many have died—"

"For the greater good?" I asked sarcastically.

"No. They died for greed, stupidity, fear, and wickedness," he said with savage coldness. "And I want the Bush family and their mafias to pay for that."

So did I, and with all my heart. I also wanted to go hunting. Or drink juice at Julia's. Or go to bed and read. Anything but sit down with Max and the tax mystic for a chat. But there was no avoiding it, so I might as well get it over. Besides, Larry had steered me to the table.

"Okay, Max," I said grimly. "When you show up it's usually bad news and hard work. So, tell me what the deal is."

"Gold," he said in his most dramatic Internet Broadcast voice. It was the voice he used to introduce economic concepts on his old show. "Bush family gold. We need it to rebuild the United States."

"You're going to need more than–"

"It's a start," he cut me off. "We believe there are other resources involved, off-shore and Swiss accounts, data for blackmail, enough to get us off the ground."

"You can't borrow from, say, France?" I asked. "They like you, Max."

"We also need to destroy the Bush family and you know they're nothing without their money," he said. "Killing them isn't enough," he added to my unspoken question. "Their poverty will be an example to anyone who might try to emulate them again."

"And prosecuting them for crimes against humanity doesn't appeal to you either?" I asked.

"Without their money to hide with, it will be easier for The Hague to find and charge them," he said. "If The Hague is so inclined. It might be more trouble than it's worth, only to rule that GW Bush is mentally unfit to stand trial. They might convict Rove, as they

214

finally did Zivota Panic, but that's a long shot. Frankly I just don't want them in the U.S. where the W cult could ever start again. Of all the countries in the world, you wouldn't think our down to earth, hard headed Southerners would build a religion out of the supposed divinity of one rich spoiled mentally challenged frat-boy, but there you have it." He sat back with a scowl.

"There's another reason we must have that gold."

I narrowed my eyes at Jane Caterham-7 but it didn't turn her into a pile of ashes.

"That gold was stolen from Hitler by Prescott Bush," she said, sounding sane if you didn't actually listen to the words. "It must be used to for good, or the sacrif–"

My gun was in her face. "Dr. Caterham-7," I said, also sounding sane when I want to. "As a historian, I want you to shut the fuck up about your insane theory of the Holocaust or I'll kill you."

She raised her eyebrows, but wisely kept her mouth shut until I put the gun away. "Really, Miss Gail," she said primly. "Your zeal for history is most impressive."

"Yeah, well," I said, looking around the table. "How do you all propose to steal this gold that might or might not exist?"

"With your help," Max said. "You're a Warlord, Nellie, you must have an army at your disposal."

"I have some guns and an attitude, Max," I said. "And that's all, pal. What about your contacts here, like the DWP?"

"The DWP has become uncharacteristically neutral in these final days, Nell," he said, kind of sadly. "I think they're playing both sides and will make a deal with whoever survives the next few weeks."

"What sides?" I asked. "They run things."

"Infrastructure, not funding," Larry chimed in. "AT&T has that in their online banking system and we're not sure who's side they're on. We've never been sure, but now that it's crunch time, I think they're going to try to keep LA county as their own fiefdom."

This made a lot of sense; it also made the situation a lot worse than I thought it was. "And I fit in where?"

"We think the MTA is in it with AT&T," he continued. "And if we have to fight them both, who knows better than you how to defeat an MTA fortress bus or besiege a fortified installation?"

"You're asking me to kick my most reliable meal tickets' asses," I said. "And then what?"

"We'll bring you back east," Max said cheerfully. "The new government will need a, um, historian. Or something."

"And leave all this?" I asked. It was a joke, but only Larry got it.

There seemed to be nothing more to say, so I decided to take a stroll before I went to bed.

I was too distracted to hunt and too restless to sit, so I strolled west on Sunset. At that hour everyone is barricaded in their places with no lights showing. The street was dark and silent, just the way I like it. I moved softly in the shadows, toward a large shadow leaning against a building ahead of me. A smaller shadow darted away farther up the block. I reached for my gun and kept my hand on it even after I'd seen it was Abilene. "Evenin'," I said softly.

"Nice night," he said, not moving.

"It's cold."

"I could put my arms around you," he offered.

I laughed. "Abilene, I don't trust you any farther

than I could throw you." I turned up my ti-tandex jacket collar. "But thanks for the thought." I turned to go.

"You know the Bush family is making a run for it through LA to the coast, don't you, Nellie?" It was more of a statement than a question.

"Yes. We are unlucky."

"You could just let them go," he said.

I laughed again. "As if I could stop them, Abi, I'm only human."

"Your brother is here."

"Family visit," I said, my hand tensing on my gun. "He came to see me because he misses me. Like you did."

It was his turn to laugh. "Yes, ma'am, but I don't want to be your brother, if you know what I mean, and I think you do!" He strolled off, chuckling.

I stood in the sheltering shadow a little longer mulling over our exchange and could only come to one conclusion: Men. They're weird.

But my head was clearer and I felt more peaceful. The moon was out, and no matter what, we get beautiful moons in LA. Even if there was no one to admire it, the LA moon would put on a good show two weeks a month. What a trouper.

I went back to my place and slept like the dead.

Several days later I got an email from Ed, the DWP guy I was seeing so much of last year, asking for a meeting at Julia's that night. This seemed fairly harmless; he's a married man after all. So I didn't dress up, but I also didn't demur when he suggested we take our carrot juices and go for a walk in the moonlight. I should have known he just wanted to be where there were no extra ears.

"Gloria Molina wants to see you," he said as we

strolled along a deserted stretch of pavement.

"Oh, not you, too, Ed," I sighed. "I don't believe in Molina. She's dead."

"I'm just the messenger, Nellie," he said. "But... well, I kind of believe in her. People say she appears when they need her and gives them courage."

I stopped in my tracks and turned to face him. "Those people are having hallucinations, Ed. They might as well see the Easter Bunny to give them courage."

"Nellie..."

"What's the deal, Ed? I don't care who wants to see me, but I do care why." I waited.

He sighed. "Okay, I don't know all of it, but it seems there are some people that Molina–" he held up a hand to restrain my outburst, "–or whoever it is, wants to stop at the coast. They have something she, or whoever, wants and wants badly. That's where you come in."

"Why?"

"You're the only person in LA who can stop an MTA bus," he said grimly.

"Oh my God, they've turned," I said, realizing I hadn't seen an MTA bus on Sunset in few days. "Why?"

"They've thrown in with AT&T," he said. "DWP brass thinks there might be a deal to turn LA over to whoever it is Molina is so worried about."

I thought I knew better, but things might have changed. AT&T was arrogant and stupid enough to think they could outwit the Bush Family Evil Empire. Or maybe they were just going to get played like everyone else around that sick clan.

"MTA never really liked the way DWP ran things, you know," Ed continued into my silence. "But we did a pretty good job with what we had, didn't we, Nell? Kept the water running and the power on, what more did anyone need?"

"Yeah, yeah," I said, thinking hard and fast. "LA is great. When is all this going down?"

"I don't know," he said. "I've just been asked to get you to a meeting." He named a time and place.

"Will you be there?" I asked, remembering that he'd saved my ass a few times.

"No, I'm just the messenger, like I said."

"But DWP is involved, right?"

"Strictly as back-up," he said, heading us back to the lights and bustle of my block. "There are bigger players involved in this one, but I don't know who." He said good night and left me at Julia's.

Bigger players than DWP? I found it hard to believe that I'd never heard of them, but I don't get out as much as I should.

I went inside to dress for my evening meeting with Santa Molina, or whoever it was. I had just slid the stiletto into the sheath at the back of the neck of my titandex catsuit when Larry materialized beside me. He's the only person on earth who can sneak up on me.

"Goin' out, huh?"

"Yeah, little hunting. Need to let off some steam," I said, bracing for him to want to go with me.

"Have fun!"

"And what will you be doing tonight?"

"Helping Alvarado and Wilshire with their writing," he said way too cheerfully. "You know they can read a little."

"I'd heard something about that," I muttered, annoyed he was taking my job. Not that it was my job... but... still...

"Know how?" He asked. I shook my head, and he told me. "They said they used to sit on either side of an old woman and she'd run her finger under the words as she read. Pretty soon they could read faster than she could."

"Ah."

"But here's the kicker," he said, smiling manically. "The stories they remember sound like they're from the Bible."

This was slightly amusing so I forced myself to chuckle, more for Larry than for me. "That's probably the only good that book ever did them."

"And please notice they took up one of the few professions it mentions."

"Yeah, well, Larry, there just aren't that many carpenter jobs out there these days," I said, and he had the grace to laugh at me.

Always leave 'em laughing, they used to say, so I did. Damn Larry, he'd put me in a good mood and it took a few blocks to shake it. But by the time I got to Sunset Junction, I was back to my usual morose and paranoid, and cracklingly-aware self. And being so, I slipped the Electrocatti and me into the shadows just past what was left of Hyperion Avenue, to let a pack of feral teens go by before they saw or heard me. Not that I was worried; even on the Electrocatti I could outrun them, and I could certainly out-gun them. I looked them over a little more carefully than usual, wondering if Wilshirado ever ran with a pack like that. Most probably they ran from them; these kids in the dark with me were damaged, dangerous and doomed. Through luck and brains, Wilshirado were at least a step above that.

Because it was safer to sit in the shadows a little longer, I used the time to mull some things over about

Wilshirado. I must be getting old because my train of thought would distract me if I didn't finish it. They were around the office more often since the houseguests had arrived. And our houseguests seemed to have a lot of time on their hands. I'd noticed Caterham-7 teaching them simple arithmetic one evening and Max taught Wilshire how to play chess. I know this because Julia Limo put a chess set on my tab with a reference to 'Dr. Max and W.' She should have just given it to W, because her brother Jim and W seemed to be getting very very cozy. On the other hand, that might be why she charged so much for it. Larry had the same instinct for teaching as I did. He'd taught me every new thing he ever learned; even after he went away to university, I got link-filled emails full of stuff he'd learned and pages of his thoughts before... before things changed. I took a few deep breaths to loosen my throat up. "Before things changed to the way they are now," I said softly. "And this is what I must deal with now." I let the past go, checked the street, the vibe, and eased my ride out of the shadows.

I was on the Electrocatti for stealth. I was going to Lincoln Heights, I'd need it just to get to the meeting. What I'd find there was another matter.

Very little of Lincoln Heights had survived the retaliatory bombing for their brave, but futile, resistance to the Occupation. Theirs had been a passionate rebellion of people who know it's better to die on your feet than live on your knees. Even Hollenbeck police division had joined with the people and fought—and died—with them. The Plaza de la Raza in Lincoln Park was an Alamo of sorts; there had been one last stand there. The siege only lasted a day. The U.S. troops set up operations across Mission in the Department of

Motor Vehicles. That being the case, most of the DMV building was spared, and this was where I was supposed to meet Molina.

As planned, I got there early and stashed the bike on the rise behind the DMV. It had survived, but the Army trashed it before they left, and it was further trashed over the years by scavengers and God knew what lived in Lincoln Park. I had on my Infra-RayBans, but had recently invested in a pair of military grade night binoculars, made in China, that were the size of opera glasses and weighed next to nothing. I flipped up my shades and took a look around.

It was quiet, too quiet. So quiet the hammer click next to my ear sounded like a rifle shot.

"Molina is waiting for you."

The voice was very soft, but so deep it carried. I looked up the speaker; his face was obscured by a ski-mask, but I recognized the tattered insignia: Hollenbeck. An officer of the doomed police force. I felt better already. If Hollenbeck was involved, there was some moral weight behind this mess, whatever it was.

I rose very slowly and handed over my Mauser, Beretta, Titanium Colt, flat flex machine gun that very quietly shot poison needles, mace, garrote, blackjack, mini-baton, brass knuckles, boot stiletto, and Bowie knife. Since he didn't frisk me very hard, I managed to keep the stiletto tucked in my catsuit's neckline. Two more shadows animated, guns drawn and pointed at me, as we made our way slowly down to the DMV building.

And then we kept going. "Hey, we're not–" A hard shove in the right kidney told me we were indeed going into Lincoln Park. Great; I've always wanted to be eaten alive.

The park had been heavily bombed, but even in

Lincoln Heights plants grow back eventually. We moved quietly over grass and past shrubs on what, in the darkness, looked like little trails. We made a little noise, more than I felt comfortable with, but then I realized we were passing sentries and even a checkpoint or two.

My escort led me to a wreck of a building, pushed aside some foliage and we went up a short flight of stairs. A big door opened into a candle-lit hallway; on the right there were doors, a few were open and I saw a very clean kitchen, rooms of bunk beds and immaculate bathrooms. I only glanced at these; what really had my full attention was a wall of candles surrounding a faded mural of Our Lady of the Americas... with an official headshot of former Los Angeles County Supervisor Gloria Molina glued over the Virgin's head. The cult of Santa Molina. And I was right in the middle of it.

But I wondered, because none of my three guards even looked at the icon, let alone paid it any obeisance. Perhaps they saw it every day, or maybe they didn't believe in Santa Molina any more than I did. However, I was about to meet someone or something claiming to be the fallen heroine.

At the end of the long hallway, the Officer knocked three times on a steel door and handed me and my weapons off to the very urbane restaurateur, Mr. Chung Wah, and his three heavily armed Asian guys. I thought these might be waiters from his restaurant, but it was too dark for me to get a good look at them,

"Very glad you could make it, Miss Gail," Mr. Chung said pleasantly.

"Yeah," I growled, and sketched a wave at Hollenbeck's back. "See ya, guys."

"This way, please," Mr. Chung said, ushering me further into the building.

We must have been underground by then, because the hallway sloped down, and had a few stairs in the steep parts. At another steel, Mr. Chung knocked twice and handed me off to another group of guys. "Mr. Chung, do you–"

"I'll be waiting for you here, Miss Gail," he said, laying a reassuring hand on my arm. "Please have faith in us."

I nodded as the door closed between us. I looked at my new six-man escort; they seemed bland, efficient and were all dressed in a familiar shade of brown. A few were in navy blue, and even wearing shorts in this cold weather. I noticed one of the brown-clad guys had a nametag: Bob. "So, Bob, what now?" I asked, and was ignored.

A dim light over another steel door went on at the end of the hallway and we headed toward it. I was ushered into a room that was reasonably well lit, at least enough to see who was in it.

"MILTY! YOU FUCKING BASTARD!" I flung myself at him like a crazy woman. Instinctively I reached for the one weapon I had on me: the stiletto in my catsuit neckline. The last thing I heard over my howl of rage, was Milty barking, 'Don't kill her!" and then blackness.

I woke up stretched out on a couch in a dim room, dizzy and with an Excedrin headache in a world where there was no Excedrin. There were two guys sitting facing me, one in brown and one in blue, their rifles across their laps, not pointed at me. Like in the nightmares I used to have, Uncle Milty was sitting next to me, but I knew this wasn't a dream because he was pressing a blood-soaked handkerchief to a vertical slice in his right cheek.

"With a little more composure, you might have

gotten my eye, Nellie," he said blandly when he saw me staring at him.

I started to sit up, but the room spun wildly, so I lay down again. "Where's Molina?" I asked, hoping Milty wasn't the end of the line.

"She's dead, like you've been saying all along," Milty said. "I'm the one that wants to see you." He paused, waiting for the question I had no intention of asking. "All right, I'll tell you why: you're going to help me save Los Angeles." He paused again, and I still didn't ask the question. "Because this city deserves to be saved. And I need the Bush family gold to save it." He paused again and, realizing I wasn't going to say anything, went into monologue mode. "These guys with the guns, the one in brown leads the UPS drivers." This was interesting—I thought I'd recognized that uniform— so I focused on the man in brown. "UPS management is not involved because that management was full of Republican swine. No, he leads the union drivers, they've been wandering in the desert and the islands of civilization out there for all these years and they'd like to settle in LA. The other gentleman in blue, wearing shorts, leads the renegade Federal Express drivers, not union men, but some of them saw the sense in organizing themselves for survival after the fall of Los Angeles. They've been stuck in the desert with UPS, often competing for the same abandoned gas. But they joined forces a few years ago and they don't like the direction AT&T is taking things any more than I do. AT&T has increased gas production when most people with vehicles are using hybrids or electrics, like you, and they've introduced a scrip, when they swore to me they'd leave the economy online."

I swung my eyes at him because I had nothing

else to swing at him. He interpreted this as a question. "Yes, it was me who formed the master plan to get LA back on its feet after the occupation destroyed it. Surprised? Who did you think got LA off its knees after the occupation? Those ninnyhammers at DWP? The idiots at AT&T? The fucktards at MTA? Well, it was me, I had the plan, the vision, and now those bureaucrat fools at AT&T and MTA are messing it up. Keeping the money all online meant we keep the economy on an even keel until it was strong enough to stand on its own. Economies are weak when your country is being invaded by your northern and southern neighbors, so of course AT&T introduces worthless paper into this fragile economy at this delicate time. Fools. I disagreed with them so violently they tried to kill me. Lincoln Heights has been my only refuge for nearly a year." He cleared this throat and softened his gaze at me. This made me queasy. "And you, you've played your part well since coming home, Nellie, first moving money around—oh, yes, you didn't realize I put you in Universal Life Insurance as a data entry clerk to keep you alive, but also to use your skills to move the e-money around. I called it insurance, in a way it was, moving the money from country to country, investing and reaping returns, and all in cyberspace, because money is only real if you believe in it. You were just one of tens of thousands believing and 10-keying the world to a higher plane of existence. And although gold is tangible, it's also symbolic, and Los Angeles needs that gold; it will buy us much credibility in the world.

"And Los Angeles deserves it, it deserves to survive and flourish. I learned that long ago, when I'd walk out at night, away from the stadium-turned-torture-chamber-and-execution-ground. This city restored my faith in humans. Do you know what kind of people you have in this City, Nell? The weak died, they always do, but the strong built new communities next to gutters still flowing with blood. The people of this city were beaten to pulp, and yet everyone I passed had a gracious nod for a stranger, if only while they watched to make sure I was not lingering. And during the food and water rationing, somehow a black economy sprang up, there was enough food for everyone and even some for barter. It was summer, wasn't it? That horrible summer, and yet God must love Los Angeles most of all because it was a cool summer, and few died of heat or thirst. Yes, I know, some say Santa Molina worked miracles all over the city to keep it going, but Molina was dead in the failed siege of this place, Plaza de la Raza, by then, so it was some other miraculous set of events that kept LA from being pounded into a paste of dust and blood. That's when I began to believe I could save myself from whatever hell was waiting from me, but only through helping Los Angeles.

"I was once like you, Nell, a little farther along, though; I was a Ph.D. candidate in medical ethics at Harvard." He looked away from me, making me wish I had a gun, even just a little one. "I was going to reconcile all the ethical issues science was kicking up as it plowed through society, if not reality itself, resolve all the conflicts between bioscience and ethics because I believed in both science and ethics and the goodness and greatness of humankind with all my heart. And then there was the stolen 2000 election, and we all thought 'this too shall pass,' and it never did. Then the fetus people fundie religiously insane maniacs took over and science was destroyed; except for the parts they liked, science was turned into black magic and scientists vilified, one or two were lynched. And these culture of life warriors were as capable of killing as any sociopath in a back alley, but they were killing for the Lord, they said, as if that made any sense. They destroyed science and ethics for me, Nell, there was nothing to live for if there wasn't a future in a world I could believe in. So I decided to believe in nothing, and to force that into others, like you and—"

"Don't," I said softly. "Don't even say his name."

"... like you. Your city gave me my faith back, Nell, I'm going to it defend to the death for that."

I didn't ask whose death. "Why me?" I asked.

The UPS guy answered: "You know how to take out an MTA fortress bus," he said. "We used to be able to ambush them for weapons, but you've gotten them too smart."

"You also know a few things about AT&T, like the layout of their interrogation center," the FedEx guy said. "We think that's where the Bush family will regroup when they get to the coast."

"Why do you think that?" I asked.

"Because between AT&T and MTA, they have the trucks and muscle to move the Bush family and their mafias to the coast and onto the ships that are coming," Milty answered. "I think the other side also has your old pal, Kevin, working for them. Much of this is far too well planned for the usual AT&T/MTA business model. Watch your back, Nellie, rumor has it that Kevin is still smarting from being bested by you in the Millie Bush and then in the Chelsea Clinton matters."

He hardly had to remind me of those insane incidents; they were still fresh in my mind. I'd beaten Kevin and his minions with skill and daring; I had outmaneuvered him in our two clashes. Kevin might possess more skills than I, but he had no daring, and that was what made me a better, more successful operative. I had been hoping Kevin was dead, because if he wasn't dead, he had to be nursing a huge grudge, and that made him very dangerous. The passion of revenge makes a man daring, if only for revenge.

"The Bush family is stuck on what's left of Route 66; the fighting out there tore up most of the infrastructure," Milty continued over my train of thought. "They'd be here if they could leave their stuff behind, but they can't, and this is the important part, this is why we can grab their gold when they get here. But only with your help."

"Why should I help you?" I asked.

"Because I'll kill you if you don't."

"That would make for a very abrupt ending."

"And then I'd switch to Larry," Milty said coldly. "He's smarter than you, just not as ruthless, and I need your ruthlessness for this."

"You go near Larry and I'll kill you, Milty, slowly."

"Not if you're dead," he said matter-of-factly. "Do we have a deal?"

"Like I have a choice? Deal." I ignored the hand he stuck out. "Tell me what else you know." The three of them ran down what I already knew: AT&T and MTA had gone insane and thrown in with the Bush family, the gold was on its way, disguised in cargo, but stuck on the bad roads of the wasteland east of the Rockies, Carlyle Group ships were either on their way or were already docked on the ocean-side of Catalina, and they thought the main Bush family and their operatives were with the gold.

I did not think that; I knew the Bushes would

leave the dangerous scut work to their lackeys. I figured the Bushes were probably in the lap of luxury in some soulless part of Europe or Asia, where their money would buy them out of whatever earthly sins anyone might ask them to atone for. But Larry was right; they were nothing without their money, and taking it from them would be the best possible revenge. Giving it to Milty made me slightly sick; I'd rather give it to Max and Caterham-7, or even the DWP, who'd do the right thing. But at the moment, as I lay listening to the intelligence Milty and his gang had scraped together, all I really wanted was to go home and drink carrot juice and talk to Larry. Home... when did I start thinking of it as home?

They finally wound down and called it a night. Milty saw me as far as the door of the room we were in.

"Nellie," he said behind me. "Can you, please, forgive me for what I did to you and–"

"Don't."

"...for what I did to you?"

"No." I sighed. "But I will think about how to do our deal."

"Do more than think about it, girl."

I suppressed a shudder; I knew that voice too well, it was the voice of the cruel master he must still be, because people just don't change that much. But I just shrugged and walked out. The truth of the moment was that he needed me alive right then more than he might like to kill me.

The USP and FedEx guys handed me off at the next door to Mr. Chung, who saw me all the way out of the building, where my Electrocatti was waiting for me. He very graciously held my things as I put all my weapons back on. He didn't ask any questions; he must have known this was bigger than the Chinatown Defense

League or Hollenbeck. I said, "thanks," and took a few deep breaths to clear my head. I had survived my meeting with Milty, but I still had to get out of Lincoln Heights in one piece.

When I got home– When I got back to my place, it was very late, and no one was up or in. This was okay. I really didn't want to see anyone just then anyway. I was asleep the second my head hit the pillow, this was a good thing; I'd need all the rest I could get because the next day my home– I mean, my building would be leveled by a tank.

I was trying to enjoy my carrot juice in the bustle of activity mornings had become. Usually I would be wishing them all, except Larry and maybe Wilshirado, gone, but there was food being cooked in the kitchen and they had all finally learned to leave me the fuck alone until at least 10:30 AM. I particularly needed this morning to think about the night before, what I would have to do, and how I might do it. My Plan A was to grab Larry and run for it: Mexico or Canada or China, didn't matter, just get the fuck out of LA, which seemed about to implode. It was on my mind to confide in him when the phone rang. I would not have answered it, but the Identificación de persona que llama said it was Mad calling. This was odd; I thought she was a late sleeper. I picked up the phone.

"Nell, there's a tank on its way to you," she said before I could say anything.

"What?"

"A tank just went past my videocámaras al aire libre de monitor de vigilancia, heading your way!" she said, starting to yell.

"Why do you think it's coming here?" I asked, pushing my dirty, crumbling net curtains out of the way.

"WHERE THE FUCK ELSE WOULD IT BE GOING?!"

I might have argued about this, but just then Julia Limo ran into the street under my window and fired a very big pistol in the air three times.

"MISS GAIL!!!"

"Fuck!" Grabbing all the guns and keys I could lay my hands on, I ran from my office. "EVERYBODY OUT THE BACK!"

Alvarado, I think, stuck her head out of the kitchen. "But breakfast–?"

"C'MON OR DIE!" She and Larry ran out and headed for the back stairs. "Where's your sister?"

"Out somewhere!"

Keeping them in front of me, I ran for the stairs. If Max, Caterham-7 and her monk were behind me, that was great; otherwise they were on their own. I didn't bother with the upstairs locks, I just shot them off with my Colt. We were downstairs at the steel door I had to use a key on when the first blast hit. I'll say this, that building was well made. We got some plaster dust in our hair, but the walls and ceiling held. I kept my cool, and got the door open, hoping there wasn't a tank waiting for us in the back.

There wasn't, but there was a pitched shoot-out between the Limos and someone in progress. We were trapped between the building, which might fall on us any second, and the bullets, which would also kill us. Brother AK-47 did us all a favor and laid down enough fire for us to get away from the building. Jim Limo covered us as we ran down the alley parallel to Sunset. Smoke was pouring out of Julia's restaurant; this did not bode well for my carrot juice supply.

Max was next to me yelling, "Nellie! We need

reinforcements! Call your bravos!"

"I don't have any bravos!" I yelled, peering around the building next door at, yes, indeed, the tank shelling my building. "I have Limos!"

"You're a Warlord, you must have troops!"

I laughed in his face. "Yeah, right, Max, dream on!"

The street was in chaos, Universal Life Insurance employees were firing from the windows when they weren't jumping from them. The Limos were putting up a good fight, but what can automatic weapons do against a tank? They were up against more than the tank; there were machine gun trucks that looked very much like the ones the MTA was testing as escorts. "Damn it, Max, we–" And then I saw it, on the other side of us: the black sedan, a Honda Accord to be exact, with tinted windows and monster tires. And the driver saw me because he took off.

It was too much; I was beyond caring. I must have been because no sane woman chases a car down Sunset Boulevard, no matter how pissed off she is. I run pretty fast and shoot pretty straight, but in the smoke and confusion, I couldn't hit the side of a barn. But I almost shot the machine gun truck that pulled up beside me, except for Larry screaming at me to get in the car. Max was on the machine gun, laying down decent cover fire for an economist.

"Where'dja-?"

"I borrowed it!" he yelled, roaring off after the Honda. "What's with that car?"

"Dunno! Let's find out!" I yelled, shooting at some opposition trying to stop us.

"Nellie!?" Larry yelled a few seconds later.

"What, Larry?"

"What do you think of Alvarado?"

"WHAT?!"

"I really like her! What do you think?"

"Um..." I shot some more while thinking. "I–" BOOM. "I think the tank is following us! Turn right!" He did. "Turn left!" Brilliant! We careened right into a pitched gun battle at Highland and Hollywood, including two MTA fortress buses. There's a lot of firepower in that end of Hollywood because it's on the border of my theoretical Warlord turf, and the local business folk were defending it with all their might. One bus was in flames, and the MTA, I now assumed it was them, was retreating, so most of the fighting was in front of Mad's library. Mad had bravos, and they were fighting like, well, bravos.

With the fight before us and the tank behind us, we figured we'd be better off on foot, so after emptying the machine gun, we used the truck for cover. Mongo recognized me and waved us into an assault formation with him and his fellow Chinese students. No good: we got pushed back onto the sidewalk in front of Mad's library entrance. I don't think it was the tank, too far way; I think it was a grenade that exploded most of what we were using for cover. Mongo and the boys zigged left away from the library, and we zigged right toward it.

"NELLIE! GET IN HERE!" Mad was standing in her own doorway, holding a Uzi and blinking in the sunlight. She gave us enough covering fire so we could get into shelter. She waved at someone, presumably Mongo, and slammed the door just as the tank pulled up outside and swung its gun at us. "Told you there was a tank coming up the street," she yelled over her shoulder as we ran like demons through her underground archive.

I made introductions on the fly. "Mad, my brother, Larry, Larry, Mad, Mad, Max, Max, Mad!" She was charmed, or as charmed as a woman running full speed can be charmed.

We got past two reinforced steel doors and who knew how many feet below the surface before the first blast came, and it still knocked us off our feet.

"Where did all this armor come from, Mad?" I asked as she slammed yet another steel reinforced door behind us. Not that I was complaining. Another blast jolted the door, but it held. Just barely. We ran on, deeper into the archive.

"Well," she panted. "I've been getting loans and bartering... with you as security on the deals."

Yet another entrepreneur taking my name in vain.

"Hey!" Larry yelled, grabbing a fat book off a shelf. "It's the William Jones book!"

"The what?" I yelled, dragging him along.

"It's the linguistics bible! No copies are supposed to exist!"

I was too busy running after Mad and Max to answer, or be impressed. The dust and smoke and noise were getting to me. Larry finally snapped out of it, and we ran faster running together.

"This way! Hurry!" Mad cried, leading us farther underground, ignoring me, or maybe not even hearing me, it was loud in there and my ears were ringing. "In here..." She pushed open a cobwebby door and we ran down a small flight of stairs. We were really and truly underground. We were in a tunnel. One with train tracks.

"Mad...?"

"It's the LA subway," she said, wearily.

"Great! We'll get out and circle around–" Max

began

"The ends are sealed," Mad cut him off. "So no one could get in this way and ambush my... MY POOR LIBRARY!" She gave way to feminine tears, and fell sobbing on Max's chest. I felt her pain. But not for long.

"So, no way in, means no way out," I said, briskly. "Larry? Logistics?"

"We're fucked, sis." He leaned against the wall and started reading the Linguists Bible by the emergency lighting. "We'll either be crushed to death or suffocate. I vote for suffocation, that way I can read a little of this book before I go."

"Oh well!" I threw my hands up. "I wish I had something to read before we die!"

The tunnel shook under a blast. "I'm leaning toward suffocation myself," Max volunteered. "But being crushed is looking more probable."

Just to get away from them, I paced the tunnel. The ends were well and truly blocked. The air vents were welded to the walls. I wondered how any air at all got down there, but, compliments of the miraculous DWP, there was a tiny stream of air blowing from them. 'There has to be a way out,' I thought. If we could just get one of these vents off... I looked around in the dim light for anything to pry the grill off. I jumped when I realized Larry was right next to me; I hadn't noticed him come up.

"Nell? Did you notice how quiet it is now?"

"Now that you mention it, it is quiet," I said. "How long...?" I shut up to listen. I thought could hear someone yelling "Miss Gail!"

"Hear that, Nell?" Max asked.

"That's Julia Limo," I said.

"We're saved!" Mad cried, wiping her eyes.

"Unless it's a trap," I added, shoving the last speed-loader into my Titanium Colt.

The cries for me, Mad, and Larry were coming closer. Someone finally yelled Max's name, which made him feel included. There was yelling in Chinese.

"Who and what was that, Mad?" I asked before she could answer.

"I don't know who it is, but they want to dig us out," she said.

"I think they should before the roof caves in," Max said, looking dubiously at the ceiling.

There was more Chinese. "It's one of my students!"

I asked if she was sure; she was, and then we all yelled for them to dig us the fuck out right fucking now.

"Oh, Miss Gail!" Julia cried and helped me out of the hole in the ground. "I was worried."

"Your shop got hit," I said. "You okay?"

"I took cover at my uncle's shop," she said, leading me through the wreckage. "We did the best we could with handguns, but..." She looked nervously at what was left of Mad's library that fronted on Hollywood. There was a wrecked tank, piles of bodies, and a solid wall three deep of UPS and FedEx armored war-trucks facing the ruins. Standing in front of the entire mess was Mr. Chung in an immaculate dove gray suit, black fedora, and matching machine gun. I turned to look a question at Julia.

"They just showed up and saved the day," she said. "Once we realized they were on our side, we chased whoever it was off pretty quick."

I nodded, and looked up and down the street; the wreckage wasn't as bad as Mad's library, but it was close. Whatever little civilization they'd built on the ruins at this end of Hollywood Boulevard was back in ruins. I was alive, but I wasn't enjoying it very much. As their Warlord, I'd failed. That made me feel bad and pissed me off as an added bonus. I looked back at the delivery war-trucks; the drivers and gunners were all staring at me.

"Okay," I said softly.

"What?" Julia yelled. "My ears are ringing."

"I said, 'Okay,'" I yelled at her.

"Okay then!" she yelled, and walked away from me.

I can't say I blamed her. Mr. Chung strolled up and suggested that since my building was rubble, we all come to Chinatown and sort things out. This was very suave; I had no choice but to accept. I collected Max and Larry, Caterham-7, her monk, Mad and her people, Alvarado and Wilshire, whom I was more than a little glad to see. "Where were you?"

Wilshire mumbled something about it being a nice day and she'd been practicing her writing and reading outside.

I thought that was damn diligent of her. "You'll have to share with your sister. All her stuff got blown up."

"Luchune!" she said, with a certain amount of awe.

I could literally dig it. We were passing the rubble of my former hom– office and residence; nothing could have survived in that crash, least of all a writing primer.

The Meng-Po-Niang looked about the same except for the statue of the goddess, which now looked somewhat like Marlene Dietrich. I asked one of the waitresses and she told me they made them in the back out of papier-mâché, thus leading me to believe this restaurant is thrashed more often than I'd imagined. It looked placid enough on the outside; even the plastic lobsters were back in their cases. Inside had more rugs and drapes than I remembered from my last visit. Mr. Chung caught me staring at a wall of drapes and explained that they hadn't finished repairing the interior walls. He assured me it would be back to the way they were very soon.

The food was just as good and I ate heartily. If Mr. Chung was going to poison me, I was ready to go. I somehow doubted it after my meeting with Milty. I wasn't expecting him, but the Company trains one to expect the unexpected. I was fully ready to make good on my vow to kill him if he came near Larry. So, I might as well have a good meal before whatever happened happened.

Things shook out very nicely in Mr. Chung's office after a really smashing lunch. Max and Larry listened carefully to what the UPS guy had to say about the where and the when of the Bush family's gold arrival. Their information jibed with mine, and it looked like things were moving faster than I'd realized. From what we knew then we had less than a week to get it together.

It was believed the gold would be transported along what was left of the 210 Freeway and then swing north on Interstate 5 and over to Oxnard and to the ships offshore. The most logical place for an ambush was where the 210 and the 5 came together. UPS's reconnaissance said the roads were a mess but passable if the drivers took care. This meant they'd have to move under cover of night.

"Why are they coming so far south?" I asked. "Why not stay north and come down the coast?"

"Your friends in at AT&T have tamed that part of

the 210 and can give them safe passage through it," the UPS guys said. "North of that, it's a wasteland. Only the city of LA had the will, manpower, money, and knowledge to rebuild. And the water. Without extra water, the outlaying compounds and farms couldn't survive."

I knew this was true as most of our food was grown in heavily guarded gardens around town, a few very heavily guarded farms near town, or shipped in from Mexico and Canada by sea. "What about sending the gold by air?" I asked.

"Not enough fuel to fly anything that big anymore, Nell," Max said. "All the military planes went overseas long ago when the Bush wars went bad and the military dissolved into chaos. Military contracting and production ground to a halt before that," he added. "Anything left on the ground, our side had captured." He turned to the UPS guy. "And I assume you delivery desert rats took care of what we didn't get at Pendleton, 29 Palms, Andrews–"

"I've forgotten the names," he said coldly. "But we got them, yes."

"MTA has helicopters," I said. "They can tow a bus into the air."

"And they're only for emergencies," Mr. Chung said. "We thought of that; they take too much fuel and can only travel short distances. The distances involved here make the tow-copter useless in this situation."

"They also make easy targets," the UPS guy added ominously. "And we've been taking out their gasoline supplies whenever we could."

I had heard something about that, but it wasn't my department at MTA. Furthermore, I knew AT&T had no air power; if they did, I knew their execs would have been swanking around in it instead of in armored limos.

"So," Larry said, making us all jump slightly. "We have one shot at the gold." He turned to the UPS guy. "How close can you know when the trucks will be in range?"

"We have people watching their progress," he said. "But communication is a little wonky lately; we think AT&T is jamming our wireless, such as it is. But we'll have enough notice to move if we're camped close to where the ambush site is."

"Makes sense," Larry said thoughtfully. "Just a matter of fighting off the escort and running down the gold trucks. If we could get them to stop, even for a few minutes, break the momentum–"

"Like if part of the road blew up in front of them?" I asked, wondering how I could get my hands on some C4. What I had was buried at Sunset and Vine.

"Exactly, sis!"

"I'd need to look at it," I said. "And I'll need C4." Mr. Chung told me that both of those things could be arranged and went to do so. I looked at the UPS guy. "And the Bush family? Where are they?"

"In hell," he said. "Or will be very soon."

I couldn't look at Larry because I'd start laughing. "No, seriously, guy; where are they?" I asked. I managed to keep a straight face.

"We have no idea," he said, and sounded really tired. "We've been following the biggest leads we can find, and in this case, those also happen to be the biggest vehicles. We lost track of the Bush family in Utah, they split up and the trails went cold after that. But we want the gold, and that's all."

I glanced at Max, who was looking very neutral at that moment. Larry was lost in the logistics of getting the gold away from the Bush family transport, not who got it afterwards. That would be Max's problem, and possibly mine, but I'd burn that bridge when I got to it.

There was shouting outside Mr. Chung's office; we all drew our guns, but put them away when Chung brought in Eustache Limo, the patriarch of the Limo clan. I'd never met him, but he had Julia with him to make introductions. He looked like God in a hipster suit and steel-toed boots.

"Señorita Gail," he said, adding an arrogant bow. "As you know, our homes and business were destroyed in an effort by unknown persons to kill you." He paused to let that sink in. "But we Limos do not despair. Where there is breath, there is hope and commerce; it is an old Limo family saying. And we are loyal; we will not desert you in your hour of need, Señorita Gail, as it has always been: our guns are your guns."

The translation was that they had nowhere to go other than to hook up with whatever I was doing. Well, I owed them; they, Mad, Wilshirado, and many others had for some incredible reason been counting on me to keep the peace, and if there was no peace, then they were counting on me to lead them to victory. Or something. It was annoying, but I figured we could use more good gun hands (and the Limos were very good gun hands), and I'd rather have them with me than somewhere else, possibly against me.

I rose, and said, "Senor Limo, I am not worthy."

You had to know him pretty well, but Larry's coughing fit sounded suspiciously like cover for laughing, the jerk.

We went back into the restaurant because Mr. Chung's office was getting too crowded. I took Mr. Chung aside. "Did you call the UPS FedEx cavalry?"

"No, they called me," he said quietly. He glanced at the UPS guy. "Do you trust them?"

"I don't have a choice," I said. "They're what I have to work with. How long have you been working with them?"

"Longer than I knew," he admitted. "Hollenbeck asked me to get you to a meeting with Molina, that's all I knew. You do realize they rescued us that night?"

"I wondered."

"Hollenbeck finally told me who they were," he said, uneasily. "But if they're working for Molina..." He gave me a hard look. "It is Molina, isn't it?"

"Yes, if it's easier to believe in Santa Molina," I said. "Or, no; it's really an aging, remorseful killer-torturer-rapist named Milton Keynes that I used to work for. But he is on your side, which is LA's side."

Mr. Chung just stared at me, which is what I would have done in his place.

"Nellie!" Larry yelled across the room. "You got transport!"

"What will you do now, Miss Gail?" Mr. Chung asked.

"I will do best I can, Mr. Chung."

I was halfway to the door when Wilshire planted herself in front of me. "Hey! When's my lesson?"

"Stay here and study with your sister," I said, trying to brush her off on Larry, who gave me a dirty look. I caved in, "Or come with me, we can do a lesson on the way." One of the UPS lieutenants gave me a weird look, but didn't say anything. It would be a long drive there and back, might as well make the most of it. Alvarado decided to study with Larry while we were gone. I could just imagine what they were studying. Wilshire and I worked on words like "car" "road" "big" "far" "cold" and so on. A travelogue of sorts.

I used a page of Wilshire's writing tablet to make a few notes at the ambush sites. The UPS guy who came with us had one site in mind, but I made him drive me around to a few others that I felt had promise. Not that any of it had much promise; it was just a bunch of barely passable fucked up highway far too out in the open for my taste. But it would do; I might not even need to blow anything up for a change.

Wilshire was very well behaved. While I skulked around the rubble, she took the LA picture book Mad gave her out of her backpack and sat quietly looking at it. I was like that once; always had something to read with me so I would be amused and not lose my temper waiting in line or waiting for anything. It had been a long time since I'd waited in line and much had changed since then.

We got back to the Meng-Po-Niang after dinner, but they fed us anyway. Then Mr. Chung opened his office to me, Larry, Max, and the UPS guy, and we began to plan in earnest.

We spent the next day arming and packing to move. These were some very well-armed and organized delivery guys. I'd run from Sunset and Vine with only my Titanium Colt, Beretta, boots, catsuit, and ti-tandex jacket; UPS outfitted me with new and improved Infra-RayBans, and a Walther pistol with a silencer. They also gave me something I'd never seen before: a very elegant Jati-Matic submachine gun. The Finns really know their design. They also had ammo for the Jati-Matic and the Walther, plus magazines for the Beretta and half a dozen speed loaders for the Colt. I was touched and impressed.

Without asking too many questions, the Limos, Hollenbeck, and Mr. Chung turned out a small, well-disciplined army and put it under the command of the UPS guy. I said good-bye to Mr. Chung and Mad; she said she'd see me later, and Mr. Chung just nodded. Frankly, he looked glad to see us go and I don't blame him; we caused him a lot of trouble and ate a lot of his food. We moved out when the sun went down.

While our side very quietly set up camouflaged camps, I took a small band out to set up the explosives. I was in a pretty good mood for once; I felt like I had enough C4 to really do some damage. And it would have been nice, except before I could lay the charges, we heard engines; big ones and a lot of them.

We hightailed it back to the ridge we'd set up on. "Fuck!" I hissed at the UPS guy. "Are they early?"

"Does it matter?" he asked, and looked at Larry. "What now, Mr. Logistics?"

"Nell?" Larry asked in stereo with Max.

"Give me a long-range rifle," I said. "One of those trucks has got to have some gasoline somewhere on it. If you've got any other shooters, bring them here." Two seconds later I had a Dragunov SVD with an infrared sight. Damn, the Russians make mighty fine guns when they put their minds to it. I also had two UPS drivers and a FedEx girl driver next to me with a similar guns. They knew what to do and were ready: aim for gas tanks, but shoot the drivers, too. "We go when we stop shooting," I said to the UPS guy. The assault was organized and ready. I really had to hand it to Uncle Milty; he was a bastard and I still wanted to kill him, but he sure knew how to recruit and manage the very acme of mayhem talent.

I told my shooters to choose targets spread out along the convoy. "Fire when I do and stop when I do," I said, and we let loose. The few trucks that had large gas tanks exploded beautifully, the rest exploded in a puny way, but they all swerved in confusion. The return fire was scattered. Several trucks made a run for it. Before I would have stopped, the UPS guy yelled, "Cease fire," and led the charge down the hill. I hopped on a borrowed BMW motorcycle and joined in.

The idea was to run down the truck with the gold. Since we didn't know which one it was, we had to stop the ones still on the run as well. The downside of that was they were loaded with people shooting at us.

God love Julia Limo; she and her brother Jim roared up beside me in a souped-up dune buggy-cum-machine-gun-truck and I jumped from the bike to it. They had grappling hooks in the back. Jim fired wisely and well while Julia gunned the buggy alongside the truck in front of us. That girl can really drive. I threw the hook and scrambled up on top of the semi-trailer. Jim switched to a handgun and picked off the guy who was on top of the truck. Julia was having issues with some outriders next to her, so Jim turned his attention to them. That was okay; I was shooting the lock off the top hatch. Or trying to. There were people inside the trailer shooting through the roof at me. Great, I was pinned between the cab and the trailer. Something had to give fairly soon before one of those bullets hit me. The cab passenger swung out and took a shot at me. I hung on for all I was worth and shot back. One of our folks came along side and shot up the cab, nearly shooting me in the process. I scrambled back on top of the trailer. The semi jerked to a stop, but stayed upright. I was beginning to think climbing on top of this truck wasn't such a great idea. Nevertheless, I opened the hatch and sprayed the inside with my Jati-Matic.

It was very very quiet. For a few minutes.

"Miss Gail?! Are you up there?" It was Julia.

"Nellie? You there?" That was Larry.

"Yeah, I'll open the truck from the inside, hang on." I swung into the interior of the trailer. Some of the lights were on and it was a pretty gory sight. But what really caught my eye was the gold, stacks and stacks of it covered with canvas. Part of the canvas was ripped from one of my bullets, and since I'd probably never get this close a look again, I flipped it back to look at the gold bar.

I thought gold wasn't supposed to shatter like that and I was damn sure it was supposed to be gold through and through, not red, as in this was gold painted clay bricks. We'd been had. Big time. I flipped the canvas back over the fake gold bricks.

Someone shot the locks off the trailer door and opened them. "Gold there?" the UPS guy yelled.

"Yeah," I said, jumping out of the trailer. "Is Larry here?" I yelled over the victory whooping and hollering. "Larry!? Larry LaRue!? Have you two seen him?" I asked Wilshirado next to me.

"I'm here, sis!"

"Larry, I gotta talk to you–" And I would've except there was a counter-attack from behind us. This would have bothered me more except we were fighting for our lives. The wave rushed us and broke through. I'm no good at hand-to-hand unless I have to be, and I was kicking ass at just that moment. The onslaught kept coming and then kept going, as if their only goal was to get past us and the crippled trucks. That would have been okay, except in the confusion, one of the twins tumbled down an incline and was swept away.

"ALVARADO!" I yelled after her.

"I'm here!"

"Shit!" I grabbed the nearest motorcycle. "Larry! Meet me at Flat Top, like the old days, at midnight." I could hear the UPS guy giving orders to move out. He thought they had the gold; he wasn't about to give chase for nothing. I would have done the same in his place.

"Nellie?" Larry put his hand on mine.

"If I'm not there by dawn, I'm dead," I was kick starting so I barely heard him ask 'why.' "Because... because she's only up to the letter 'V'." That would have to hold him until I could explain it, if I ever could. I roared off into the blackness after Wilshire.

There was a lot of dust and a lot of dark and soon there were a lot of semi-trucks going in the same direction as me. I didn't come across Wilshire's body along the way, so I was assuming she was with these people, whoever they were. I was low on fuel so I climbed aboard one of the slower-moving trucks. My arms were killing me; one climb I can do, two is murder. Anyway, at least no one was shooting at me, so I could wonder about the counter attack. Had they circled back behind us? Unlikely, we'd shot most of the original convoy outriders. Then where did these new fighters come from? Were they stragglers from the original convoy? And how did they know where we'd be and when? None of it made much sense, unless one of our people had betrayed us. Caterham-7 sprang to mind, but she was the least likely because, though she was nuts, she was firmly on our side and nuts. Mad? Why would she? Mr. Chung? Same question. I couldn't suspect the Limos because they were out there getting their asses shot off with us.

Clinging to the top of a semi-trailer is not the best place to think. I gave up wondering and just watched what I could see of the scenery go by. Mainly I watched the other vehicles: three or four big trucks, like the one I was on, a fair number of motorcycles and SUVs with machine guns mounted on them, lots of gas engines. Very wasteful: not many outfits in LA had those kind of resources to burn; certainly not the MTA. The MTA were city fighters. These vehicles were for power and for distance.

And it was a distance; I was freezing in my titandex catsuit and jacket by the time we got to the warehouse. Good thing tired people don't look up or they would have seen me climbing into the forest of cross-beams in the pitched roof. I'd been here before. It was the AT&T warehouse and torture complex in Calabasas. I caught sight of Wilshire, being led away by a driver; I was momentarily distracted by one of the trucks below having the camouflage pulled off, revealing AT&T emblazoned on the side. 'That confirms it,' I thought, following Wilshire and her guard across the echoing, chaotic space below. I looked at the guard again; it was no guard, it was Harve de Grace in a business suit, alive and still working for the wrong side. They were in a hurry down there. I'd have to move fast to save her. I knew I could scare de Grace to death, but I'd still have to get a jump on him.

Wilshire and de Grace moved through the warehouse from the big rooms packed with men, women and vehicles, to a smaller one. The ceiling was lower, but I was able to squeeze through the partition and conceal myself in the shadows. I got the Walther and silencer out as de Grace brought Wilshire in and then left.

"Luchune! I made it!" she sang happily.

Everything stopped when I saw who was in the room: Kevin.

My old enemy. I'd beaten him twice before

because he was arrogant enough to underestimate me and what I'd be willing to fight for. Shouldn't old Kev still be sulking somewhere? And yet, here he was, in the middle of my action again. His puffed-up wafer-thin ego must still be smarting from the Sara Lee and Chelsea Clinton missions.

How interesting. Kevin was the most dangerous free-lance functionary I knew—soulless, ruthless, expeditious and efficient. I put the gun away and stayed very still. It was quiet in the room, which was more like a garage—a garage containing a black Honda Accord with monster tires—I didn't want them to hear me moving around.

"Well?" Kevin asked in that creepy voice he has.

"All set," Wilshire said. She sounded arrogant and sure of herself. "They fell for it, just like you said they would!"

"Yes, that will buy us enough time to get to the ships."

I couldn't see his face, but I was sure he was smiling his creepy smile.

So... that was that. But what in God's name had possessed her? I'd think about it after I was out of there.

De Grace came back in. "We're ready to move the gold, sir," he said, with that weasely little voice of his.

"Excellent. Go ahead. I'll be along very soon." He waited until de Grace was gone, and then a little longer. Doors opened and big engines started in the next room. Kevin and Wilshire were quiet until the trucks pulled out. "And Nellie Gail?" He asked.

"Luchune," Wilshire snarled. "She's dead. Someone shot her next to me."

"Good work, Wilshire," he said. He pulled out a gun with a silencer and quietly shot her.

I stopped breathing, and then sighed. How very Kevin; how very foolish of Wilshire to trust him. But how could she know? She was just a kid. Was...

"Why'd ya shoot her?" Abilene strolled in liked he owed the joint. "She was a sweet little piece."

God damn, it was like old home week in here tonight.

"She'd served her purpose," Kevin said. "Are they gone?"

"Yup. So, where's the gold?"

The car was between me and whatever Kevin was doing to the fender. Abilene laughed and said something about Kev being an evil genius. Then Kevin asked Abilene to move Wilshire's body out of the way so they could leave. How little they knew Kevin. He shot Abilene in the back.

Kevin is the one person on earth you should never turn your back on, especially if he's holding a gun. Well, I had a gun, too, a Walther with a silencer. It occurred to me that I should have left Kevin alive so I'd have a worthy adversary. But could I really take a guy named Kevin seriously as a worthy adversary? Nah. Should I say something? Give him a chance to defend himself? Nah. Did he give Wilshire any kind of chance to defend herself? Nah.

I dropped down onto the roof of the car as Kevin was dragging Abilene's body into the shadows with Wilshire's and shot him in the back of the head. He fell neatly face down half in the shadows and tarps he was concealing Wilshire and Abilene in. Like they teach you in the Company, I walked over and put another bullet in his heart, just to make sure. It was disgusting, but I gave him a quick frisk. I found a wallet, but no car keys, so I was hoping they were in the car. I glanced at Wilshire;

she was dead.

I walked back to the Honda Accord and looked at the fender Kevin had done something to. He'd scratched off some of the black paint; it was gold underneath. The keys were on the seat. I started the car and pulled out into the night. Nobody shot at me. "What a scam, Kevin," I said to myself, heading the Honda Accord south. "Anyone who'd trust you is a fool or a madman or both. You were made to scam the Bush family. I'm glad I lived to see it. And you didn't live to see it." I was also glad for the big tires and four-wheel drive this weird hybrid had as the roads were still very fucked up from Calabasas down to LA.

The car was extremely quiet, had an infrared windshield and lights, and I was moving so stealthily, I startled and ran over a few scavengers along the way. I took the only route available to me, winding down parts of the 101 and then down what there was of San Fernando Road. I had time to rifle through Kevin's briefcase; it had one page with six numbered Swiss bank accounts and their passwords on it. I had no way of knowing if these were Bush Swiss bank accounts but I had a strong hunch they were. Things must really have been bad for Kevin to try to rip off the Bush family on this level: like he had absolutely nothing to lose and they were hard up enough to trust him. He must have realized they'd throw him away like a candy wrapper once he got them out of California, so it was worth the risk. He'd just underestimated me again.

Or had he? Did he think he could beat me with Wilshire's help? Well, he damn near did.

I should have killed Wilshire; she deserved to killed by someone better than Kevin. I had felt nothing but a certain amount of disappointment when he killed her. She'd betrayed me and now she could never tell me why. Wilshire didn't do things for no reason. There was probably a really interesting explanation I'd never get now. Was it something I said or did? Did Kevin and Abilene have a better deal for her? Why?

'Why? Luchune. Why not?' I could just hear her say it. Damn her, she'd gambled again and lost this time. Luchune. Fucking luchune.

I got to the base of Flat Top a little after midnight. I parked in a secluded spot—the driveway of a bombed house—as close to the top as I could and walked up. Larry was there; Alvarado was with him. I took out the Walther because it would be quiet and pointed it at her before either of them could say anything. "You knew."

"Please Miss Gail—" she begged.

"You knew," I said, my hand completely still, holding the gun loosely. "But you didn't tell us."

Alvarado fell to her knees. "Please, Miss Gail. I begged her not to—"

"She's dead."

"I begged her, because you were so good to us—" She was sobbing.

"Then, why?" I could feel Larry looking at me, putting it together for himself.

"I begged her but she said it's what you'd do," she was groveling at my feet and choking on her sobs. "Please Miss Gail, I begged her but she was my sister, she was all I ever had." She was crying too hard to go on.

'...all I ever had.' Well, I could understand that. Never taking my eyes off her, I pointed the gun at the sky above us and stepped away. I handed the gun to Larry. "This is your problem," I said and walked away from him.

He'd have to shoot one of us; there was no way we could both survive Wilshire's betrayal. Was it what I would have done in Wilshire's place? Maybe. But I hope I would have survived it.

There was a muffled shot, and then a second shot. I knew he'd shot Alvarado again, just to make sure. He was Company trained like I was.

"You've got to have trust in a relationship," he said when he was next to me. He put his arm around me and we walked down to where I'd parked the car. "Well, Nellie–"

"Alison."

"Well, Alison," he said, giving me a one-armed squeeze. "At least we got a nice Toyota–"

"Honda. Honda Accord."

"We got a nice Honda Accord out of it. Here's your gun."

"Thanks. Um, Larry? About this Honda Accord..."

We wound up in Lincoln Heights after Mr. Chung helped us contact the UPS guys. They were glad to see us and the gold. I was forced to trade away one of the Swiss bank accounts for safe passage to Europe for me and Larry. No sign of Milty and a good thing, too; he must have realized getting me and Larry out of LA was the best thing he could do for himself.

When the dust settled, the new U.S. was very much like the old 13 colonies U.S. Canada took over the area from the Great Lakes to the Pacific and down to south of San Francisco. Mexico took back what they'd lost in the Mexican American war, plus the rest of California and quite a bit of Louisiana. They built a very big wall on their eastern and northern border and guarded it vigilantly. Most of the Southern U.S. was left a wasteland; too much fighting, starvation, AIDS, and the atrocities of the Christianists had left it a haunted, ravaged place. The new U.S. government had abandoned it. They allowed crazy people to go there to die and exiled incorrigibles to it, but otherwise they guarded the line separating it from civilization with the same care and ferocity the Mexicans did. It would be left as an Autonomous Zone to see what, if anything, developed there. That region didn't have any oil, so there wasn't much chance of the wrong people organizing it. The new U.S. really didn't have any enemies; it was so beaten up and the new leadership was so good, or at least realistic, the world came to its rescue. Except Saudi Arabia, which had been recognized as the second biggest problem in the world and partitioned by its neighbors, so it no longer existed. The U.S. would never be what it was, but the wages of fear are death, or, at the very least, downsizing.

The exiled brain and art power, the heart and soul of the United States, turned out to be a very forgiving bunch and came back to rebuild. I thought they were nuts, but love makes you do crazy things.

The scum that was left in our military—because all the good ones were dead, ground up in the Bush war machine—either turned themselves in or were rounded up by professional and amateur bounty hunters and handed over to the authorities. The worst of them, like the Butchers of New York and those responsible for massacres in Chicago, Detroit, Atlanta, and Los Angeles, were handed over to the World Court for Crimes Against Humanity. However, most were so pathetic, they were released and vanished, probably into to the Autonomous Zone where they could play soldiers for a while longer and then eventually die of disease, starvation, or unnatural causes; all the things our government had kept somewhat under control until the Bush family decided to destroy the rule of law and take the money and run. In its last years, the Bush administration seemed to think their best bet was to unleash the psychotics of the military on their own citizens. Well, it worked for a while. But that was in the past and the country was trying to heal itself. I read on the internet that starvation and cannibalism were such a serious problem in the Autonomous Zone, some very fine people tried to organize a way to at least feed it, but after some study realized things just needed to run their course down there.

The biggest bounty was for any member of the Bush family, but they were never seen or heard from again. It was as if without their money, they simply ceased to exist and that made a perfect kind of sense. Larry was right as usual; without their money, they're nothing.

I never saw any of the LA crowd again, but I did get a mysterious postcard from Shanghai a few years later with a picture of Zhou En-Lai and a note about it being too soon to tell if the American experiment was a success. I found this puzzling and vaguely threatening at the same time. I figured it was from Mad, and I was glad she was in China where she wanted to be, and way far on the other side of the steppe from me. I didn't count her as an enemy; of everyone in LA, she would have most understood why I did what I did. Anyway, I had enough enemies after I left LA, but most of them stayed the fuck away from me, and those that didn't, didn't last very long.

Uncle Milty merged back into the fabric of Los Angeles, where he was inaccessible and might be doing good works in penance for the past. I knew this because I'd looked into having him killed. It wouldn't change the past, but it would tie up a loose end for me. Eventually I gave up on the project. If I ever had the right opportunity to kill him, I would. However, that would involve a trip to LA, and that was unlikely.

I almost felt bad about the Limos, but I saw an Internet Broadcast that LA recently elected Julia Limo as Mayor, so they must have landed on their feet more or less. I suppose the city is in good, if rather stingy hands now.

Dr. Jane Caterham-7 returned to public service as the head of the newly organized U.S. Revenue Service. Because there were no taxes to collect yet, she was in charge of managing the money that generous and forgiving nations sent in for reconstruction. Based on what I read on the internet, she was doing a great job of rebuilding the U.S. or what was left of it.

Dr. Max blamed everything that went wrong with that last mission in Los Angeles on me and Larry. However, that didn't stop him from revamping the monetary system and getting the Bank of the United States on its feet with money from a Bush Swiss account he said mysteriously appeared on his computer one day. Believing this to be a loaves-and-fishes-like miracle or some other kind of sign from God or Whatever, he retired to a Trappist monastery in Pennsylvania that had been transplanted from Tennessee before the mass psychosis south of the Mason Dixon line got too deep. Taking a vow of silence, he wrote very angry poetry about linguists and historians and published it on the internet. I don't know how much he wrote and published, but this was such a pale anemic shadow of his former glory on "Dr. Max's Live Nude Economics," I had to stop reading after a half a dozen poems. Larry kept reading; he said the poetry got better after a while, and either Max got it out of his system or the abbot cut off his internet access because eventually he stopped posting.

Larry finally did his experiment on the palatization of the letter "t" and got his doctorate in linguistics at the Sorbonne. For weeks afterward he wandered around the Left Bank muttering "Monsieur le Doctor La Rue," and laughing softly. He snapped out of it in time to marry a very chic and perfectly nice Parisienne, and produce three kids in five years. The European grass does not grow under Monsieur le Doctor La Rue's feet.

My world was finished. In a stabilized and healing U.S. and a world feeling more secure because of it, the time for gunslingers like me was past. The dead, like Laguna Woods and Abilene, and even the functionary bastards like Kevin, were forgotten. The living either vanished or were rehabilitated to blend in with a more peaceful society. There was nothing in the U.S.A. 2.0 for Nellie Gail but death, or worse: decline.

Of course I was never seen or heard from again. However, Alison LaRue received her doctorate in history from the University of Heidelberg after her successful defense of her dissertation: "Causes and consequences of the developed West's genocide against the people of Iraq, 1991-2010."

I love LA.

I wish it well.

But I don't miss it.

The End

Afterward

Yes, I was very angry the week I wrote "The Way we Live Now at Sunset and Vine." I wrote it in five days starting on September 7, 2003 when our unduly elected President Bush lied to us again:

> "Our strategy in Iraq will require new resources. We have conducted a thorough assessment of our military and reconstruction needs in Iraq, and also in Afghanistan. I will soon submit to Congress a request for $87 billion. The request will cover ongoing military and intelligence operations in Iraq, Afghanistan and elsewhere, which we expect will cost $66 billion over the next year. This budget request will also support our commitment to helping the Iraqi and Afghan people rebuild their own nations, after decades of oppression and mismanagement. We will provide funds to help them improve security. And we will help them to restore basic services, such as electricity and water, and to build new schools, roads, and medical clinics. This effort is essential to the stability of those nations, and therefore, to our own security. Now and in the future, we will support our troops and we will keep our word to the more than 50 million people of Afghanistan and Iraq."

That night in 2003, as I read to this speech on my computer, I could not know that over four thousand American soldiers would die in the service of a government that was unworthy of their sacrifice, that more than 100,000 Iraqis would die, that Abu Ghraib would question my faith in our military and humanity, that billions would go missing somewhere between Halliburton and, well, Halliburton. I could not know the America I was raised to love would promote torture, despotism, fear, greed, slavery, rape, murder, and more murder for the goals of one small group of men who'd come to power, legally or not, but who'd turned the tragic events of September 11, 2001 into an opportunity to sweep away any moral or legal obstacles to their plans to rule through fear, because they could not govern through consent. And so they did. And so they continue to do so. Monstrous men—Cheney, Bush and Rumsfeld—and their minions not much less monstrous than themselves.

But that night in September 2003 I could not know any of this, I could only go cold with rage and fury that the moral and fiscal consequences of Bush's murderous Iraq invasion were going to sow horror in my country for generations and that it was so fucking unnecessary. I was too angry to cry, to furious to move, and the only thing I could do was open a word processing window and pound out the first five thousand words of part one of Darkness at Sunset and Vine, "The Way we Live Now at Sunset and Vine," which is twenty thousand words, more or less. I wrote it in five days and somehow managed to work my 9–5 job as well. This story poured out of me in a torrent of fury and sorrow in between bouts of pounding on my desk and howling with rage. I am not a patriot. I love my country because it's mine. I hadn't realized how much I loved it, and writing a story might not seem like much of a fight for something one loves, but it was the only fight

I had in me at that moment. Even a California girl will turn and fight with whatever is at hand when her back is against the surf. And this is how I felt in September 2003. Nine years later, I've calmed down a little, but I've only banked my fire with hope and sadness, it could flare up again with the right provocation.

At the time I was writing "The Way we Live Now at Sunset and Vine," my beloved California, for various insane and greedy reasons, was in the throes of recalling Governor Gray Davis, an unlucky and mediocre bureaucrat. Maybe I was just kidding myself, but at the time it seemed like the recall could go either way and I wrote the story as if Davis had won the recall, but the Bush family sent troops into California to install Schwarzenegger as governor. Would Californians fight this kind of invasion? For the purposes of fiction, I said yes, but looking around at the suckers like Darryl Issa and the clowns who elected Schwarzenegger and then re-elected him, I wonder. At one point in the second novella, The End of History at Sunset and Vine, Nellie's dinner date (yeah, I know, Nellie on a date, laugh riot, right?) opines that he didn't like what happened to his State. Nellie politely refrains from saying out loud that she thinks her State got what it deserved. It's too long and complicated to go into in this screed, but through overuse of the referendum mechanism, which means we vote more than Switzerland, a manipulative, if not malevolent business culture and media, and just being stupid and greedy, California has bankrupted its government, painted itself into a corner, tied its hands, and knocked over a candle to set the house on fire, which the under-funded emergency services aren't going to get to in time. But, hey dude! Arnold Schwarzenegger is our governor, and the only thing that stands between our citizenry and complete moral, physical and financial collapse is the California Nurses Association and a couple of unions. But, hey, dude! Arnold Schwarzenegger is our governor, and– oh, just fucking, never mind.

The Enron scandal was also a factor in Governor Davis' downfall, but that wasn't clear to most people until after he was ousted. Most people still think he was a big loser because he couldn't control energy prices and, in truth, he couldn't control them under the deregulated system most of California adopted in the mid-1990s, led by Republican governor Pete Wilson, who governed under some kind of curse so powerful that California experienced nothing but catastrophe after disaster, including, but not limited to, earthquakes, weeks of wildfires, urban rioting, and energy deregulation during his terms in Sacramento. I wrote quite a bit on how LA and parts of the State I liked might survive through the good management of a few farsighted individuals and the brute force and street smarts of the rest of the citizens determined to stay in what would be left of a post-Federal occupation Los Angeles. The fate of Los Angeles and California were very much on my mind in the aftermath of the Enron free-market assault on my foolish State. During the 1990s energy deregulation madness in California, the head of the Los Angeles Department of Water and Power, Mr. David Freeman, refused to deregulate our utilities. It was not mandatory and, being an intelligent man who could remember longer than last week and might have done some reading on the history of unrestrained capitalism, he could see deregulating a vital service was not just a bad idea, it was a really fucking stupid idea. So he refused to do it. Our DWP has flaws, but deregulation is not one of them. This is why the DWP is keeping the lights on and the water flowing and raking a percentage off the top of every dollar circulating on the net in the City of Angels in 2016. How would they do it? They'd hire thugs like Nellie to protect their aqueducts and power stations, as well as dig up alternative energy sources that were getting dusty through disuse. The original El Pueblo de Nuestra Señora la Reina de Los Angeles de Porciúncula founded in 1781 had (and likely still has) enough water to support about 14,000 souls. The Los Angeles Nellie lives in is about that half that number, and I surmised that the DWP could find a way to support that many paying customers with electricity and water. In parts two and three of the "Darkness at Sunset and Vine" trilogy, I expound on the Metropolitan Transit Authority's role in policing their bus routes and how AT&T keeps the internet working, but nearly destroys everything in a further grab for power, but I digress.

However clever these novellas might sound nine years later, at the time I was writing them it was painful. These novellas are my plea to my country, which seems hell bent on destroying everything that's ever been good about it, to stop, please stop, before it's too late. Why, America, why does it even seem possible that such things as happen in "Darkness at Sunset and Vine" could ever occur, but with a less happy ending? Why have you handed yourself to the monsters of the Bush family and their mafias? Why? Are we too numb, too stupid, to beaten down to fight for the only things that mean anything in this crazy mixed up world? To fight for our freedom, our future, and the ideals Americans have been willing to die for for over 200 years? Have we forgotten that it's better to die on our feet than live on our knees?

Or did we never really know it? Or will we just not care? Until it really is too late?

It's 2012, Occupy America has shaken things up more than I'd ever hope things could be shaken up again. 4.6 billion dollars moved from major banks to credit unions and community banks on November 5, 2011. Occupy America says they have no demands but their message is clear: the United States must run fairly and equitably for everyone, not just the 1% with all the money. It's a simple enough message; let's hope D.C. hears it correctly. It is, after all, an election year.

Ginger Mayerson
Los Angeles
March 2012

Acknowledgements

Many many thanks to Lynn Loper, Jane Seaton, and Laurel Sutton for editing the snarling and teeth gnashing and for their calm and calming input on this work. I am indebted to them for their support and friendship through this and many other adventures. Everyone should have friends and editors like Lynn, Jane, and Laurel.

Thank you to Robin Austin for the lovely cover and Nancy Lilly and Deana Swart for the final proofreads.

Dr. Kelly S. Taylor has thanked me for allowing her to produce Part 1 of the trilogy in 2008, and I'm very grateful to her for understanding and realizing my work so brilliantly on stage. I'm also very grateful for her introduction to this book.

And if you made it this far, here's a drawing of Nellie by the fabulous Molly Kiely. Thanks, Molly.

Molly Kiely, 2004

www.ingramcontent.com/pod-product-compliance
Lightning Source LLC
Chambersburg PA
CBHW072206170626
46813CB00003B/814